THE DIAL PRESS
1 Dag Hammarskjold Plaza
245 EAST 47 STREET • NEW YORK, N.Y. 10017

SFWA CIRCULATING BOOK PLAN

UNACCOMPANIED SONATA

UNACCOMPANIED SONATA &
OTHER STORIES

ORSON SCOTT CARD

 A QUANTUM BOOK

The Dial Press · New York

Published by
The Dial Press
1 Dag Hammarskjold Plaza
New York, New York 10017

"Ender's Game," "I Put My Blue Genes On," and "The Monkeys Thought 'Twas All in Fun" first appeared in *Analog*; "Kingsmeat" in *Analog Yearbook*; "Deep Breathing Exercises," "Quietus," and "Unaccompanied Sonata" in *Omni*; "Closing the Timelid" and "Mortal Gods" in *The Magazine of Fantasy & Science Fiction*; "Eumenides in the Fourth Floor Lavatory" in *Chrysalis IV* edited by Roy Torgeson; and "Tin Men" in *The Anthology of Speculative Poetry*, No. 4, February 1980.

Manufactured in the United States of America

First printing

Library of Congress Cataloging in Publication Data
Card, Orson Scott.
  Unaccompanied sonata & other stories.
  CONTENTS: Bova, B. Introduction.—Ender's game.—Kingsmeat.—Deep breathing exercises. [etc.]
  1. Science fiction, American. I. Title.
PS3553.A655U5   813'.54   80-20448
ISBN 0-8037-9175-5

To François Camoin,
the good teacher,
who removed the guilt
from Eumenides

Contents

Tin Men

I saw an old loop at the museum,
The flat kind they put on a screen.
It was a dream,
Or, if you will, a lie,
Of men with boyish grins
Bursting from impossibly bright spaceships
To rescue naked women
And stride unhindered on dusty planets
And, yes, destroy evil, which always sneered
And made stupid mistakes
And clearly deserved to die.

They believed in destiny, no doubt,
And thought, because the worlds looked small,
They could be harvested by reaching out;
Because the road from proteins in the sea
Looked infinite, they thought the road ahead
Was also straight and infinitely long.
They were wrong.

Oh, there's no sign the road will end—
They just weren't counting on our little bend.
These tin men, star men, never lacked for heart.
But in their dreams they ended voyages
We have neither wit nor will to start.
And when we set our hands
To killing evil at its source,
We traced it through its tortuous course:
We found it shyly hiding in our glands,
Where all our wishing could not have it dead;
It rises hungry with us in the morning
And returns in darkness with us to our bed.

—Orson Scott Card

UNACCOMPANIED SONATA

Introduction:
An Open Letter to the Author

Dear Scott:

Success has a thousand fathers, it's quite true. But, as the editor who first "discovered" you, I think that I'm entitled to a bit more parental pride than most. So you'll excuse me if I wax expansive about this publication of your collection of short stories.

It's a special landmark in the career of a writer, you know, to have a story collection published. Book publishers have learned through bitter experience that novels sell better than most anthologies and single-author collections. It is only when a large number of readers recognize a writer's name, and will buy books bearing that name, that a publisher will risk a story collection. Even then, the publishers prefer novels. A writer must really be a hot property, a bright star, before a publisher willingly takes the chance of bringing out a collection of his stories. The fact that yours is a very new name among the top writers in the country makes this story collection especially noteworthy.

I remember the first story of yours that I ever laid eyes on. It was "Ender's Game." It's a great satisfaction to see it leading this book. I recall quite well that afternoon in the office of *Analog* magazine when I was reading through the slushpile, doing that chore that every editor dreads—wading through the dismal stack of manuscripts from totally unknown writers—when "Ender's Game" turned up. It was a joy to read

then, and an even bigger joy to see again after all
these years.

All these years! It was only August 1977 when
"Ender's Game" was published in *Analog*. You've
come a long way, baby. In a very short time.

I've never seen readers react so strongly to
someone's first story. The mail that came in to *Analog*
as a result of "Ender's Game" correctly identified you
as an important new writer. And, of course, by the
time the 1978 World Science Fiction Convention met
in Phoenix, you easily scooped up the John W.
Campbell Award for the Best New Writer of the Year.

A truly impressive beginning to a writing career. But what impressed me even more (long before
Phoenix) was your second story, and your third, and
the next few after those. Each of them was a quantum
leap above the previous tale in polish, depth, ability.
With each new story you showed that you were growing, learning, reaching new heights as a writer, rang-
ing farther and deeper into the souls of your characters.

By the time I became editor of *Omni* magazine,
your stories had already outgrown the narrow conven-
tions of "hard-core" science fiction. You were ready for
that big, international audience that *Omni* reaches.
And then some. Let me tell you, when the *proofread-
ers* come running into the editor's office with tears in
their eyes to say how much they enjoyed reading a
story—that's writing!

Stories such as "Quietus" and "Deep Breathing
Exercises" and especially "Unaccompanied Sonata"
drew an enormous, heartfelt response from readers all
around the world. You hit people where they lived,
with those stories.

I know you've published several novels and
many more short stories. I know you've written plays

and film scripts, and that you're deeply into work on "the big one," a major historical novel.

Still, your origins are in the field we call science fiction. It's a field we both know and love. Yet I must give you a fatherly warning about science fiction, and a bit of unsolicited advice.

Science fiction, as a subdivision of contemporary American letters, is in a stage of immense flux and turmoil. You are as aware of that fact as I am, perhaps. But what you may not realize is that you, more than any other writer in the field today, epitomize the transition that science fiction is going through.

Long before you were born, generations before, American science fiction somehow got misplaced into a literary ghetto. Some of the best work by our best writers was ignored for decades by the rest of the world because it was published under the label of "science fiction," which the majority of readers took to mean "incomprehensible gibberish."

They were wrong, of course. But their indifference to science fiction (including the early works of writers such as Heinlein, Asimov, and Clarke) created a ghetto wall around science fiction writers—and readers.

Today those walls have been demolished. But many—too many—science fiction writers and readers still huddle together where the ghetto used to be, unwilling or perhaps unable to step out into the larger, grander, more demanding world.

You, Scott, have already taken your first steps into that bigger world. The stories in this book prove that. True, your earliest stories were published in "hard-core" science fiction magazines. Your first novels were sold from the science fiction shelves of bookstores.

But as the stories in this volume show, you are a powerful writer whose work can be understood and enjoyed by *any* reader. Your stories deal with people, living, breathing, bleeding people who love and fear and hate and laugh. Readers can weep for your characters, rejoice with them, thrill over them.

This means that you have already gone far beyond the usual fare of science fiction. You are a writer for all the people, not merely the narrow spectrum of readers who want nothing more than "hard-core" science fiction.

And that's what I must warn you about. The science fiction community is a lovely, warm nest, filled (for the most part) with good-hearted people whose common interest is science fiction. But there are forces within that community that can beguile a writer into betraying his own capabilities. Many a writer has found it so safe and comfortable within the old science fiction ghetto that he (or she) continues to write nothing but the same tired old sagas, year after year after year. Such writers stop growing. Worse, they deny their talents to the rest of the reading world. Worse still, some of them are my very dearest friends.

I know there have already been pressures put on you by the self-appointed guardians of science fiction "purity." You have succeeded too fast, as far as they are concerned. Unable to write the way you do, jealous of your swift rise in the marketplace, they have made a concerted effort to take you down a notch or two, with personal attacks and jaundiced reviews in the fan magazines.

These so-called critics are the denizens of darkness who don't have the brains or heart to accept the powerful stories you write. Terrified of real emotion, they insist on reading nothing more demanding than rehashes of the tales they read when they were children, about stainless-steel heroes who conquer the world in phallus-shaped spaceships. They never understood any depth of characterization beyond the prepubertal level, and they never will.

If they can, they will drag you down to their level. Don't let them do it. You owe the reading public the benefit of your talents.

More than any writer in sight today, Scott, you exemplify what is best in science fiction: bold imagination blended with realistic human characterizations. Humanism plus technology. Brains and heart. That is the wave of the future, not merely for American literature, but for the whole world's salvation, as well.

Be true to yourself and to your talent and to all of us who enjoy reading your work. Fear nothing. Long after all of us are gone, the work itself will survive, and that is the only monument that a writer should care about.

I know I don't have to tell you to keep writing; I've never seen a writer who works as hard at his task as you do.

But I will make one final fatherly demand on you: You are a very young writer, and your best and most creative days still lie ahead of you. So, good as these stories in this volume are, I expect you to do better in the future. And I know you will.

Ad astra,
Ben Bova
Manhattan, March 1980

Ender's Game

"Whatever your gravity is when you get to the door, remember—the enemy's gate is *down*. If you step through your own door like you're out for a stroll, you're a big target and you deserve to get hit. With more than a flasher." Ender Wiggins paused and looked over the group. Most were just watching him nervously. A few understanding. A few sullen and resisting.

First day with this army, all fresh from the teacher squads, and Ender had forgotten how young new kids could be. He'd been in it for three years, they'd had six months—nobody over nine years old in the whole bunch. But they were his. At eleven, he was half a year early to be a commander. He'd had a toon of his own and knew a few tricks, but there were forty in his new army. Green. All marksmen with a flasher, all in top shape, or they wouldn't be here—but they were all just as likely as not to get wiped out first time into battle.

"Remember," he went on, "they can't see you till you get through that door. But the second you're out, they'll be on you. So hit that door the way you want to be when they shoot at you. Legs up under you, going straight *down*." He pointed at a sullen kid who looked like he was only seven, the smallest of them all. "Which way is down, greenoh!"

"Toward the enemy door." The answer was quick. It was also surly, as if to say, Yeah, yeah, now get on with the important stuff.

"Name, kid?"

"Bean."

"Get that for size or for brains?"

Bean didn't answer. The rest laughed a little. Ender had chosen right. This kid *was* younger than the rest, must have been advanced because he was sharp. The others didn't like him much, they were happy to see him taken down a little. Like Ender's first commander had taken him down.

"Well, Bean, you're right onto things. Now I tell you this, nobody's gonna get through that door without a good chance of getting hit. A lot of you are going to be turned into cement somewhere. Make sure it's your legs. Right? If only your legs get hit, then only your legs get frozen, and in nullo that's no sweat." Ender turned to one of the dazed ones. "What're legs for? Hmmm?"

Blank stare. Confusion. Stammer.

"Forget it. Guess I'll have to ask Bean here."

"Legs are for pushing off walls." Still bored.

"Thanks, Bean. Get that, everybody?" They all got it, and didn't like getting it from Bean. "Right. You can't *see* with legs, you can't *shoot* with legs, and most of the time they just get in the way. If they get frozen sticking straight out you've turned yourself into a blimp. No way to hide. So how do legs go?"

A few answered this time, to prove that Bean wasn't the only one who knew anything. "Under you. Tucked up under."

"Right. A shield. You're kneeling on a shield, and the shield is your own legs. And there's a trick to the suits. Even when your legs are flashed you can *still* kick off. I've never seen anybody do it but me—but you're all gonna learn it."

Ender Wiggins turned on his flasher. It glowed faintly green in his hand. Then he let himself rise in the weightless workout room, pulled his legs under him as though he were kneeling, and flashed both of them. Immediately his suit stiffened at the knees and ankles, so that he couldn't bend at all.

"Okay, I'm frozen, see?"

He was floating a meter above them. They all looked up at him, puzzled. He leaned back and caught one of the handholds on the wall behind him, and pulled himself flush against the wall.

"I'm stuck at a wall. If I had legs, I'd use legs, and string myself out like a string *bean,* right?"

They laughed.

"But I don't have legs, and that's *better,* got it? Because of this." Ender jackknifed at the waist, then straightened out violently. He was across the workout room in only a moment. From the other side he called to them. "Got that? I didn't use hands, so I still had use of my flasher. *And* I didn't have my legs floating five feet behind me. Now watch it again."

He repeated the jackknife, and caught a handhold on the wall near them. "Now, I don't just want you to do that when they've flashed your legs. I want you to do that when you've still got legs, because it's better. And because they'll never be expecting it. All right now, everybody up in the air and kneeling."

Most were up in a few seconds. Ender flashed the stragglers, and they dangled, helplessly frozen, while the others laughed. "When I give an order, you move. Got it? When we're at a door and they clear it, I'll be giving you orders in two seconds, as soon as I see the setup. And when I give the order you better be out there, because whoever's out there first is going to win, unless he's a fool. I'm not. And you better not be, or I'll have you back in the teacher squads." He saw more than a few of them gulp, and the frozen ones looked at him with fear. "You guys who are hanging there. You watch. You'll thaw out in about fifteen minutes, and let's see if you can catch up to the others."

For the next half hour Ender had them jack-knifing off walls. He called a stop when he saw that they all had the basic idea. They were a good group, maybe. They'd get better.

"Now you're warmed up," he said to them, "we'll start working."

Ender was the last one out after practice, since he stayed to help some of the slower ones improve on technique. They'd had good teachers, but like all armies they were uneven, and some of them could be a real drawback in battle. Their first battle might be weeks away. It might be tomorrow. A schedule was never printed. The commander just woke up and found a note by his bunk, giving him the time of his battle and the name of his opponent. So for the first while he was going to drive his boys until they were in top shape—all of them. Ready for anything, at any time. Strategy was nice, but it was worth nothing if the soldiers couldn't hold up under the strain.

He turned the corner into the residence wing and found himself face to face with Bean, the seven-year-old he had picked on all through practice that day. Problems. Ender didn't want problems right now.

"Ho, Bean."

"Ho, Ender."

Pause.

"Sir," Ender said softly.

"We're not on duty."

"In my army, Bean, we're always on duty." Ender brushed past him.

Bean's high voice piped up behind him. "I know what you're doing, Ender, sir, and I'm warning you."

Ender turned slowly and looked at him. "Warning me?

"I'm the best man you've got. But I'd better be treated like it."

"Or what?" Ender smiled menacingly.

"Or I'll be the worst man you've got. One or the other."

"And what do you want? Love and kisses?" Ender was getting angry now.

Bean was unworried. "I want a toon."

Ender walked back to him and stood looking down into his eyes. "I'll give a toon," he said, "to the boys who prove they're worth something. They've got to be good soldiers, they've got to know how to take orders, they've got to be able to think for themselves in a pinch, and they've got to be able to keep respect. That's how I got to be a commander. That's how you'll get to be a toon leader. Got it?"

Bean smiled. "That's fair. *If* you actually work that way, I'll be a toon leader in a month."

Ender reached down and grabbed the front of his uniform and shoved him into the wall. "When I say I work a certain way, Bean, then that's the way I work."

Bean just smiled. Ender let go of him and walked away, and didn't look back. He was sure, without looking, that Bean was still watching, still smiling, still just a little contemptuous. He might make a good toon leader at that. Ender would keep an eye on him.

Captain Graff, six foot two and a little chubby, stroked his belly as he leaned back in his chair. Across his desk sat Lieutenant Anderson, who was earnestly pointing out high points on a chart.

"Here it is, Captain," Anderson said. "Ender's

already got them doing a tactic that's going to throw off everyone who meets it. Doubled their speed."

Graff nodded.

"And you know his test scores. He thinks well, too."

Graff smiled. "All true, all true, Anderson, he's a fine student, shows real promise."

They waited.

Graff sighed. "So what do you want me to do?"

"Ender's the one. He's got to be."

"He'll never be ready in time, Lieutenant. He's eleven, for heaven's sake, man, what do you want, a miracle?"

"I want him into battles, every day starting tomorrow. I want him to have a year's worth of battles in a month."

Graff shook his head. "That would have his army in the hospital."

"No, sir. He's getting them into form. And we need Ender."

"Correction, Lieutenant. We need somebody. You think it's Ender."

"All right, I think it's Ender. Which of the commanders if it isn't him?"

"I don't know, Lieutenant." Graff ran his hands over his slightly fuzzy bald head. "These are children, Anderson. Do you realize that? Ender's army is nine years old. Are we going to put them against the older kids? Are we going to put them through hell for a month like that?"

Lieutenant Anderson leaned even farther over Graff's desk.

"Ender's test scores, Captain!"

"I've seen his bloody test scores! I've watched him in battle, I've listened to tapes of his training sessions, I've watched his sleep patterns, I've heard tapes of his conversations in the corridors and in the bathrooms, I'm more aware of Ender Wiggins than you could possibly imagine! And against all the arguments, against his obvious qualities, I'm weighing one thing. I have this picture of Ender a year from now, if you have your way. I see him completely useless, worn down, a failure, because he was pushed farther than he or any living person could go. But it doesn't weigh enough, does it, Lieutenant, because there's a war on, and our best talent is gone, and the biggest battles are ahead. So give Ender a battle every day this week. And then bring me a report."

Anderson stood and saluted. "Thank you, sir."

He had almost reached the door when Graff called his name. He turned and faced the captain.

"Anderson," Captain Graff said. "Have you been outside, lately I mean?"

"Not since last leave, six months ago."

"I didn't think so. Not that it makes any difference. But have you ever been to Beaman Park, there in the city? Hmm? Beautiful park. Trees. Grass. No nullo, no battles, no worries. Do you know what else there is in Beaman Park?"

"What, sir?" Lieutenant Anderson asked.

"Children," Graff answered.

"Of course children," said Anderson.

"I mean children. I mean kids who get up in the morning when their mothers call them and they go to school and then in the afternoons they go to Beaman Park and play. They're happy, they smile a lot, they laugh, they have fun. Hmmm?"

"I'm sure they do, sir."

"Is that all you can say, Anderson?"

Anderson cleared his throat. "It's good for children to have fun, I think, sir. I know I did when I was a boy. But right now the world needs soldiers. And this is the way to get them."

Graff nodded and closed his eyes. "Oh, indeed, you're right, by statistical proof and by all the important theories, and dammit they work and the system is right but all the same Ender's older than I am. He's not a child. He's barely a person."

"If that's true, sir, then at least we all know that Ender is making it possible for the others of his age to be playing in the park."

"And Jesus died to save all men, of course." Graff sat up and looked at Anderson almost sadly. "But we're the ones," Graff said, "we're the ones who are driving in the nails."

Ender Wiggins lay on his bed staring at the ceiling. He never slept more than five hours a night—but the lights went off at 2200 and didn't come on again until 0600. So he stared at the ceiling and thought.

He'd had his army for three and a half weeks. Dragon Army. The name was assigned, and it wasn't a lucky one. Oh, the charts said that about nine years ago a Dragon Army had done fairly well. But for the next six years the name had been attached to inferior armies, and finally, because of the superstition that was beginning to play about the name, Dragon Army was retired. Until now. And now, Ender thought, smiling, Dragon Army was going to take them by surprise.

The door opened quietly. Ender did not turn his head. Someone stepped softly into his room, then left with the sound of the door shutting. When soft steps died away Ender rolled over and saw a white slip of paper lying on the floor. He reached down and picked it up.

"Dragon Army against Rabbit Army, Ender Wiggins and Carn Carby, 0700."

The first battle. Ender got out of bed and

quickly dressed. He went rapidly to the rooms of each of his toon leaders and told them to rouse their boys. In five minutes they were all gathered in the corridor, sleepy and slow. Ender spoke softly.

"First battle, 0700 against Rabbit Army. I've fought them twice before but they've got a new commander. Never heard of him. They're an older group, though, and I know a few of their old tricks. Now wake up. Run, doublefast, warmup in workroom three."

For an hour and a half they worked out, with three mock battles and calisthenics in the corridor out of the nullo. Then for fifteen minutes they all lay up in the air, totally relaxing in the weightlessness. At 0650 Ender roused them and they hurried into the corridor. Ender led them down the corridor, running again, and occasionally leaping to touch a light panel on the ceiling. The boys all touched the same light panel. And at 0658 they reached their gate to the battleroom.

The members of toons C and D grabbed the first eight handholds in the ceiling of the corridor. Toons A, B, and E crouched on the floor. Ender hooked his feet into two handholds in the middle of the ceiling, so he was out of everyone's way.

"Which way is the enemy's door?" he hissed.

"Down!" they whispered back, and laughed.

"Flashers on." The boxes in their hands glowed green. They waited for a few seconds more, and then the grey wall in front of them disappeared and the battleroom was visible.

Ender sized it up immediately. The familiar open grid of most early games, like the monkey bars at the park, with seven or eight boxes scattered through the grid. They called the boxes *stars*. There were enough of them, and in forward enough positions, that they were worth going for. Ender decided this in a second, and he hissed, "Spread to near stars. E hold!"

The four groups in the corners plunged through the forcefield at the doorway and fell down into the battleroom. Before the enemy even appeared through the opposite gate Ender's army had spread from the door to the nearest stars.

Then the enemy soldiers came through the door. From their stance Ender knew they had been in a different gravity, and didn't know enough to disorient themselves from it. They came through standing up, their entire bodies spread and defenseless.

"Kill 'em, E!" Ender hissed, and threw himself out the door knees first, with his flasher between his legs and firing. While Ender's group flew across the room the rest of Dragon Army lay down a protecting fire, so that E group reached a forward position with only one boy frozen completely, though they had all lost the use of their legs—which didn't impair them in the least. There was a lull as Ender and his opponent, Carn Carby, assessed their positions. Aside from Rabbit Army's losses at the gate, there had been few casualties, and both armies were near full strength. But Carn had no originality—he was in a four-corner spread that any five-year-old in the teacher squads might have thought of. And Ender knew how to defeat it.

He called out, loudly, "E covers A, C down. B, D angle east wall." Under E toon's cover, B and D toons lunged away from their stars. While they were still exposed, A and C toons left their stars and drifted toward the near wall. They reached it together, and together jackknifed off the wall. At double the normal speed they appeared behind the enemy's stars, and opened fire. In a few seconds the battle was over, with the enemy almost entirely frozen, including the commander, and the rest scattered to the corners. For the

next five minutes, in squads of four, Dragon Army
cleaned out the dark corners of the battleroom and
shepherded the enemy into the center, where their
bodies, frozen at impossible angles, jostled each other.
Then Ender took three of his boys to the enemy gate
and went through the formality of reversing the one-
way field by simultaneously touching a Dragon Army
helmet at each corner. Then Ender assembled his
army in vertical files near the knot of frozen Rabbit
Army soldiers.

Only three of Dragon Army's soldiers were im-
mobile. Their victory margin—38 to 0—was ridicu-
lously high, and Ender began to laugh. Dragon Army
joined him, laughing long and loud. They were still
laughing when Lieutenant Anderson and Lieutenant
Morris came in from the teachergate at the south end
of the battleroom.

Lieutenant Anderson kept his face stiff and un-
smiling, but Ender saw him wink as he held out his
hand and offered the stiff, formal congratulations that
were ritually given to the victor in the game.

Morris found Carn Carby and unfroze him,
and the thirteen-year-old came and presented himself
to Ender, who laughed without malice and held out
his hand. Carn graciously took Ender's hand and
bowed his head over it. It was that or be flashed again.

Lieutenant Anderson dismissed Dragon Army,
and they silently left the battleroom through the
enemy's door—again part of the ritual. A light was
blinking on the north side of the square door, indicat-
ing where the gravity was in that corridor. Ender,
leading his soldiers, changed his orientation and went
through the forcefield and into gravity on his feet. His
army followed him at a brisk run back to the workroom. When they got there they formed up into
squads, and Ender hung in the air, watching them.

"Good first battle," he said, which was excuse

enough for a cheer, which he quieted. "Dragon Army did all right against Rabbits. But the enemy isn't always going to be that bad. And if that had been a good army we would have been smashed. We still would have won, but we would have been smashed. Now let me see B and D toons out here. Your takeoff from the stars was way too slow. If Rabbit Army knew how to aim a flasher, you all would have been frozen solid before A and C even got to the wall."

They worked out for the rest of the day.

That night Ender went for the first time to the commanders' mess hall. No one was allowed there until he had won at least one battle, and Ender was the youngest commander ever to make it. There was no great stir when he came in. But when some of the other boys saw the Dragon on his breast pocket, they stared at him openly, and by the time he got his tray and sat at an empty table, the entire room was silent, with the other commanders watching him. Intensely self-conscious, Ender wondered how they all knew, and why they all looked so hostile.

Then he looked above the door he had just come through. There was a huge scoreboard across the entire wall. It showed the win/loss record for the commander of every army; that day's battles were lit in red. Only four of them. The other three winners had barely made it—the best of them had only two men whole and eleven mobile at the end of the game. Dragon Army's score of thirty-eight mobile was embarrassingly better.

Other new commanders had been admitted to the commanders' mess hall with cheers and congratulations. Other new commanders hadn't won thirty-eight to zero.

Ender looked for Rabbit Army on the scoreboard. He was surprised to find that Carn Carby's score to date was eight wins and three losses. Was he

that good? Or had he only fought against inferior
armies? Whichever, there was still a zero in Carn's
mobile and whole columns, and Ender looked down
from the scoreboard grinning. No one smiled back,
and Ender knew that they were afraid of him, which
meant that they would hate him, which meant that
anyone who went into battle against Dragon Army
would be scared and angry and less competent. Ender
looked for Carn Carby in the crowd, and found him
not too far away. He stared at Carby until one of the
other boys nudged the Rabbit commander and
pointed to Ender. Ender smiled again and waved
slightly. Carby turned red, and Ender, satisfied,
leaned over his dinner and began to eat.

At the end of the week Dragon Army had
fought seven battles in seven days. The score stood 7
wins and 0 losses. Ender had never had more than five
boys frozen in any game. It was no longer possible for
the other commanders to ignore Ender. A few of them
sat with him and quietly conversed about game strategies that Ender's opponents had used. Other much
larger groups were talking with the commanders that
Ender had defeated, trying to find out what Ender
had done to beat them.

In the middle of the meal the teacher door
opened and the groups fell silent as Lieutenant Anderson stepped in and looked over the group. When he
located Ender he strode quickly across the room and
whispered in Ender's ear. Ender nodded, finished his
glass of water, and left with the lieutenant. On the
way out, Anderson handed a slip of paper to one of
the older boys. The room became very noisy with conversation as Anderson and Ender left.

Ender was escorted down corridors he had
never seen before. They didn't have the blue glow of
the soldier corridors. Most were wood paneled, and

the floors were carpeted. The doors were wood, with nameplates on them, and they stopped at one that said "Captain Graff, supervisor." Anderson knocked softly, and a low voice said, "Come in."

They went in. Captain Graff was seated behind a desk, his hands folded across his pot belly. He nodded, and Anderson sat. Ender also sat down. Graff cleared his throat and spoke.

"Seven days since your first battle, Ender."

Ender did not reply.

"Won seven battles, one every day."

Ender nodded.

"Scores unusually high, too."

Ender blinked.

"Why?" Graff asked him.

Ender glanced at Anderson, and then spoke to the captain behind the desk. "Two new tactics, sir. Legs doubled up as a shield, so that a flash doesn't immobilize. Jackknife takeoffs from the walls. Superior strategy, as Lieutenant Anderson taught, think places, not spaces. Five toons of eight instead of four of ten. Incompetent opponents. Excellent toon leaders, good soldiers."

Graff looked at Ender without expression. Waiting for what, Ender wondered. Lieutenant Anderson spoke up.

"Ender, what's the condition of your army?"

Do they want me to ask for relief? Not a chance, he decided. "A little tired, in peak condition, morale high, learning fast. Anxious for the next battle."

Anderson looked at Graff. Graff shrugged slightly and turned to Ender.

"Is there anything you want to know?"

Ender held his hands loosely in his lap. "When are you going to put us up against a good army?"

Graff's laughter rang in the room, and when it stopped, Graff handed a piece of paper to Ender.

"Now," the captain said, and Ender read the paper: "Dragon Army against Leopard Army, Ender Wiggins and Pol Slattery, 2000."

Ender looked up at Captain Graff. "That's ten minutes from now, sir."

Graff smiled. "Better hurry, then, boy."

As Ender left he realized Pol Slattery was the boy who had been handed his orders as Ender left the mess hall.

He got to his army five minutes later. Three toon leaders were already undressed and lying naked on their beds. He sent them all flying down the corridors to rouse their toons, and gathered up their suits himself. When all his boys were assembled in the corridor, most of them still getting dressed, Ender spoke to them.

"This one's hot and there's no time. We'll be late to the door, and the enemy'll be deployed right outside our gate. Ambush, and I've never heard of it happening before. So we'll take our time at the door. A and B toons, keep your belts loose, and give your flashers to the leaders and seconds of the other toons."

Puzzled, his soldiers complied. By then all were dressed, and Ender led them at a trot to the gate. When they reached it the forcefield was already on one-way, and some of his soldiers were panting. They had had one battle that day and a full workout. They were tired.

Ender stopped at the entrance and looked at the placement of the enemy soldiers. Some of them were grouped not more than twenty feet out from the gate. There was no grid, there were no stars. A big empty space. Where were most of the enemy soldiers? There should have been thirty more.

"They're flat against this wall," Ender said, "where we can't see them."

He took A and B toons and made them kneel,

their hands on their hips. Then he flashed them, so that their bodies were frozen rigid.

"You're shields," Ender said, and then had boys from C and D kneel on their legs and hook both arms under the frozen boys' belts. Each boy was holding two flashers. Then Ender and the members of E toon picked up the duos, three at a time, and threw them out the door.

Of course, the enemy opened fire immediately. But they mainly hit the boys who were already flashed, and in a few moments pandemonium broke out in the battleroom. All the soldiers of Leopard Army were easy targets as they lay pressed flat against the wall or floated, unprotected, in the middle of the battleroom; and Ender's soldiers, armed with two flashers each, carved them up easily. Pol Slattery reacted quickly, ordering his men away from the wall, but not quickly enough—only a few were able to move, and they were flashed before they could get a quarter of the way across the battleroom.

When the battle was over Dragon Army had only twelve boys whole, the lowest score they had ever had. But Ender was satisfied. And during the ritual of surrender Pol Slattery broke form by shaking hands and asking, "Why did you wait so long getting out of the gate?"

Ender glanced at Anderson, who was floating nearby. "I was informed late," he said. "It was an ambush."

Slattery grinned, and gripped Ender's hand again. "Good game."

Ender didn't smile at Anderson this time. He knew that now the games would be arranged against him, to even up the odds. He didn't like it.

It was 2150, nearly time for lights out, when Ender knocked at the door of the room shared by

Bean and three other soldiers. One of the others opened the door, then stepped back and held it wide. Ender stood for a moment, then asked if he could come in. They answered, of course, of course, come in, and he walked to the upper bunk, where Bean had set down his book and was leaning on one elbow to look at Ender.

"Bean, can you give me twenty minutes?"

"Near lights out," Bean answered.

"My room," Ender answered. "I'll cover for you."

Bean sat up and slid off his bed. Together he and Ender padded silently down the corridor to Ender's room. Bean entered first, and Ender closed the door behind them.

"Sit down," Ender said, and they both sat on the edge of the bed, looking at each other.

"Remember four weeks ago, Bean? When you told me to make you a toon leader?"

"Yeah."

"I've made five toon leaders since then, haven't I? And none of them was you."

Bean looked at him calmly.

"Was I right?" Ender asked.

"Yes, sir," Bean answered.

Ender nodded. "How have you done in these battles?"

Bean cocked his head to one side. "I've never been immobilized, sir, and I've immobilized forty-three of the enemy. I've obeyed orders quickly, and I've commanded a squad in mop-up and never lost a soldier."

"Then you'll understand this." Ender paused, then decided to back up and say something else first.

"You know you're early, Bean, by a good half year. I was, too, and I've been made a commander six months early. Now they've put me into battles after only three weeks of training with my army. They've given me eight battles in seven days. I've already had more battles than boys who were made commander four months ago. I've won more battles than many who've been commanders for a year. And then tonight. You know what happened tonight."

Bean nodded. "They told you late."

"I don't know what the teachers are doing. But my army is getting tired, and I'm getting tired, and now they're changing the rules of the game. You see, Bean, I've looked in the old charts. No one has ever destroyed so many enemies and kept so many of his own soldiers whole in the history of the game. I'm unique—and I'm getting unique treatment."

Bean smiled. "You're the best, Ender."

Ender shook his head. "Maybe. But it was no accident that I got the soldiers I got. My worst soldier could be a toon leader in another army. I've got the best. They've loaded things my way—but now they're loading it all against me. I don't know why. But I know I have to be ready for it. I need your help."

"Why mine?"

"Because even though there are some better soldiers than you in Dragon Army—not many, but some—there's nobody who can think better and faster than you." Bean said nothing. They both knew it was true.

Ender continued, "I need to be ready, but I can't retrain the whole army. So I'm going to cut every toon down by one, including you. With four others you'll be a special squad under me. And you'll learn to do some new things. Most of the time you'll be in the regular toons just like you are now. But when I need you. See?"

Bean smiled and nodded. "That's right, that's good, can I pick them myself?"

"One from each toon except your own, and you can't take any toon leaders."

"What do you want us to do?"

"Bean, I don't know. I don't know what they'll throw at us. What would you do if suddenly our flashers didn't work, and the enemy's did? What would you do if we had to face two armies at once? The only thing I know is—there may be a game where we don't even try for score. Where we just go for the enemy's gate. That's when the battle is technically won—four helmets at the corners of the gate. I want you ready to do that any time I call for it. Got it? You take them for two hours a day during regular workout. Then you and I and your soldiers, we'll work at night after dinner."

"We'll get tired."

"I have a feeling we don't know what tired is." Ender reached out and took Bean's hand, and gripped it. "Even when it's rigged against us, Bean. We'll win."

Bean left in silence and padded down the corridor.

Dragon Army wasn't the only army working out after hours now. The other commanders had finally realized they had some catching up to do. From early morning to lights out soldiers all over Training and Command Center, none of them over fourteen years old, were learning to jackknife off walls and use each other as living shields.

But while other commanders mastered the techniques that Ender had used to defeat them, Ender and Bean worked on solutions to problems that had never come up.

There were still battles every day, but for a while they were normal, with grids and stars and sudden plunges through the gate. And after the battles,

Ender and Bean and four other soldiers would leave the main group and practice strange maneuvers. Attacks without flashers, using feet to physically disarm or disorient an enemy. Using four frozen soldiers to reverse the enemy's gate in less than two seconds. And one day Bean came to workout with a 300-meter cord.

"What's that for?"

"I don't know yet." Absently Bean spun one end of the cord. It wasn't more than an eighth of an inch thick, but it could have lifted ten adults without breaking.

"Where did you get it?"

"Commissary. They asked what for. I said to practice tying knots."

Bean tied a loop in the end of the rope and slid it over his shoulders.

"Here, you two, hang on to the wall here. Now don't let go of the rope. Give me about fifty yards of slack." They complied, and Bean moved about ten feet from them along the wall. As soon as he was sure they were ready, he jackknifed off the wall and flew straight out, fifty yards. Then the rope snapped taut. It was so fine that it was virtually invisible, but it was strong enough to force Bean to veer off at almost a right angle. It happened so suddenly that he had inscribed a perfect arc and hit the wall hard before most of the other soldiers knew what had happened. Bean did a perfect rebound and drifted quickly back to where Ender and the others waited for him.

Many of the soldiers in the five regular squads hadn't noticed the rope, and were demanding to know how it was done. It was impossible to change direction that abruptly in nullo. Bean just laughed.

"Wait till the next game without a grid! They'll never know what hit them."

They never did. The next game was only two hours later, but Bean and two others had become pretty good at aiming and shooting while they flew at ridiculous speeds at the end of the rope. The slip of paper was delivered, and Dragon Army trotted off to the gate, to battle with Griffin Army. Bean coiled the rope all the way.

When the gate opened, all they could see was a large brown star only fifteen feet away, completely blocking their view of the enemy's gate.

Ender didn't pause. "Bean, give yourself fifty feet of rope and go around the star." Bean and his four soldiers dropped through the gate and in a moment Bean was launched sideways away from the star. The rope snapped taut, and Bean flew forward. As the rope was stopped by each edge of the star in turn, his arc became tighter and his speed greater, until when he hit the wall only a few feet away from the gate he was barely able to control his rebound to end up behind the star. But he immediately moved all his arms and legs so that those waiting inside the gate would know that the enemy hadn't flashed him anywhere.

Ender dropped through the gate, and Bean quickly told him how Griffin Army was situated. "They've got two squares of stars, all the way around the gate. All their soldiers are under cover, and there's no way to hit any of them until we're clear to the bottom wall. Even with shields, we'd get there at half strength and we wouldn't have a chance."

"They moving?" Ender asked.

"Do they need to?"

"I would." Ender thought for a moment. "This one's tough. We'll go for the gate, Bean."

Griffin Army began to call out to them.

"Hey, is anybody there!"

"Wake up, there's a war on!"

"We wanna join the picnic!"

They were still calling when Ender's army came out from behind their star with a shield of fourteen frozen soldiers. William Bee, Griffin Army's commander, waited patiently as the screen approached, his men waiting at the fringes of their stars for the moment when whatever was behind the screen became visible. About ten yards away the screen suddenly exploded as the soldiers behind it shoved the screen north. The momentum carried them south twice as fast, and at the same moment the rest of Dragon Army burst from behind their star at the opposite end of the room, firing rapidly.

William Bee's boys joined battle immediately, of course, but William Bee was far more interested in what had been left behind when the shield disappeared. A formation of four frozen Dragon Army soldiers was moving headfirst toward the Griffin Army gate, held together by another frozen soldier whose feet and hands were hooked through their belts. A sixth soldier hung to his waist and trailed like the tail of a kite. Griffin Army was winning the battle easily, and William Bee concentrated on the formation as it approached the gate. Suddenly the soldier trailing in back moved—he wasn't frozen at all! And even though William Bee flashed him immediately, the damage was done. The formation drifted to the Griffin Army gate, and their helmets touched all four corners simultaneously. A buzzer sounded, the gate reversed, and the frozen soldier in the middle was carried by momentum right through the gate. All the flashers stopped working, and the game was over.

The teachergate opened and Lieutenant Anderson came in. Anderson stopped himself with a slight movement of his hands when he reached the center of the battleroom. "Ender," he called, breaking protocol. One of the frozen Dragon soldiers near the south wall tried to call through jaws that were clamped shut by the suit. Anderson drifted to him and unfroze him.

Ender was smiling.

"I beat you again, sir," Ender said.

Anderson didn't smile. "That's nonsense, Ender," Anderson said softly. "Your battle was with William Bee of Griffin Army."

Ender raised an eyebrow.

"After that maneuver," Anderson said, "the rules are being revised to require that all of the enemy's soldiers must be immobilized before the gate can be reversed."

"That's all right," Ender said. "It could only work once, anyway." Anderson nodded, and was turning away when Ender added, "Is there going to be a new rule that armies be given equal positions to fight from?"

Anderson turned back around. "If you're in one of the positions, Ender, you can hardly call them equal, whatever they are."

William Bee counted carefully and wondered how in the world he had lost when not one of his soldiers had been flashed and only four of Ender's soldiers were even mobile.

And that night as Ender came into the commanders' mess hall, he was greeted with applause and cheers, and his table was crowded with respectful commanders, many of them two or three years older than he was. He was friendly, but while he ate he wondered what the teachers would do to him in his next battle. He didn't need to worry. His next two battles were easy victories, and after that he never saw the battleroom again.

It was 2100 and Ender was a little irritated to hear someone knock at his door. His army was exhausted, and he had ordered them all to be in bed after 2030. The last two days had been regular battles, and Ender was expecting the worst in the morning.

It was Bean. He came in sheepishly, and saluted.

Ender returned his salute and snapped, "Bean, I wanted everybody in bed."

Bean nodded but didn't leave. Ender considered ordering him out. But as he looked at Bean it occurred to him for the first time in weeks just how young Bean was. He had turned eight a week before, and he was still small and—no, Ender thought, he wasn't young. Nobody was young. Bean had been in battle, and with a whole army depending on him he had come through and won. And even though he was small, Ender could never think of him as young again.

Ender shrugged and Bean came over and sat on the edge of the bed. The younger boy looked at his hands for a while, and finally Ender grew impatient and asked, "Well, what is it?"

"I'm transferred. Got orders just a few minutes ago."

Ender closed his eyes for a moment. "I knew they'd pull something new. Now they're taking— where are you going?"

"Rabbit Army."

"How can they put you under an idiot like Carn Carby!"

"Carn was graduated. Support squads."

Ender looked up. "Well, who's commanding Rabbit then?"

Bean held his hands out helplessly.

"Me," he said.

Ender nodded, and then smiled. "Of course. After all, you're only four years younger than the regular age."

"It isn't funny," Bean said. "I don't know what's going on here. First all the changes in the game. And now this. I wasn't the only one transferred, either, Ender. Ren, Peder, Brian, Wins, Younger. All commanders now."

Ender stood up angrily and strode to the wall. "Every damn toon leader I've got!" he said, and whirled to face Bean. "If they're going to break up my army, Bean, why did they bother making me a commander at all?"

Bean shook his head. "I don't know. You're the best, Ender. Nobody's ever done what you've done. Nineteen battles in fifteen days, sir, and you won every one of them, no matter what they did to you."

"And now you and the others are commanders. You know every trick I've got, I trained you, and who am I supposed to replace you with? Are they going to stick me with six greenohs?"

"It stinks, Ender, but you know that if they gave you five crippled midgets and armed you with a roll of toilet paper you'd win."

They both laughed, and then they noticed that the door was open.

Lieutenant Anderson stepped in. He was followed by Captain Graff.

"Ender Wiggins," Graff said, holding his hands across his stomach.

"Yes sir," Ender answered.

"Orders."

Anderson extended a slip of paper. Ender read it quickly, then crumpled it, still looking at the air where the paper had been. After a few moments he asked, "Can I tell my army?"

"They'll find out," Graff answered. "It's better not to talk to them after orders. It makes it easier."

"For you or for me?" Ender asked. He didn't wait for an answer. He turned quickly to Bean, took his hand for a moment, and then headed for the door.

"Wait," Bean said. "Where are you going? Tactical or Support School?"

"Command School," Ender answered, and then he was gone and Anderson closed the door.

Command School, Bean thought. Nobody went to Command School until they had gone through three years of Tactical. But then, nobody went to Tactical until they had been through at least five years of Battle School. Ender had only had three.

The system was breaking up. No doubt about it, Bean thought. Either somebody at the top was going crazy, or something was going wrong with the war—the real war, the one they were training to fight in. Why else would they break down the training system, advance somebody—even somebody as good as Ender—straight to Command School? Why else would they ever have an eight-year-old greenoh like Bean command an army?

Bean wondered about it for a long time, and then he finally lay down on Ender's bed and realized that he'd never see Ender again, probably. For some reason that made him want to cry. But he didn't cry, of course. Training in the preschools had taught him how to force down emotions like that. He remembered how his first teacher, when he was three, would have been upset to see his lip quivering and his eyes full of tears.

Bean went through the relaxing routine until he didn't feel like crying anymore. Then he drifted off to sleep. His hand was near his mouth. It lay on his pillow hesitantly, as if Bean couldn't decide whether to bite his nails or suck on his fingertips. His forehead was creased and furrowed. His breathing was quick and light. He was a soldier, and if anyone had asked him what he wanted to be when he grew up, he wouldn't have known what they meant.

There's a war on, they said, and that was excuse enough for all the hurry in the world. They said it like a password and flashed a little card at every ticket counter and customs check and guard station. It got them to the head of every line.

Ender Wiggins was rushed from place to place so quickly he had no time to examine anything. But he did see trees for the first time. He saw men who were not in uniform. He saw women. He saw strange animals that didn't speak, but that followed docilely behind women and small children. He saw suitcases and conveyor belts and signs that said words he had never heard of. He would have asked someone what the words meant, except that purpose and authority surrounded him in the persons of four very high officers who never spoke to each other and never spoke to him.

Ender Wiggins was a stranger to the world he was being trained to save. He did not remember ever leaving Battle School before. His earliest memories were of childish war games under the direction of a teacher, of meals with other boys in the grey and green uniforms of the armed forces of his world. He did not know that the grey represented the sky and the green represented the great forests of his planet. All he knew of the world was from vague references to "outside."

And before he could make any sense of the strange world he was seeing for the first time, they enclosed him again within the shell of the military, where nobody had to say There's a war on anymore because no one within the shell of the military forgot it for a single instant of a single day.

They put him in a spaceship and launched him to a large artificial satellite that circled the world.

This space station was called Command School. It held the ansible.

On his first day Ender Wiggins was taught

about the ansible and what it meant to warfare. It meant that even though the starships of today's battles were launched a hundred years ago, the commanders of the starships were men of today, who used the ansible to send messages to the computers and the few men on each ship. The ansible sent words as they were spoken, orders as they were made. Battleplans as they were fought. Light was a pedestrian.

For two months Ender Wiggins didn't meet a single person. They came to him namelessly, taught him what they knew, and left him to other teachers. He had no time to miss his friends at Battle School. He only had time to learn how to operate the simulator, which flashed battle patterns around him as if he were in a starship at the center of the battle. How to command mock ships in mock battles by manipulating the keys on the simulator and speaking words into the ansible. How to recognize instantly every enemy ship and the weapons it carried by the pattern that the simulator showed. How to transfer all that he learned in the nullo battles at Battle School to the starship battles at Command School.

He had thought the game was taken seriously before. Here they hurried him through every step, were angry and worried beyond reason every time he forgot something or made a mistake. But he worked as he had always worked, and learned as he had always learned. After a while he didn't make any more mistakes. He used the simulator as if it were a part of himself. Then they stopped being worried and gave him a teacher.

Maezr Rackham was sitting cross-legged on the floor when Ender awoke. He said nothing as Ender got up and showered and dressed, and Ender did not bother to ask him anything. He had long since learned that when something unusual was going on, he would often find out more information faster by waiting than by asking.

Maezr still hadn't spoken when Ender was ready and went to the door to leave the room. The door didn't open. Ender turned to face the man sitting on the floor. Maezr was at least forty, which made him the oldest man Ender had ever seen close up. He had a day's growth of black and white whiskers that grizzled his face only slightly less than his close-cut hair. His face sagged a little and his eyes were surrounded by creases and lines. He looked at Ender without interest.

Ender turned back to the door and tried again to open it.

"All right," he said, giving up. "Why's the door locked?"

Maezr continued to look at him blankly.

Ender became impatient. "I'm going to be late. If I'm not supposed to be there until later, then tell me so I can go back to bed." No answer. "Is it a guessing game?" Ender asked. No answer. Ender decided that maybe the man was trying to make him angry, so he went through a relaxing exercise as he leaned on the door, and soon he was calm again. Maezr didn't take his eyes off Ender.

For the next two hours the silence endured, Maezr watching Ender constantly, Ender trying to pretend he didn't notice the old man. The boy became more and more nervous, and finally ended up walking from one end of the room to the other in a sporadic pattern.

He walked by Maezr as he had several times before, and Maezr's hand shot out and pushed Ender's left leg into his right in the middle of a step. Ender fell flat on the floor.

He leaped to his feet immediately, furious. He

found Maezr sitting calmly, cross-legged, as if he had never moved. Ender stood poised to fight. But the other's immobility made it impossible for Ender to attack, and he found himself wondering if he had only imagined the old man's hand tripping him up.

The pacing continued for another hour, with Ender Wiggins trying the door every now and then. At last he gave up and took off his uniform and walked to his bed.

As he leaned over to pull the covers back, he felt a hand jab roughly between his thighs and another hand grab his hair. In a moment he had been turned upside down. His face and shoulders were being pressed into the floor by the old man's knee, while his back was excruciatingly bent and his legs were pinioned by Maezr's arm. Ender was helpless to use his arms, and he couldn't bend his back to gain slack so he could use his legs. In less than two seconds the old man had completely defeated Ender Wiggins.

"All right," Ender gasped. "You win."

Maezr's knee thrust painfully downward.

"Since when," Maezr asked in a soft, rasping voice, "do you have to tell the enemy when he has won?"

Ender remained silent.

"I surprised you once, Ender Wiggins. Why didn't you destroy me immediately afterward? Just because I looked peaceful? You turned your back on me. Stupid. You have learned nothing. You have never had a teacher."

Ender was angry now. "I've had too many damned teachers, how was I supposed to know you'd turn out to be a —" Ender hunted for a word. Maezr supplied one.

"An enemy, Ender Wiggins," Maezr whispered. "I am your enemy, the first one you've ever had who was smarter than you. There is no teacher but the enemy, Ender Wiggins. No one but the enemy will ever tell you what the enemy is going to do. No one but the enemy will ever teach you how to destroy and conquer. I am your enemy, from now on. From now on I am your teacher."

Then Maezr let Ender's legs fall to the floor. Because the old man still held Ender's head to the floor, the boy couldn't use his arms to compensate, and his legs hit the plastic surface with a loud crack and a sickening pain that made Ender wince. Then Maezr stood and let Ender rise.

Slowly the boy pulled his legs under him, with a faint groan of pain, and he knelt on all fours for a moment, recovering. Then his right arm flashed out. Maezr quickly danced back and Ender's hand closed on air as his teacher's foot shot forward to catch Ender on the chin.

Ender's chin wasn't there. He was lying flat on his back, spinning on the floor, and during the moment that Maezr was off balance from his kick Ender's feet smashed into Maezr's other leg. The old man fell on the ground in a heap.

What seemed to be a heap was really a hornet's nest. Ender couldn't find an arm or a leg that held still long enough to be grabbed, and in the meantime blows were landing on his back and arms. Ender was smaller—he couldn't reach past the old man's flailing limbs.

So he leaped back out of the way and stood poised near the door.

The old man stopped thrashing about and sat up, cross-legged again, laughing. "Better, this time, boy. But slow. You will have to be better with a fleet than you are with your body or no one will be safe with you in command. Lesson learned?"

Ender nodded slowly.

Maezr smiled. "Good. Then we'll never have

such a battle again. All the rest with the simulator. I will program your battles, I will devise the strategy of your enemy, and you will learn to be quick and discover what tricks the enemy has for you. Remember, boy. From now on the enemy is more clever than you. From now on the enemy is stronger than you. From now on you are always about to lose."

Then Maezr's face became serious again. "You will be about to lose, Ender, but you will win. You will learn to defeat the enemy. He will teach you how."

Maezr got up and walked toward the door. Ender stepped back out of the way. As the old man touched the handle of the door, Ender leaped into the air and kicked Maezr in the small of the back with both feet. He hit hard enough that he rebounded onto his feet, as Maezr cried out and collapsed on the floor.

Maezr got up slowly, holding on to the door handle, his face contorted with pain. He seemed disabled, but Ender didn't trust him. He waited warily. And yet in spite of his suspicion he was caught off guard by Maezr's speed. In a moment he found himself on the floor near the opposite wall, his nose and lip bleeding where his face had hit the bed. He was able to turn enough to see Maezr open the door and leave. The old man was limping and walking slowly.

Ender smiled in spite of the pain, then rolled over onto his back and laughed until his mouth filled with blood and he started to gag. Then he got up and painfully made his way to the bed. He lay down and in a few minutes a medic came and took care of his injuries.

As the drug had its effect and Ender drifted off to sleep he remembered the way Maezr limped out of his room and laughed again. He was still laughing softly as his mind went blank and the medic pulled the blanket over him and snapped off the light. He

slept until pain woke him in the morning. He
dreamed of defeating Maezr.

The next day Ender went to the simulator
room with his nose bandaged and his lip still puffy.
Maezr was not there. Instead, a captain who had
worked with him before showed him an addition that
had been made. The captain pointed to a tube with a
loop at one end. "Radio. Primitive, I know, but it
loops over your ear and we tuck the other end into
your mouth like this."

"Watch it," Ender said as the captain pushed
the end of the tube into his swollen lip.

"Sorry. Now you just talk."

"Good. Who to?"

The captain smiled. "Ask and see."

Ender shrugged and turned to the simulator.
As he did a voice reverberated through his skull. It
was too loud for him to understand, and he ripped the
radio off his ear.

"What are you trying to do, make me deaf?"

The captain shook his head and turned a dial
on a small box on a nearby table. Ender put the radio
back on.

"Commander," the radio said in a familiar
voice.

Ender answered, "Yes."

"Instructions, sir?"

The voice was definitely familiar. "Bean?"
Ender asked.

"Yes, sir."

"Bean, this is Ender."

Silence. And then a burst of laughter from the
other side. Then six or seven more voices laughing,
and Ender waited for silence to return. When it did,
he asked, "Who else?"

A few voices spoke at once, but Bean drowned

them out. "Me, I'm Bean, and Peder, Wins, Younger, Lee, and Vlad."

Ender thought for a moment. Then he asked what the hell was going on. They laughed again.

"They can't break up the group," Bean said. "We were commanders for maybe two weeks, and here we are at Command School, training with the simulator, and all of a sudden they told us we were going to form a fleet with a new commander. And that's you."

Ender smiled. "Are you boys any good?"

"If we aren't, you'll let us know."

Ender chuckled a little. "Might work out. A fleet."

For the next ten days Ender trained his toon leaders until they could maneuver their ships like precision dancers. It was like being back in the battleroom again, except that now Ender could always see everything, and could speak to his toon leaders and change their orders at any time.

One day as Ender sat down at the control board and switched on the simulator, harsh green lights appeared in the space—the enemy.

"This is it," Ender said. "X, Y, bullet, C, D, reserve screen, E, south loop, Bean, angle north."

The enemy was grouped in a globe, and outnumbered Ender two to one. Half of Ender's force was grouped in a tight, bulletlike formation, with the rest in a flat circular screen—except for a tiny force under Bean that moved off the simulator, heading behind the enemy's formation. Ender quickly learned the enemy's strategy: whenever Ender's bullet formation came close, the enemy would give way, hoping to draw Ender inside the globe where he would be surrounded. So Ender obligingly fell into the trap, bringing his bullet to the center of the globe.

The enemy began to contract slowly, not wanting to come within range until all their weapons could be brought to bear at once. Then Ender began to work in earnest. His reserve screen approached the outside of the globe, and the enemy began to concentrate his forces there. Then Bean's force appeared on the opposite side, and the enemy again deployed ships on that side.

Which left most of the globe only thinly defended. Ender's bullet attacked, and since at the point of attack it outnumbered the enemy overwhelmingly, he tore a hole in the formation. The enemy reacted to try to plug the gap, but in the confusion the reserve force and Bean's small force attacked simultaneously, while the bullet moved to another part of the globe. In a few more minutes the formation was shattered, most of the enemy ships destroyed, and the few survivors rushing away as fast as they could go.

Ender switched the simulator off. All the lights faded. Maezr was standing beside Ender, his hands in his pockets, his body tense. Ender looked up at him.

"I thought you said the enemy would be smart," Ender said.

Maezr's face remained expressionless. "What did you learn?"

"I learned that a sphere only works if your enemy's a fool. He had his forces so spread out that I outnumbered him whenever I engaged him."

"And?"

"And," Ender said, "you can't stay committed to one pattern. It makes you too easy to predict."

"Is that all?" Maezr asked quietly.

Ender took off his radio. "The enemy could have defeated me by breaking the sphere earlier."

Maezr nodded. "You had an unfair advantage."

Ender looked up at him coldly. "I was outnumbered two to one."

Maezr shook his head. "You have the ansible.

The enemy doesn't. We include that in the mock battles. Their messages travel at the speed of light."

Ender glanced toward the simulator. "Is there enough space to make a difference?"

"Don't you know?" Maezr asked. "None of the ships was ever closer than thirty thousand kilometers to any other."

Ender tried to figure the size of the enemy's sphere. Astronomy was beyond him. But now his curiosity was stirred.

"What kind of weapons are on those ships? To be able to strike so fast?"

Maezr shook his head. "The science is too much for you. You'd have to study many more years than you've lived to understand even the basics. All you need to know is that the weapons work."

"Why do we have to come so close to be in range?"

"The ships are all protected by forcefields. A certain distance away the weapons are weaker and can't get through. Closer in the weapons are stronger than the shields. But the computers take care of all that. They're constantly firing in any direction that won't hurt one of our ships. The computers pick targets, aim; they do all the detail work. You just tell them when and get them in a position to win. All right?"

"No." Ender twisted the tube of the radio around his fingers. "I have to know how the weapons work."

"I told you, it would take—"

"I can't command a fleet—not even on the simulator—unless I know." Ender waited a moment, then added, "Just the rough idea."

Maezr stood up and walked a few steps away. "All right, Ender. It won't make any sense, but I'll try. As simply as I can." He shoved his hands into his pockets. "It's this way, Ender. Everything is made up of atoms, little particles so small you can't see them with your eyes. These atoms, there are only a few different types, and they're all made up of even smaller particles that are pretty much the same. These atoms can be broken, so that they stop being atoms. So that this metal doesn't hold together anymore. Or the plastic floor. Or your body. Or even the air. They just seem to disappear, if you break the atoms. All that's left is the pieces. And they fly around and break more atoms. The weapons on the ships set up an area where it's impossible for atoms of anything to stay together. They all break down. So things in that area—they disappear."

Ender nodded. "You're right, I don't understand it. Can it be blocked?"

"No. But it gets wider and weaker the farther it goes from the ship, so that after a while a forcefield will block it. OK? And to make it strong at all, it has to be focused, so that a ship can only fire effectively in maybe three or four directions at once."

Ender nodded again, but he didn't really understand, not well enough. "If the pieces of the broken atoms go breaking more atoms, why doesn't it just make everything disappear?"

"Space. Those thousands of kilometers between the ships, they're empty. Almost no atoms. The pieces don't hit anything, and when they finally do hit something, they're so spread out they can't do any harm." Maezr cocked his head quizzically. "Anything else you need to know?"

"Do the weapons on the ships—do they work against anything besides ships?"

Maezr moved in close to Ender and said firmly, "We only use them against ships. Never anything else.

If we used them against anything else, the enemy would use them against us. Got it?"

Maezr walked away, and was nearly out the door when Ender called to him.

"I don't know your name yet," Ender said blandly.

"Maezr Rackham."

"Maezr Rackham," Ender said, "I defeated you."

Maezr laughed.

"Ender, you weren't fighting me today," he said. "You were fighting the stupidest computer in the Command School, set on a ten-year-old program. You don't think I'd use a sphere, do you?" He shook his head. "Ender, my dear little fellow, when you fight me you'll know it. Because you'll lose." And Maezr left the room.

Ender still practiced ten hours a day with his toon leaders. He never saw them, though, only heard their voices on the radio. Battles came every two or three days. The enemy had something new every time, something harder—but Ender coped with it. And won every time. And after every battle Maezr would point out mistakes and show Ender that he had really lost. Maezr only let Ender finish so that he would learn to handle the end of the game.

Until finally Maezr came in and solemnly shook Ender's hand and said, "That, boy, was a good battle."

Because the praise was so long in coming, it pleased Ender more than praise had ever pleased him before. And because it was so condescending, he resented it.

"So from now on," Maezr said, "we can give you hard ones."

From then on Ender's life was a slow nervous breakdown.

He began fighting two battles a day, with problems that steadily grew more difficult. He had been trained in nothing but the game all his life, but now the game began to consume him. He woke in the morning with new strategies for the simulator and went fitfully to sleep at night with the mistakes of the day preying on him. Sometimes he would wake up in the middle of the night crying for a reason he didn't remember. Sometimes he woke with his knuckles bloody from biting them. But every day he went impassively to the simulator and drilled his toon leaders until the battles, and drilled his toon leaders after the battles, and endured and studied the harsh criticism that Maezr Rackham piled on him. He noted that Rackham perversely criticized him more after his hardest battles. He noted that every time he thought of a new strategy the enemy was using it within a few days. And he noted that while his fleet always stayed the same size, the enemy increased in numbers every day.

He asked his teacher.

"We are showing you what it will be like when you really command. The ratios of enemy to us."

"Why does the enemy always outnumber us?"

Maezr bowed his grey head for a moment, as if deciding whether to answer. Finally he looked up and reached out his hand and touched Ender on the shoulder. "I will tell you, even though the information is secret. You see, the enemy attacked us first. He had good reason to attack us, but that is a matter for politicians, and whether the fault was ours or his, we could not let him win. So when the enemy came to our worlds, we fought back, hard, and spent the finest of our young men in the fleets. But we won, and the enemy retreated."

Maezr smiled ruefully. "But the enemy was not through, boy. The enemy would never be through. They came again, with more numbers, and it was harder to beat them. And another generation of young men was spent. Only a few survived. So we came up with a plan—the big men came up with the plan. We knew that we had to destroy the enemy once and for all, totally, eliminate his ability to make war against us. To do that we had to go to his home worlds—his home world, really, since the enemy's empire is all tied to his capital world."

"And so?" Ender asked.

"And so we made a fleet. We made more ships than the enemy ever had. We made a hundred ships for every ship he had sent against us. And we launched them against his twenty-eight worlds. They started leaving a hundred years ago. And they carried on them the ansible, and only a few men. So that someday a commander could sit on a planet somewhere far from the battle and command the fleet. So that our best minds would not be destroyed by the enemy."

Ender's question had still not been answered. "Why do they outnumber us?"

Maezr laughed. "Because it took a hundred years for our ships to get there. They've had a hundred years to prepare for us. They'd be fools, don't you think, boy, if they waited in old tugboats to defend their harbors. They have new ships, great ships, hundreds of ships. All we have is the ansible, that and the fact that they have to put a commander with every fleet, and when they lose—and they will lose—they lose one of their best minds every time."

Ender started to ask another question.

"No more, Ender Wiggins. I've told you more than you ought to know as it is."

Ender stood angrily and turned away. "I have a right to know. Do you think this can go on forever, pushing me through one school and another and never telling me what my life is for? You use me and the others as a tool, someday we'll command your ships, someday maybe we'll save your lives, but I'm not a computer, and I have to *know!*"

"Ask me a question, then, boy," Maezr said, "and if I can answer, I will."

"If you use your best minds to command the fleets, and you never lose any, then what do you need me for? Who am I replacing, if they're all still there?"

Maezr shook his head. "I can't tell you the answer to that, Ender. Be content that we will need you, soon. It's late. Go to bed. You have a battle in the morning."

Ender walked out of the simulator room. But when Maezr left by the same door a few moments later, the boy was waiting in the hall.

"All right, boy," Maezr said impatiently, "what is it? I don't have all night and you need to sleep."

Ender wasn't sure what his question was, but Maezr waited. Finally Ender asked softly, "Do they live?"

"Does who live?"

"The other commanders. The ones now. And before me."

Maezr snorted. "Live. Of course they live. He wonders if they live." Still chuckling, the old man walked off down the hall. Ender stood in the corridor for a while, but at last he was tired and he went off to bed. They live, he thought. They live, but he can't tell me what happens to them.

That night Ender didn't wake up crying. But he did wake up with blood on his hands.

Months wore on with battles every day, until at last Ender settled into the routine of the destruction of himself. He slept less every night, dreamed more, and he began to have terrible pains in his stomach. They put him on a very bland diet, but soon he didn't even have an appetite for that. "Eat," Maezr said, and Ender would mechanically put food in his mouth. But if nobody told him to eat he didn't eat.

One day as he was drilling his toon leaders the room went black and he woke up on the floor with his face bloody where he had hit the controls.

They put him to bed then, and for three days he was very ill. He remembered seeing faces in his dreams, but they weren't real faces, and he knew it even while he thought he saw them. He thought he saw Bean sometimes, and sometimes he thought he saw Lieutenant Anderson and Captain Graff. And then he woke up and it was only his enemy, Maezr Rackham.

"I'm awake," he said to Maezr.

"So I see," Maezr answered. "Took you long enough. You have a battle today."

So Ender got up and fought the battle and he won it. But there was no second battle that day, and they let him go to bed earlier. His hands were shaking as he undressed.

During the night he thought he felt hands touching him gently, and he dreamed he heard voices saying, "How long can he go on?"

"Long enough."

"So soon?"

"In a few days, then he's through."

"How will he do?"

"Fine. Even today, he was better than ever."

Ender recognized the last voice as Maezr Rackham's. He resented Rackham's intruding even in his sleep.

He woke up and fought another battle and won.

Then he went to bed.

He woke up and won again.

And the next day was his last day in Command School, though he didn't know it. He got up and went to the simulator for the battle.

Maezr was waiting for him. Ender walked slowly into the simulator room. His step was slightly shuffling, and he seemed tired and dull. Maezr frowned.

"Are you awake, boy?" If Ender had been alert, he would have cared more about the concern in his teacher's voice. Instead, he simply went to the controls and sat down. Maezr spoke to him.

"Today's game needs a little explanation, Ender Wiggins. Please turn around and pay strict attention."

Ender turned around, and for the first time he noticed that there were people at the back of the room. He recognized Graff and Anderson from Battle School, and vaguely remembered a few of the men from Command School—teachers for a few hours at some time or another. But most of the people he didn't know at all.

"Who are they?"

Maezr shook his head and answered, "Observers. Every now and then we let observers come in to watch the battle. If you don't want them, we'll send them out."

Ender shrugged. Maezr began his explanation. "Today's game, boy, has a new element. We're staging this battle around a planet. This will complicate things in two ways. The planet isn't large, on the scale we're using, but the ansible can't detect anything on the other side of it—so there's a blind spot. Also, it's against the rules to use weapons against the planet itself. All right?"

"Why, don't the weapons work against planets?"

Maezr answered coldly, "There are rules of war, Ender, that apply even in training games."

Ender shook his head slowly. "Can the planet attack?"

Maezr looked nonplussed for a moment, then smiled. "I guess you'll have to find that one out, boy. And one more thing. Today, Ender, your opponent isn't the computer. I am your enemy today, and today I won't be letting you off so easily. Today is a battle to the end. And I'll use any means I can to defeat you."

Then Maezr was gone, and Ender expressionlessly led his toon leaders through maneuvers. Ender was doing well, of course, but several of the observers shook their heads, and Graff kept clasping and unclasping his hands, crossing and uncrossing his legs. Ender would be slow today, and today Ender couldn't afford to be slow.

A warning buzzer sounded, and Ender cleared the simulator board, waiting for today's game to appear. He felt muddled today, and wondered why people were there watching. Were they going to judge him today? Decide if he was good enough for something else? For another two years of grueling training, another two years of struggling to exceed his best? Ender was twelve. He felt very old. And as he waited for the game to appear, he wished he could simply lose it, lose the battle badly and completely so that they would remove him from the program, punish him however they wanted, he didn't care, just so he could sleep.

Then the enemy formation appeared, and Ender's weariness turned to desperation.

The enemy outnumbered him a thousand to one, the simulator glowed green with them, and Ender knew that he couldn't win.

And the enemy was not stupid. There was no formation that Ender could study and attack. Instead the vast swarms of ships were constantly moving, constantly shifting from one momentary formation to another, so that a space that for one moment was empty was immediately filled with a formidable enemy force. And even though Ender's fleet was the largest he had ever had, there was no place he could deploy it where he would outnumber the enemy long enough to accomplish anything.

And behind the enemy was the planet. The planet, which Maezr had warned him about. What difference did a planet make, when Ender couldn't hope to get near it? Ender waited, waited for the flash of insight that would tell him what to do, how to destroy the enemy. And as he waited, he heard the observers behind him begin to shift in their seats, wondering what Ender was doing, what plan he would follow. And finally it was obvious to everyone that Ender didn't know what to do, that there was nothing to do, and a few of the men at the back of the room made quiet little sounds in their throats.

Then Ender heard Bean's voice in his ear. Bean chuckled and said, "Remember, the enemy's gate is *down*." A few of the other toon leaders laughed, and Ender thought back to the simple games he had played and won in Battle School. They had put him against hopeless odds there, too. And he had beaten them. And he'd be damned if he'd let Maezr Rackham beat him with a cheap trick like outnumbering him a thousand to one. He had won a game in Battle School by going for something the enemy didn't expect, something against the rules—he had won by going against the enemy's gate.

And the enemy's gate was down.

Ender smiled, and realized that if he broke this rule they'd probably kick him out of school, and that way he'd win for sure: He would never have to play a game again.

He whispered into the microphone. His six commanders each took a part of the fleet and launched themselves against the enemy. They pursued erratic courses, darting off in one direction and then another. The enemy immediately stopped his aimless maneuvering and began to group around Ender's six fleets.

Ender took off his microphone, leaned back in his chair, and watched. The observers murmured out loud, now. Ender was doing nothing—he had thrown the game away.

But a pattern began to emerge from the quick confrontations with the enemy. Ender's six groups lost ships constantly as they brushed with each enemy force—but they never stopped for a fight, even when for a moment they could have won a small tactical victory. Instead they continued on their erratic course that led, eventually, down. Toward the enemy planet.

And because of their seemingly random course the enemy didn't realize it until the same time that the observers did. By then it was too late, just as it had been too late for William Bee to stop Ender's soldiers from activating the gate. More of Ender's ships could be hit and destroyed, so that of the six fleets only two were able to get to the planet, and those were decimated. But those tiny groups *did* get through, and they opened fire on the planet.

Ender leaned forward now, anxious to see if his guess would pay off. He half expected a buzzer to sound and the game to be stopped, because he had broken the rule. But he was betting on the accuracy of the simulator. If it could simulate a planet, it could simulate what would happen to a planet under attack.

It did.

The weapons that blew up little ships didn't blow up the entire planet at first. But they did cause terrible explosions. And on the planet there was no space to dissipate the chain reaction. On the planet the chain reaction found more and more fuel to feed it.

The planet's surface seemed to be moving back and forth, but soon the surface gave way in an immense explosion that sent light flashing in all directions. It swallowed up Ender's entire fleet. And then it reached the enemy ships.

The first simply vanished in the explosion. Then, as the explosion spread and became less bright, it was clear what happened to each ship. As the light reached them they flashed brightly for a moment and disappeared. They were all fuel for the fire of the planet.

It took more than three minutes for the explosion to reach the limits of the simulator, and by then it was much fainter. All the ships were gone, and if any had escaped before the explosion reached them, they were few and not worth worrying about. Where the planet had been there was nothing. The simulator was empty.

Ender had destroyed the enemy by sacrificing his entire fleet and breaking the rule against destroying the enemy planet. He wasn't sure whether to feel triumphant at his victory or defiant at the rebuke he was certain would come. So instead he felt nothing. He was tired. He wanted to go to bed and sleep.

He switched off the simulator, and finally heard the noise behind him.

There were no longer two rows of dignified military observers. Instead there was chaos. Some of them were slapping each other on the back; some of them were bowed, head in hands; others were openly weeping. Captain Graff detached himself from the group and came to Ender. Tears streamed down his face, but he was smiling. He reached out his arms, and to Ender's surprise he embraced the boy, held him tightly, and whispered, "Thank you, thank you, thank you, Ender."

Soon all the observers were gathered around the bewildered child, thanking him and cheering him and patting him on the shoulder and shaking his hand. Ender tried to make sense of what they were saying. Had he passed the test after all? Why did it matter so much to them?

Then the crowd parted and Maezr Rackham walked through. He came straight up to Ender Wiggins and held out his hand.

"You made the hard choice, boy. But heaven knows there was no other way you could have done it. Congratulations. You beat them, and it's all over."

All over. Beat them. "I beat *you*, Maezr Rackham."

Maezr laughed, a loud laugh that filled the room. "Ender Wiggins, you never played me. You never played a *game* since I was your teacher."

Ender didn't get the joke. He had played a great many games, at a terrible cost to himself. He began to get angry.

Maezr reached out and touched his shoulder. Ender shrugged him off. Maezr then grew serious and said, "Ender Wiggins, for the last months you have been the commander of our fleets. There were no games. The battles were real. Your only enemy was *the* enemy. You won every battle. And finally today you fought them at their home world, and you destroyed their world, their fleet, you destroyed them completely, and they'll never come against us again. You did it. You."

Real. Not a game. Ender's mind was too tired to cope with it all. He walked away from Maezr, walked silently through the crowd that still whispered

thanks and congratulations to the boy, walked out of
the simulator room and finally arrived in his bedroom
and closed the door.

He was asleep when Graff and Maezr Rackham
found him. They came in quietly and roused him. He
awoke slowly, and when he recognized them he turned
away to go back to sleep.

"Ender," Graff said. "We need to talk to you."

Ender rolled back to face them. He said nothing.

Graff smiled. "It was a shock to you yesterday, I
know. But it must make you feel good to know you
won the war."

Ender nodded slowly.

"Maezr Rackham here, he never played against
you. He only analyzed your battles to find out your
weak spots, to help you improve. It worked, didn't
it?"

Ender closed his eyes tightly. They waited. He
said, "Why didn't you tell me?"

Maezr smiled. "A hundred years ago, Ender, we
found out some things. That when a commander's life
is in danger he becomes afraid, and fear slows down
his thinking. When a commander knows that he's killing people, he becomes cautious or insane, and neither of those help him do well. And when he's mature,
when he has responsibilities and an understanding of
the world, he becomes cautious and sluggish and can't
do his job. So we trained children, who didn't know
anything but the game, and never knew when it
would become real. That was the theory, and you
proved that the theory worked."

Graff reached out and touched Ender's shoulder. "We launched the ships so that they would all
arrive at their destination during these few months.
We knew that we'd probably have only one good

commander, if we were lucky. In history it's been very rare to have more than one genius in a war. So we planned on having a genius. We were gambling. And you came along and we won."

Ender opened his eyes again and they realized that he was angry. "Yes, you won."

Graff and Maezr Rackham looked at each other. "He doesn't understand," Graff whispered.

"I understand," Ender said. "You needed a weapon, and you got it, and it was me."

"That's right," Maezr answered.

"So tell me," Ender went on, "how many people lived on that planet that I destroyed."

They didn't answer him. They waited awhile in silence, and then Graff spoke. "Weapons don't need to understand what they're pointed at, Ender. We did the pointing, and so we're responsible. You just did your job."

Maezr smiled. "Of course, Ender, you'll be taken care of. The government will never forget you. You served us all very well."

Ender rolled over and faced the wall, and even though they tried to talk to him, he didn't answer them. Finally they left.

Ender lay in his bed for a long time before anyone disturbed him again. The door opened softly. Ender didn't turn to see who it was. Then a hand touched him softly.

"Ender, it's me, Bean."

Ender turned over and looked at the little boy who was standing by his bed.

"Sit down," Ender said.

Bean sat. "That last battle, Ender. I didn't know how you'd get us out of it."

Ender smiled. "I didn't. I cheated. I thought they'd kick me out."

"Can you believe it! We won the war. The

whole war's over, and we thought we'd have to wait till we grew up to fight in it, and it was us fighting it all the time. I mean, Ender, we're little kids. I'm a little kid, anyway." Bean laughed and Ender smiled. Then they were silent for a little while, Bean sitting on the edge of the bed, Ender watching him out of half-closed eyes.

Finally Bean thought of something else to say.

"What will we do now that the war's over?" he said.

Ender closed his eyes and said, "I need some sleep, Bean."

Bean got up and left and Ender slept.

Graff and Anderson walked through the gates into the park. There was a breeze, but the sun was hot on their shoulders.

"Abba Technics? In the capital?" Graff asked.

"No, in Biggock County. Training division," Anderson replied. "They think my work with children is good preparation. And you?"

Graff smiled and shook his head. "No plans. I'll be here for a few more months. Reports, winding down. I've had offers. Personnel development for DCIA, executive vice-president for U and P, but I said no. Publisher wants me to do memoirs of the war. I don't know."

They sat on a bench and watched leaves shivering in the breeze. Children on the monkey bars were laughing and yelling, but the wind and the distance swallowed their words. "Look," Graff said, pointing. A little boy jumped from the bars and ran near the bench where the two men sat. Another boy followed him, and holding his hands like a gun he made an explosive sound. The child he was shooting at didn't stop. He fired again.

"I got you! Come back here!"

The other little boy ran on out of sight.

"Don't you know when you're dead?" The boy shoved his hands in his pockets and kicked a rock back to the monkey bars. Anderson smiled and shook his head. "Kids," he said. Then he and Graff stood up and walked on out of the park.

Kingsmeat

The gatekeeper recognized him and the gate fell away. The Shepherd put his axe and his crook into the bag at his belt and stepped out onto the bridge. As always he felt a rush of vertigo as he walked the narrow arch over the foaming acid of the moat. Then he was across and striding down the road to the village.

A child was playing with a dog on a grassy hillside. The Shepherd looked up at him, his fine dark face made bright by his eyes. The boy shrank back, and the Shepherd heard a woman's voice cry out, "Back here, Derry, you fool!" The Shepherd walked on down the road as the boy retreated among the hayricks on the far slope. The Shepherd could hear the scolding: "Play near the castle again, and he'll make kingsmeat of you."

Kingsmeat, thought the Shepherd. How the king does get hungry. The word had come down through the quick grapevine—steward to cook to captain to guard to shepherd and then he was dressed and out the door only minutes after the king had muttered, "For supper, what is your taste?" and the queen had fluttered all her arms and said, "Not stew again, I hope," and the king had murmured as he picked up the computer printouts of the day, "Breast in butter," and so now the Shepherd was out to harvest from the flock.

The village was still in the distance when the Shepherd began to pass the people. He remembered the time, back when the king had first made his tastes known, when there had been many attempts to evade the villagers' duties to the king. Now they only watched, perhaps hiding the unblemished members of the flock, sometimes thrusting them forward to end the suspense; but mostly the Shepherd saw the old legless, eyeless, or armless men and women who hobbled about their duties with those limbs that were still intact.

Those with fingers thatched or wove; those with eyes led those whose hands were their only contact with the world; those with arms rode the backs of those with legs; and all of them took their only solace in sad and sagging beds, producing, after a suitable interval, children whose miraculous wholeness made them gods to a surprised and wondering mother, made them hated reminders to a father whose tongue had fallen from his mouth, or whose toes had somehow been mislaid, or whose buttocks were a scar, his legs a useless reminder of hams long since dropped off.

"Ah, such beauty," a woman murmured, pumping the bellows at the bread-oven fire. There was a sour grunt from the legless hag who shoveled in the loaves and turned them with a wooden shovel. It was true, of course, for the Shepherd was never touched, no indeed. (No indeed, came the echo from the midnight fires of Unholy Night, when dark tales frightened children half out of their wits, dark tales that the shrunken grown-ups knew were true, were inevitable, were tomorrow.) The Shepherd had long dark hair, and his mouth was firm but kind, and his eyes flashed sunlight even in the dark, it seemed, while his hands were soft from bathing, large and strong and dark and smooth and fearful.

And the Shepherd walked into the village to a house he had noted the last time he came. He went to the door and immediately heard a sigh from every other house, and silence from the one that he had picked.

He raised his hand before the door and it opened, as it had been built to do: for all things that opened served the Shepherd's will, or at least served the bright metal ball the king had implanted in his hand. Inside the house it was dark, but not too dark to see the white eyes of an old man who lay in a hammock, legs dangling bonelessly. The man could see his future in the Shepherd's eyes—or so he thought, at least, until the Shepherd walked past him into the kitchen.

There a young woman, no older than fifteen, stood in front of a cupboard, her hands clenched to do violence. But the Shepherd only shook his head and raised his hand, and the cupboard answered him and opened however much she pushed against it, revealing a murmuring baby wrapped in sound-smothering blankets. The Shepherd only smiled and shook his head. His smile was kind and beautiful, and the woman wanted to die.

He stroked her cheek and she sighed softly, moaned softly, and then he reached into his bag and pulled out his shepherd's crook and leaned the little disc against her temple and she smiled. Her eyes were dead but her lips were alive and her teeth showed. He laid her on the floor, carefully opened her blouse, and then took his axe from his bag.

He ran his finger around the long, narrow cylinder and a tiny light shone at one end. Then he touched the axe's glowing tip to the underside of her breast and drew a wide circle. Behind the axe a tiny red line followed, and the Shepherd took hold of the breast and it came away in his hand. Laying it aside, he stroked the axe lengthwise and the light changed to a dull blue. He passed the axe over the red wound, and the blood gelled and dried and the wound began to heal.

He placed the breast into his bag and repeated the process on the other side. Through it the woman watched in disinterested amusement, the smile still playing at her lips. She would smile like that for days before the peace wore off.

When the second breast was in his bag, the Shepherd put away the axe and the crook and carefully buttoned the woman's blouse. He helped her to her feet, and again passed his deft and gentle hand across her cheek. Like a baby rooting she turned her lips toward his fingers, but he withdrew his hand.

As he left, the woman took the baby from the cupboard and embraced it, cooing softly. The baby nuzzled against the strangely harsh bosom and the woman smiled and sang a lullaby.

The Shepherd walked through the streets, the bag at his belt jostling with his steps. The people watched the bag, wondering what it held. But before the Shepherd was out of the village the word had spread, and the looks were no longer at the bag but rather at the Shepherd's face. He looked neither to the left nor to the right, but he felt their gazes and his eyes grew soft and sad.

And then he was back at the moat, across the narrow bridge, through the gate, and into the high dark corridors of the castle.

He took the bag to the cook, who looked at him sourly. The Shepherd only smiled at him and took his crook from the bag. In a moment the cook was docile, and calmly he began to cut the red flesh into thin slices, which he lightly floured and then placed in a pan of simmering butter. The smell was strong and sweet, and the flecks of milk sizzled in the pan.

The Shepherd stayed in the kitchen, watching, as the cook prepared the king's meal. Then he followed to the door of the dining hall as the steward entered the king's presence with the steaming slices on a tray. The king and queen ate silently, with severe but gracious rituals of shared servings and gifts of finest morsels.

And at the end of the meal the king murmured a word to the steward, who beckoned both the cook and the Shepherd into the hall.

The cook, the steward, and the Shepherd knelt before the king, who reached out three arms to touch their heads. Through long practice they accepted his touch without recoiling, without even blinking, for they knew such things displeased him. After all, it was a great gift that they could serve the king: their services kept them from giving kingsmeat from their own flesh, or from decorating with their skin the tapestried walls of the castle or the long train of a hunting-cape.

The king's armtips still touched the heads of the three servants when a shudder ran through the castle and a low warning tone began to drone.

The king and queen left the table and with deliberate dignity moved to the consoles and sat. There they pressed buttons, setting in motion all the unseeable defenses of the castle.

After an hour of exhausting concentration they recognized defeat and pulled their arms back from the now-useless tasks they had been doing. The fields of force that had long held the thin walls of the castle to their delicate height now lapsed, the walls fell, and a shining metal ship settled silently in the middle of the ruins.

The side of the skyship opened and out of it came four men, weapons in their hands and anger in their eyes. Seeing them, the king and queen looked sadly at each other and then pulled the ritual knives from their resting place behind their heads and simultaneously plunged them between one another's eyes.

They died instantly, and the twenty-two-year conquest of Abbey Colony was at an end.

Dead, the king and queen looked like sad squids lying flat and empty on a fisherman's deck, not at all like conquerors of planets and eaters of men. The men from the skyship walked to the corpses and made certain they were dead. Then they looked around and realized for the first time that they were not alone.

For the Shepherd, the steward, and the cook stood in the ruins of the palace, their eyes wide with unbelief.

One of the men from the ship reached out a hand.

"How can you be alive?" he asked.

They did not answer, not knowing really what the question meant.

"How have you survived here, when—"

And then there were no words, for they looked beyond the palace, across the moat to the crowd of colonists and sons of colonists who stood watching them. And seeing them there without arms and legs and eyes and breasts and lips, the men from the ship emptied their hands of weapons and filled their palms with tears and then crossed the bridge to grieve among the delivered ones' rejoicing.

There was no time for explanations, nor was there a need. The colonists crept and hobbled and, occasionally, walked across the bridge to the ruined palace and formed a circle around the bodies of the king and queen. Then they set to work, and within an hour the corpses were lying in the pit that had been the foundation of the castle, covered with urine and feces and stinking already of decay.

Then the colonists turned to the servants of the king and queen.

The men from the ship had been chosen on a

distant world for their judgment, speed, and skill, and before the mob had found its common mind, before they had begun to move, there was a forcefence around the steward, the cook, the gatekeeper, and the guards. Even around the Shepherd, and though the crowd mumbled its resentment, one of the men from the ship patiently explained in soothing tones that whatever crimes were done would be punished in due time, according to Imperial justice.

The fence stayed up for a week as the men from the ship worked to put the colony in order, struggling to interest the people in the fields that once again belonged completely to them. At last they gave up, realizing that justice could not wait. They took the machinery of the court out of the ship, gathered the people together, and began the trial.

The colonists waited as the men from the ship taped a metal plate behind each person's right ear. Even the servants in their prison and the men from the ship were fitted with them, and then the trial began, each person testifying directly from his memory into the minds of every other person.

The court first heard the testimony of the men from the ship. The people closed their eyes and saw men in a huge starship, pushing buttons and speaking rapidly into computers. Finally expressions of relief, and four men entering a skyship to go down.

The people saw that it was not their world, for here there were no survivors. Instead there was just a castle, just a king and queen, and when they were dead, just fallow fields and the ruins of a village abandoned many years before.

They saw the same scene again and again. Only Abbey Colony had any human beings left alive.

Then they watched as bodies of kings and queens on other worlds were cut open. A chamber within the queen split wide, and there in a writing

mass of life lived a thousand tiny fetuses, many-armed
and bleeding in the cold air outside the womb. Thirty
years of gestation, and then two by two they would
have continued to conquer and rape other worlds in
an unstoppable epidemic across the galaxy.

But in the womb it was stopped, and the fetuses were sprayed with a chemical and soon they lay
still and dried into shriveled balls of grey skin.

The testimony of the men from the ship ended,
and the court probed the memories of the colonists:

A screaming from the sky, and a blast of light,
and then the king and queen descending without
machinery. But the devices follow quickly, and the
people are beaten by invisible whips and forced into a
pen that they watched grow from nothing into a dark,
tiny room that they barely fit into, standing.

Heavy air, impossible to breathe. A woman
fainting, then a man, and the screams and cries deaf-
ening. Sweat until bodies are dry, heat until bodies
are cold, and then a trembling through the room.

A door, and then the king, huger than any had
thought, his many arms revolting. Vomit on your back
from the man behind, then your own vomit, and your
bladder empties in fear. The arms reach, and screams
are all around, screams in all throats, screams until all
voices are silenced. Then one man plucked writhing
from the crowd, the door closed again, darkness back,
and the stench and heat and terror greater than before.

Silence. And in the distance a drawn-out cry of
agony.

Silence. Hours. And then the open door again,
the king again, the scream again.

The third time the king is in the door and out
of the crowd walks one who is not screaming, whose
shirt is caked with stale vomit but who is not vomit-

ing, whose eyes are calm and whose lips are at peace
and whose eyes shine. The Shepherd, though known
then by another name.

He walks to the king and reaches out his hand,
and he is not seized. He is led, and he walks out, and
the door closes.

Silence. Hours. And still no scream.

And then the pen is gone, into the nothing it
seemed to come from, and the air is clear and the sun
is shining and the grass is green. There is only one
change: the castle, rising high and delicately and
madly in an upward tumble of spires and domes. A
moat of acid around it. A slender bridge.

And then back to the village, all of them. The
houses are intact, and it is almost possible to forget.

Until the Shepherd walks through the village
streets. He is still called by the old name—what was
the name? And the people speak to him, ask him,
what is in the castle, what do the king and queen
want, why were we imprisoned, why are we free.

But the Shepherd only points to a baker. The
man steps out, the Shepherd touches him on the temple with his crook, and the man smiles and walks
toward the castle.

Four strong men likewise sent on their way,
and a boy, and another man, and then the people
begin to murmur and shrink back from the Shepherd.
His face is still beautiful, but they remember the
scream they heard in the pen. They do not want to go
to the castle. They do not trust the empty smiles of
those who go.

And then the Shepherd comes again, and
again, and limbs are lost from living men and women.
There are plans. There are attacks. But always the
Shepherd's crook or the Shepherd's unseen whip stop
them. Always they return crippled to their houses.
And they wait. And they hate.

And there are many who wish they had died in the first terrified moments of the attack. But never once does the Shepherd kill.

The testimony of the people ended, and the court let them pause before the trial went on. They needed time to dry their eyes of the tears their memories shed. They needed time to clear their throats of the thickness of silent cries.

And then they closed their eyes again and watched the testimony of the Shepherd. This time there were not many different views; they all watched through one pair of eyes:

The pen again, crowds huddled in terror. The door opens, as before. Only this time all of them walk toward the king in the door, and all of them hold out a hand, and all of them feel a cold tentacle wrap around and lead them from the pen.

The castle grows closer, and they feel the fear of it. But also there is a quietness, a peace that is pressed down on the terror, a peace that holds the face calm and the heart to its normal beat.

The castle. A narrow bridge, and acid in a moat. A gate opens. The bridge is crossed with a moment of vertigo when the king seems about to push, about to throw his prey into the moat.

And then the vast dining hall, and the queen at the console, shaping the world according to the pattern that will bring her children to life.

You stand alone at the head of the table, and the king and queen sit on high stools and watch you. You look at the table and see enough to realize why the others screamed. You feel a scream rise in your throat, knowing that you, and then all the others, will be torn like that, will be half-devoured, will be left in a pile of gristle and bone until all are gone.

And then you press down the fear, and you watch.

The king and queen raise and lower their arms, undulating them in syncopated patterns. They seem to be conversing. Is there meaning in the movements?

You will find out. You also extend an arm, and try to imitate the patterns that you see.

They stop moving and watch you.

You pause for a moment, unsure. Then you undulate your arms again.

They move in a flurry of arms and soft sounds. You also imitate the soft sounds.

And then they come for you. You steel yourself, vow that you will not scream, knowing that you will not be able to stop yourself.

A cold arm touches you and you grow faint. And then you are led from the room, away from the table, and it grows dark.

They keep you for weeks. Amusement. You are kept alive to entertain them when they weary of their work. But as you imitate them you begin to learn, and they begin to teach you, and soon a sort of stammering language emerges, they speaking slowly with their loose arms and soft voices, you with only two arms trying to imitate, then initiate words. The strain of it is killing, but at last you tell them what you want to tell them, what you must tell them before they become bored and look at you again as meat.

You teach them how to keep a herd.

And so they make you a shepherd, with only one duty: to give them meat in a never-ending supply. You have told them you can feed them and never run out of manflesh, and they are intrigued.

They go to their surgical supplies and give you a crook so there will be no pain or struggle, and an axe for the butchery and healing, and on a piece of decaying flesh they show you how to use them. In your hand they implant the key that commands every hinge in the village. And then you go into the colony and proceed to murder your fellowmen bit by bit in order to keep them all alive.

You do not speak. You hide from their hatred in silence. You long for death, but it does not come, because it cannot come. If you died, the colony would die, and so to save their lives you continue a life not worth living.

And then the castle falls and you are finished and you hide the axe and the crook in a certain place in the earth and wait for them all to kill you.

The trial ended.

The people pulled the plates from behind their ears, and blinked unbelieving at the afternoon sunlight. They looked at the beautiful face of the Shepherd and their faces wore unreadable expressions.

"The verdict of the court," a man from the ship read as the others moved through the crowd collecting witness plates, "is that the man called Shepherd is guilty of gross atrocities. However, these atrocities were the sole means of keeping alive those very persons against whom the atrocities were perpetrated. Therefore, the man called Shepherd is cleared of all charges. He is not to be put to death, and instead shall be honored by the people of Abbey Colony at least once a year and helped to live as long as science and prudence can keep a man alive."

It was the verdict of the court, and despite their twenty-two years of isolation the people of Abbey Colony would never disobey Imperial law.

Weeks later the work of the men from the ship was finished. They returned to the sky. The people governed themselves as they had before.

Somewhere between stars three of the men in the ship gathered after supper. "A shepherd, of all things," said one.

"A bloody good one, though," said another.

The fourth man seemed to be asleep. He was not, however, and suddenly he sat up and cried out, "My God, what have we done!"

Over the years Abbey Colony thrived, and a new generation grew up strong and uncrippled. They told their children's children the story of their long enslavement, and freedom was treasured, freedom and strength and wholeness and life.

And every year, as the court had commanded, they went to a certain house in the village carrying gifts of grain and milk and meat. They lined up outside the door, and one by one entered to do honor to the Shepherd.

They walked by the table where he was propped so he could see them. Each came in and looked into the beautiful face with the gentle lips and the soft eyes. There were no large strong hands now, however. Only a head and a neck and a spine and ribs and a loose sac of flesh that pulsed with life. The people looked over his naked body and saw the scars. Here had been a leg and a hip, right? Yes, and here he had once had genitals, and here shoulders and arms.

How does he live? asked the little ones, wondering.

We keep him alive, the older ones answered. The verdict of the court, they said year after year. We'll keep him as long as science and prudence can keep a man alive.

Then they set down their gifts and left, and at the end of the day the Shepherd was moved back to his hammock, where year after year he looked out the window at the weathers of the sky. They would, perhaps, have cut out his tongue, but since he never spoke they didn't think of it. They would, perhaps, have cut out his eyes, but they wanted him to see them smile.

Deep Breathing Exercises

If Dale Yorgason weren't so easily distracted, he might never have noticed the breathing. But he was on his way upstairs to change clothes, noticed the headline on the paper, and got deflected; instead of climbing the stairs, he sat on them and began to read. He could not even concentrate on that, however. He began to hear all the sounds of the house. Brian, their two-year-old son, was upstairs, breathing heavily in sleep. Colly, his wife, was in the kitchen, kneading bread and also breathing heavily.

Their breath was exactly in unison. Brian's rasping breath upstairs, thick with the mucus of a child's sleep; Colly's deep breaths as she labored with the dough. It set Dale to thinking, the newspaper forgotten. He wondered how often people did that— breathed perfectly together for minutes on end. He began to wonder about coincidence.

And then, because he was easily distracted, he remembered that he had to change his clothes and went upstairs. When he came down in his jeans and sweatshirt, ready for a good game of outdoor basketball now that it was spring, Colly called to him. "I'm out of cinnamon, Dale!"

"I'll get it on the way home!"

"I need it *now!*" Colly called.

"We have two cars!" Dale yelled back, then closed the door. He briefly felt bad about not helping her out, but reminded himself that he was already running late and it wouldn't hurt her to take Brian with her and get outside the house; she never seemed to get out of the house anymore.

His team of friends from Allways Home Products, Inc., won the game, and he came home deliciously sweaty. No one was there. The bread dough had risen impossibly, was spread all over the counter and dropping in large chunks onto the floor. Colly had obviously been gone too long. He wondered what could have delayed her.

Then came the phone call from the police, and he did not have to wonder anymore. Colly had a habit of inadvertently running stop signs.

The funeral was well attended because Dale had a large family and was well liked at the office. He sat between his own parents and Colly's parents. The speakers droned on, and Dale, easily distracted, kept thinking of the fact that of all the mourners there, only a few were there in private grief. Only a few had actually known Colly, who preferred to avoid office functions and social gatherings; who stayed home with Brian most of the time being a perfect housewife and reading books and being, in the end, solitary. Most of the people at the funeral had come for Dale's sake, to comfort him. Am I comforted? he asked himself. Not by my friends—they had little to say, were awkward and embarrassed. Only his father had had the right instinct, just embracing him and then talking about everything except Dale's wife and son who were dead, so mangled in the accident that the coffin was never opened for anyone. There was talk of the fishing in Lake Superior this summer; talk of the bastards at Continental Hardware who thought that the 65-year retirement rule ought to apply to the president of the company; talk of nothing at all. But it was good enough. It distracted Dale from his grief.

Now, however, he wondered whether he had

really been a good husband for Colly. Had she really been happy, cooped up in the house all day? He had tried to get her out, get her to meet people, and she had resisted. But in the end, as he wondered whether he knew her at all, he could not find an answer, not one he was sure of. And Brian—he had not known Brian at all. The boy was smart and quick, speaking in sentences when other children were still struggling with single words; but what had he and Dale ever had to talk about? All Brian's companionship had been with his mother; all Colly's companionship had been with Brian. In a way it was like their breathing—the last time Dale had heard them breathe—in unison, as if even the rhythms of their bodies were together. It pleased Dale somehow to think that they had drawn their last breath together, too, the unison continuing to the grave; now they would be lowered into the earth in perfect unison, sharing a coffin as they had shared every day since Brian's birth.

Dale's grief swept over him again, surprising him because he had thought he had cried as much as he possibly could, and now he discovered there were more tears waiting to flow. He was not sure whether he was crying because of the empty house he would come home to, or because he had always been somewhat closed off from his family; was the coffin, after all, just an expression of the way their relationship had always been? It was not a productive line of thought, and Dale let himself be distracted. He let himself notice that his parents were breathing together.

Their breaths were soft, hard to hear. But Dale heard, and looked at them, watched their chests rise and fall together. It unnerved him—was unison breathing more common than he had thought? He listened for others, but Colly's parents were not breathing together, and certainly Dale's breaths were at his own rhythm. Then Dale's mother looked at him, smiled, and nodded to him in an attempt at silent communication. Dale was not good at silent communication; meaningful pauses and knowing looks always left him baffled. They always made him want to check his fly. Another distraction, and he did not think of breathing again.

Until at the airport, when the plane was an hour late in arriving because of technical difficulties in Los Angeles. There was not much to talk to his parents about; even his father's chatter failed him, and they sat in silence most of the time, as did most of the other passengers. Even a stewardess and the pilot sat near them, waiting silently for the plane to arrive.

It was in one of the deeper silences that Dale noticed that his father and the pilot were both swinging their crossed legs in unison. Then he listened, and realized there was a strong sound in the gate waiting area, a rhythmic soughing of many of the passengers inhaling and exhaling together. Dale's mother and father, the pilot, the stewardess, several other passengers, all were breathing together. It unnerved him. How could this be? Brian and Colly had been mother and son; Dale's parents had been together for years. But why should half the people in the waiting area breathe together?

He pointed it out to his father.

"Kind of strange, but I think you're right," his father said, rather delighted with the odd event. Dale's father loved odd events.

And then the rhythm broke, and the plane taxied close to the windows, and the crowd stirred and got ready to board, even though the actual boarding was surely half an hour off.

The plane broke apart at landing. About half the people in the airplane survived. However, the entire crew and several passengers, including Dale's parents, were killed when the plane hit the ground.

It was then that Dale realized that the breathing was not a result of coincidence, or of people's closeness during their lives. It was a messenger of death; they breathed together *because* they were going to draw their last breath together. He said nothing about this thought to anyone else, but whenever he got distracted from other things, he tended to speculalte on this. It was better than dwelling on the fact that he, a man to whom family had been very important, was now completely without family; that the only people with whom he was completely himself, completely at ease, were gone, and there was no more ease for him in the world. Much better to wonder whether his knowledge might be used to save lives. After all, he often thought, reasoning in a circular pattern that never seemed to end, if I notice this again, I should be able to alert someone, to warn someone, to save their lives. Yet if I were going to save their lives, would they then breathe in unison? If my parents had been warned, and changed flights, he thought, they wouldn't have died, and therefore wouldn't have breathed together, and so I wouldn't have been able to warn them, and so they *wouldn't* have changed flights, and so they *would* have died, and so they *would* have breathed in unison, and so I would have noticed and warned them. . . .

More than anything that had ever passed through his mind before, this thought engaged him, and he was not easily distracted from it. It began to hurt his work; he slowed down, made mistakes, because he concentrated only on breathing, listening constantly to the secretaries and other executives in his company, waiting for the fatal moment when they would breathe in unison.

He was eating alone at a restaurant when he heard it again. The sighs of breath came all together, from every table near him. It took him a few moments to be sure; then he leaped from the table and walked briskly outside. He did not stop to pay, for the breathing was still in unison at every table right to the door of the restaurant.

The maître d', predictably, was annoyed at his leaving without paying, and called out to him. Dale did not answer. "Wait! You didn't pay!" cried the man, following Dale out into the street.

Dale did not know how far he had to go for safety from whatever danger faced everyone in the restaurant; he ended up having no choice in the matter. The maître d' stopped him on the sidewalk, only a few doors down from the restaurant, tried to pull him back toward the place, Dale resisting all the way.

"You can't leave without paying! What do you think you're doing?"

"I can't go back," Dale shouted. "I'll pay you! I'll pay you right here!" And he fumbled in his wallet for the money as a huge explosion knocked him and the maître d' to the ground. Flame erupted from the restaurant, and people screamed as the building began crumbling from the force of the explosion. It was impossible that anyone still inside the building could be alive.

The maître d', his eyes wide with horror, stood up as Dale did, and looked at him with dawning understanding. "You knew!" the maître d' said. "You knew!"

Dale was acquitted at the trial—phone calls from a radical group and the purchase of a large quantity of explosives in several states led to indictment and conviction of someone else. But at the trial enough was said to convince Dale and several psychiatrists that something was seriously wrong with him. He was voluntarily committed to an institution, where Dr. Howard Rumming spent hours in conversation with Dale, trying to understand his madness, his fixation on breathing as a sign of coming death.

"I'm sane in every other way, aren't I, Doctor?" Dale asked, again and again.

And repeatedly the doctor answered, "What is sanity? Who has it? How can *I* know?"

Dale soon found that the mental hospital was not an unpleasant place to be. It was a private institution, and a lot of money had gone into it; most of the people there were voluntary commitments, which mean that conditions had to remain excellent. It was one of the things that made Dale grateful for his father's wealth. In the hospital he was safe; the only contact with the outside world was on the television. Gradually, meeting people and becoming attached to them in the hospital, he began to relax, to lose his obsession with breathing, to stop listening quite so intently for the sound of inhalation and exhalation, the way that different people's breathing rhythms fit together. Gradually he began to be his old, distractable self.

"I'm nearly cured, Doctor," Dale announced one day in the middle of a game of backgammon.

The doctor sighed. "I know it, Dale. I have to admit it—I'm disappointed. Not in your cure, you understand. It's just that you've been a breath of fresh air, you should pardon the expression." They both laughed a little. "I get so tired of middle-aged women with fashionable nervous breakdowns."

Dale was gammoned—the dice were all against him. But he took it well, knowing that next time he was quite likely to win handily—he usually did. Then he and Dr. Rumming got up from their table and walked toward the front of the recreation room, where the television program had been interrupted by a special news bulletin. The people around the television looked disturbed; news was never allowed on the hospital television, and only a bulletin like this could creep in. Dr. Rumming intended to turn it off immediately, but then heard the words being said.

". . . from satellites fully capable of destroying every major city in the United States. The President was furnished with a list of fifty-four cities targeted by the orbiting missiles. One of these, said the communique, will be destroyed immediately to show that the threat is serious and will be carried out. Civil defense authorities have been notified, and citizens of the fifty-four cities will be on standby for immediate evacuation." There followed the normal parade of special reports and deep background, but the reporters were all afraid.

Dale's mind could not stay on the program, however, because he was distracted by something far more compelling. Every person in the room was breathing in perfect unison, including Dale. He tried to break out of the rhythm, and couldn't.

It's just my fear, Dale thought. Just the broadcast, making me think that I hear the breathing.

A Denver newsman came on the air then, overriding the network broadcast. "Denver, ladies and gentlemen, is one of the targeted cities. The city has asked us to inform you that orderly evacuation is to begin immediately. Obey all traffic laws, and drive east from the city if you live in the following neighborhoods. . . ."

Then the newsman stopped, and, breathing heavily, listened to something coming through his earphone.

The newsman was breathing in perfect unison with all the people in the room.

"Dale," Dr. Rumming said.

Dale only breathed, feeling death poised above him in the sky.

"Dale, can you hear the breathing?"

Dale heard the breathing.

The newsman spoke again. "Denver is definitely the target. The missiles have already been launched. Please leave immediately. Do not stop for any reason. It is estimated that we have less than—less than three minutes. My God," he said, and got up from his chair, breathing heavily, running out of the range of the camera. No one turned any equipment off in the station—the tube kept on showing the local news set, the empty chairs, the tables, the weather map.

"We can't get out in time," Dr. Rumming said to the inmates in the room. "We're near the center of Denver. Our only hope is to lie on the floor. Try to get under tables and chairs as much as possible." The inmates, terrified, complied with the voice of authority.

"So much for my cure," Dale said, his voice trembling. Rumming managed a half-smile. They lay together in the middle of the floor, leaving the furniture for everyone else because they knew that the furniture would do no good at all.

"You definitely don't belong here," Rumming told him. "I never met a saner man in all my life."

Dale was distracted, however. Instead of his impending death he thought of Colly and Brian in their coffin. He imagined the earth being swept away in a huge wind, and the coffin being ashed immediately in the white explosion from the sky. The barrier is coming down at last, Dale thought, and I will be with them as completely as it is possible to be. He thought of Brian learning to walk, crying when he fell; he remembered Colly saying, "Don't pick him up every time he cries, or he'll just learn that crying gets results." And so for three days Dale had listened to Brian cry and cry, and never lifted a hand to help the boy. Brian learned to walk quite well, and quickly. But now, suddenly, Dale felt again that irresistible impulse to pick him up, to put his pathetically red and weeping face on his shoulder, to say, That's all right, Daddy's holding you.

"That's all right, Daddy's holding you," Dale said aloud, softly. Then there was a flash of white so bright that it could be seen as easily through the walls as through the window, for there were no walls, and all the breath was drawn out of their bodies at once, their voices robbed from them so suddenly that they all involuntarily shouted and then, forever, were silent. Their shout was taken up in a violent wind that swept the sound, wrung from every throat in perfect unison, upward into the clouds forming over what had once been Denver.

And in the last moment, as the shout was drawn from his lungs and the heat took his eyes out of his face, Dale realized that despite all his foreknowledge, the only life he had ever saved was that of a maître d'hôtel, whose life, to Dale, didn't mean a thing.

Closing the Timelid

Gemini lay back in his cushioned chair and slid the box over his head. It was pitch black inside, except the light coming from down around his shoulders.

"All right, I'm pulling us over," said Orion. Gemini braced himself. He heard the click of a switch (or of someone's teeth clinking shut in surprise?) and the timelid closed down on him, shut out the light, and green and orange and another, nameless color beyond purple danced at the edges of his eyes.

And he stood, abruptly, in thick grass at the side of a road. A branch full of leaves brushed heavily against his back with the breeze. He moved forward, looking for—

The road, just as Orion had said. About a minute to wait, then.

Gemini slid awkwardly down the embankment, covering his hands with dirt. To his surprise it was moist and soft, clinging. He had expected it to be hard. That's what you get for believing pictures in the encyclopedia, he thought. And the ground gave gently under his feet.

He glanced behind him. Two furrows down the bank showed his path. I have made a mark in this world after all, he thought. It'll make no difference, but there is a sign of me in this time when men could still leave signs.

Then dazzling lights far up the road. The truck was coming. Gemini sniffed the air. He couldn't smell anything—and yet the books all stressed how smelly gasoline engines had been. Perhaps it was too far.

Then the lights swerved away. The curve. In a moment it would be here, turning just the wrong way on the curving mountain road until it would be too late.

Gemini stepped out into the road, a shiver of anticipation running through him. Oh, he had been under the timelid several times before. Like everyone, he had seen the major events. Michelangelo doing the Sistine Chapel. Handel writing the *Messiah* (everyone strictly forbidden to hum *any* tunes). The premiere performance of *Love's Labour's Lost*. And a few offbeat things that his hobby of history had sent him to: the assassination of John F. Kennedy, a politician; the meeting between Lorenzo d'Medici and the King of Naples; Jeanne d'Arc's death by fire—grisly.

And now, at last, to experience in the past something he was utterly unable to live through in the present.

Death.

And the truck careened around the corner, the lights sweeping the far embankment and then swerving in, brilliantly lighting Gemini for one instant before he leaped up and in, toward the glass (how horrified the face of the driver, how bright the lights, how harsh the metal) and then

agony. Ah, agony in a tearing that made him feel, for the first time, every particle of his body as it screamed in pain. Bones shouting as they splintered like old wood under a sledgehammer. Flesh and fat slithering like jelly up and down and sideways. Blood skittering madly over the surface of the truck. Eyes popping open as the brain and skull crushed forward, demanding to be let through, let by, let fly. No no no no no, cried Gemini inside the last fragment of his mind. No no no no no, make it stop!

And green and orange and more-than-purple dazzled the sides of his vision. A twist of his insides, a shudder of his mind, and he was back, snatched from death by the inexorable mathematics of the timelid. He felt his whole, unmarred body rushing back, felt every particle, yes, as clearly as when it had been hit by the truck, but now with pleasure—pleasure so complete that he didn't even notice the mere orgasm his body added to the general symphony of joy.

The timelid lifted. The box was slid back. And Gemini lay gasping, sweating, yet laughing and crying and longing to sing.

What was it like? the others asked eagerly, crowding around. What is it like, what is it, is it like—

"It's like nothing. It's." Gemini had no words. "It's like everything God promised the righteous and Satan promised the sinners rolled into one." He tried to explain about the delicious agony, the joy passing all joys, the—

"Is it better than fairy dust?" asked one man, young and shy, and Gemini realized that the reason he was so retiring was that he was undoubtedly dusting tonight.

"After this," Gemini said, "dusting is no better than going to the bathroom."

Everyone laughed, chattered, volunteered to be next ("Orion knows how to throw a party"), as Gemini left the chair and the timelid and found Orion a few meters away at the controls.

"Did you like the ride?" Orion asked, smiling gently at his friend.

Gemini shook his head. "Never again," he said.

Orion looked disturbed for a moment, worried. "That bad for you?"

"Not bad. Strong. I'll never forget it. I've never

felt so—alive, Orion. Who would have thought it. Death being so—"

"Bright," Orion said, supplying the word. His hair hung loosely and clean over his forehead—he shook it out of his eyes. "The second time is better. You have more time to appreciate the dying."

Gemini shook his head. "Once is enough for me. Life will never be bland again." He laughed. "Well, time for somebody else, yes?"

Harmony had already lain down on the chair. She had removed her clothing, much to the titillation of the other party-goers, saying, "I want nothing between me and the cold metal." Orion made her wait, though, while he corrected the setting. While he worked, Gemini thought of a question. "How many times have you done this, Orion?"

"Often enough," the man answered, studying the holographic model of the timeclip. And Gemini wondered then if death could not, perhaps, be as addictive as fairy dust, or cresting, or pitching in.

Rod Bingley finally brought the truck to a halt, gasping back the shock and horror. The eyes were still resting there in the gore on the windshield. Only they seemed real. The rest was road-splashing, mud flipped by the weather and the tires.

Rod flung open the door and ran around the front of the truck, hoping to do—what? There was no hope that the man was alive. But perhaps some identification. A nuthouse freak, turned loose in weird white clothes to wander the mountain roads? But there was no hospital near here.

And there was no body on the front of his truck.

He ran his hand across the shiny metal, the clean windshield. A few bugs on the grill.

Had this dent in the metal been there before?

Rod couldn't remember. He looked all around the truck. Not a sign of anything. Had he imagined it?

He must have. But it seemed so real. And he hadn't drunk anything, hadn't taken any uppers—no trucker in his right mind *ever* took stay-awakes. He shook his head. He felt creepy. *Watched*. He glanced back over his shoulder. Nothing but the trees bending slightly in the wind. Not even an animal. Some moths already gathering in the headlights. That's all.

Ashamed of himself for being afraid at nothing, he nevertheless jumped into the cab quickly and slammed the door shut behind him and locked it. The key turned in the starter. And he had to force himself to look up through that windshield. He half-expected to see those eyes again.

The windshield was clear. And because he had a deadline to meet, he pressed on. The road curved away infinitely before him.

He drove more quickly, determined to get back to civilization before he had another hallucination.

And as he rounded a curve, his lights sweeping the trees on the far side of the road, he thought he glimpsed a flash of white to the right, in the middle of the road.

The lights caught her just before the truck did, a beautiful girl, naked and voluptuous and eager. Madly eager, standing there, legs broadly apart, arms wide. She dipped, then jumped up as the truck caught her, even as Rod smashed his foot into the brake, swerved the truck to the side. Because he swerved she ended up, not centered, but caught on the left side, directly in front of Rod, one of her arms flapping crazily around the edge of the cab, the hand rapping on the glass of the side window. She, too, splashed.

Rod whimpered as the truck again came to a halt. The hand had dropped loosely down to the woman's side, so it no longer blocked the door. Rod got out quickly, swung himself around the open door, and touched her.

Body warm. Hand real. He touched the buttock nearest him. It gave softly, sweetly, but under it Rod could feel that the pelvis was shattered. And then the body slopped free of the front of the truck, slid to the oil-and-gravel surface of the road

and disappeared.

Rod took it calmly for a moment. She fell from the front of the truck, and then there was nothing there. Except a faint (and new, definitely new!) crack in the windshield, there was no sign of her.

Rodney screamed.

The sound echoed from the cliff on the other side of the chasm. The trees seemed to swell the sound, making it louder among the trunks. An owl hooted back.

And finally Rod got back into the truck and drove again, slowly, but erratically, wondering what, please God tell me what the hell's the matter with my mind.

Harmony rolled off the couch, panting and shuddering violently.

"Is it better than sex?" one of the men asked her. One who had doubtless tried, but failed, to get into her bed.

"It *is* sex," she answered. "But it's better than sex with *you*."

Everyone laughed. What a wonderful party. Who could top this? The would-be hosts and hostesses despaired, even as they clamored for a chance at the timelid.

But the crambox opened then, buzzing with the police override. "We're busted!" somebody shrieked gaily, and everyone laughed and clapped.

The policeman was young, and she seemed

unused to the forceshield, walking awkwardly as she stepped into the middle of the happy room.

"Orion Overweed?" she asked, looking around.

"I," answered Orion, from where he sat at the controls, looking wary, Gemini beside him.

"Officer Mercy Manwool, Los Angeles Timesquad."

"Oh no," somebody muttered.

"You have no jurisdiction here," Orion said.

"We have a reciprocal enforcement agreement with the Canadian Chronospot Corporation. And we have reason to believe you are interfering with timetracks in the eighth decade of the twentieth century." She smiled curtly. "We have witnessed two suicides, and by making a careful check of your recent use of your private timelid, we have found several others. Apparently you have a new way to pass the time, Mr. Overweed."

Orion shrugged. "It's merely a passing fancy. But I am not interfering with timetracks."

She walked over to the controls and reached unerringly for the coldswitch. Orion immediately snagged her wrist with his hand. Gemini was surprised to see how the muscles of his forearm bulged with strength. Had he been playing some kind of *sport*? It would be just like Orion, of course, behaving like one of the lower orders—

"A warrant," Orion said.

She withdrew her arm. "I have an official complaint from the Timesquad's observation team. That is sufficient. I must interrupt your activity."

"According to law," Orion said, "you must show cause. Nothing we have done tonight will in any way change history."

"That truck is not robot-driven," she said, her voice growing strident. "There's a man in there. You are changing his life."

Orion only laughed. "Your observers haven't done their homework. I have. Look."

He turned to the controls and played a speeded-up sequence, focused always on the shadow image of a truck speeding down a mountain road. The truck made turn after turn, and since the hologram was centered perpetually on the truck, it made the surrounding scenery dance past in a jerky rush, swinging left and right, up and down as the truck banked for turns or struck bumps.

And then, near the bottom of the chasm between mountains, the truck got on a long, slow curve that led across the river on a slender bridge.

But the bridge wasn't there.

And the truck, unable to stop, skidded and swerved off the end of the truncated road, hung in the air over the chasm, then toppled, tumbled, banging against first this side, then that side of the ravine. It wedged between two outcroppings of rock more than ten meters above the water. The cab of the truck was crushed completely.

"He dies," Orion said. "Which means that anything we do with him before his death and after his last possible contact with another human being is legal. According to the code."

The policeman turned red with anger.

"I saw your little games with airplanes and sinking ships. But this is cruelty, Mr. Overweed."

"Cruelty to a dead man is, by definition, not cruelty. I don't change history. And Mr. Rodney Bingley is dead, has been for more than four centuries. I am doing no harm to any living man. And you owe me an apology."

Officer Mercy Manwool shook her head. "I think you're as bad as the Romans, who threw people into circuses to be torn by lions—"

"I know about the Romans," Orion said coldly,

"and I know whom they threw. In this case, however, I am throwing my friends. And retrieving them very safely through the full retrieval and reassembly feature of the Hamburger Safety Device built inextricably into every timelid. And you owe me an apology."

She drew herself erect. "The Los Angeles Timesquad officially apologizes for making improper allegations about the activities of Orion Overweed."

Orion grinned. "Not exactly heartfelt, but I accept it. And while you're here, may I offer you a drink?"

"Nonalcoholic," she said instantly, and then looked away from him at Gemini, who was watching her with sad but intent eyes. Orion went for glasses and to try to find something nonalcoholic in the house.

"You performed superbly," Gemini said.

"And you, Gemini," she said softly (voicelessly), "were the first subject to travel."

Gemini shrugged. "Nobody said anything about my not taking part."

She turned her back on him. Orion came back with the drink. He laughed. "Coca-Cola," he said. "I had to import it all the way from Brazil. They still drink it there, you know. Original recipe." She took it and drank.

Orion sat back at the controls.

"Next!" he shouted, and a man and woman jumped on the couch together, laughing as the others slid the box over their head.

Rod had lost count. At first he had tried to count the curves. Then the white lines in the road, until a new asphalt surface covered them. Then stars. But the only number that stuck in his head was nine.

9
NINE
Oh God, he prayed silently, what is happening

to me, what is happening to me, change this night, let me wake up, whatever is happening to me make it *stop*.

A grey-haired man was standing beside the road, urinating. Rod slowed to a crawl. Slowed until he was barely moving. Crept past the man so slowly that if he had even twitched Rod could have stopped the truck. But the grey-haired man only finished, dropped his robe, and waved gaily to Rod. At that moment Rod heaved a sigh of relief and sped up.

Dropped his robe. The man was wearing a robe. Except for this gory night men did not wear *robes*. And at that moment he caught through his side mirror the white flash of the man throwing himself under the rear tires. Rod slammed on the brake and leaned his head against the steering wheel and wept loud, wracking sobs that shook the whole cab, that set the truck rocking slightly on its heavy-duty springs.

For in every death Rod saw the face of his wife after the traffic accident (not my fault!) that had killed her instantly and yet left Rod to walk away from the wreck without a scratch on him.

I was not supposed to live, he thought at the time, and thought now. I was not supposed to live, and now God is telling me that I am a murderer with my wheels and my motor and my steering wheel.

And he looked up from the wheel.

Orion was still laughing at Hector's account of how he fooled the truck driver into speeding up.

"He thought I was conking into the bushes at the side of the road!" he howled again, and Orion burst into a fresh peal of laughter at his friend.

"And then a backflip into the road, under his tires! How I wish I could see it!" Orion shouted. The other guests were laughing, too. Except Gemini and Officer Manwool.

"You can see it, of course," Manwool said softly. Her words penetrated through the noise, and Orion shook his head. "Only on the holo. And that's not very good, not a good image at all."

"It'll do," she said.

And Gemini, behind Orion, murmured, "Why not, Orry?"

The sound of the old term of endearment was startling to Orion, but oddly comforting. Did Gemini, then, treasure those memories as Orion did? Orion turned slowly, looked into Gemini's sad, deep eyes. "Would you like to see it on the holo?" he asked.

Gemini only smiled. Or rather, twitched his lips into that momentary piece of a smile that Orion knew from so many years before (only forty years, but forty years was back into my childhood, when I was only thirty and Gemini was—what?—fifteen. Helot to my Spartan; Slav to my Hun) and Orion smiled back. His fingers danced over the controls.

Many of the guests gathered around, although others, bored with the coming and going in the time-lid, however extravagant it might be as a party entertainment ("Enough energy to light all of Mexico for an hour," said the one with the giddy laugh who had already promised her body to four men and a woman and was now giving it to another who would not wait), occupied themselves with something decadent and delightful and distracting in the darker corners of the room.

The holo flashed on. The truck crept slowly down the road, its holographic image flickering.

"Why does it do that?" someone asked, and Orion answered mechanically, "There aren't as many chronons as there are photons, and they have a lot more area to cover."

And then the image of a man flickering by the side of the road. Everyone laughed as they realized it was Hector, conking away with all his heart. Then another laugh as he dropped his robe and waved. The truck sped up, and then a backflip by the manfigure, under the wheels. The body flopped under the doubled back tires, then lay limp and shattered in the road as the truck came to a stop only a few meters ahead. A few moments later, the body disappeared.

"Brilliantly done, Hector!" Orion shouted again. "Better than you told it!" Everyone applauded in agreement, and Orion reached over to flip off the holo. But Officer Manwool stopped him.

"Don't turn it off, Mr. Overweed," she said. "Freeze it, and move the image."

Orion looked at her for a moment, then shrugged and did as she said. He expanded the view, so that the truck shrank. And then he suddenly stiffened, as did the guests close enough and interested enough to notice. Not more than ten meters in front of the truck was the ravine, where the broken bridge waited.

"He can see it," somebody gasped. And Officer Manwool slipped a lovecord around Orion's wrist, pulled it taut, and fastened the loose end to her workbelt.

"Orion Overweed, you're under arrest. That man can see the ravine. He will not die. He was brought to a stop in plenty of time to notice the certain death ahead of him. He will live—with a knowledge of whatever he saw tonight. And already you have altered the future, the present, and all the past from his time until the present."

And for the first time in all his life, Orion realized that he had reason to be afraid.

"But that's a capital offense," he said lamely.

"I only wish it included torture," Officer Manwool said heatedly, "the kind of torture you put that poor truck driver through!"

And then she started to pull Orion out of the room.

Rod Bingley lifted his eyes from the steering wheel and stared uncomprehendingly at the road ahead. The truck's lights illuminated the road clearly for many meters. And for five seconds or thirty minutes or some other length of time that was both brief and infinite he did not understand what it meant.

He got out of the cab and walked to the edge of the ravine, looking down. For a few minutes he felt relieved.

Then he walked back to the truck and counted the wounds in the cab. The dents on the grill and the smooth metal. Three cracks in the windshield.

He walked back to where the man had been urinating. Sure enough, though there was no urine, there was an indentation in the ground where the hot liquid had struck, speckles in the dirt where it had splashed.

And in the fresh asphalt, laid, surely, that morning (but then why no warning signs on the bridge? Perhaps the wind tonight blew them over), his tire tracks showed clearly. Except for a manwidth stretch where the left rear tires had left no print at all.

And Rodney remembered the dead, smashed faces, especially the bright and livid eyes among the blood and broken bone. They all looked like Rachel to him, Rachel who had wanted him to—to what? Couldn't he even remember the dreams anymore?

He got back into the cab and gripped the steering wheel. His head spun and ached, but he felt himself on the verge of a marvelous conclusion, a simple answer to all of this. There was evidence, yes, even though the bodies were gone, there was evidence that he had hit those people. He had not imagined it.

They must, then, be (he stumbled over the word, even in his mind, laughed at himself as he concluded:) angels. Jesus sent them, he knew it, as his mother had taught him, destroying angels teaching him the death that he had brought to his wife while daring, himself, to walk away scatheless.

It was time to even up the debt.

He started the engine and drove, slowly, deliberately toward the end of the road. And as the front tires bumped off and a sickening moment passed when he feared that the truck would be too heavy for the driving wheels to push along the ground, he clasped his hands in front of his face and prayed, aloud: "Forward!"

And then the truck slid forward, tipped downward, hung in the air, and fell. His body pressed into the back of the truck. His clasped hands struck his face. He meant to say, "Into thy hands I commend my spirit," but instead he screamed, "No no no no no," in an infinite negation of death that, after all, didn't do a bit of good once he was committed into the gentle, unyielding hands of the ravine. They clasped and enfolded him, pressed him tightly, closed his eyes and pillowed his head between the gas tank and the granite.

"Wait," Gemini said.

"Why the hell should we?" Officer Manwool said, stopping at the door with Orion following docilely on the end of the lovecord. Orion, too, stopped, and looked at the policeman with the adoring expression all lovecord captives wore.

"Give the man a break," Gemini said.

"He doesn't deserve one," she said. "And neither do you."

"I say give the man a break. At least wait for the proof."

She snorted. "What more proof does he need, Gemini? A signed statement from Rodney Bingley that Orion Overweed is a bloody hitler?"

Gemini smiled and spread his hands. "We didn't actually *see* what Rodney did next, did we? Maybe he was struck by lightning two hours later, before he saw anybody—I mean, you're required to show that damage did happen. And I don't feel any change to the present—"

"You know that changes aren't felt. They aren't even known, since we wouldn't remember anything other than how things actually happened!"

"At least," Gemini said, "watch what happens and see whom Rodney tells."

So she led Orion back to the controls, and at her instructions Orion lovingly started the holo moving again.

And they all watched as Rodney Bingley walked to the edge of the ravine, then walked back to the truck, drove it to the edge and over into the chasm, and died on the rocks.

As it happened, Hector hooted in joy. "He died after all! Orion didn't change a damned thing, not one damned thing!"

Manwool turned on him in disgust. "You make me sick," she said.

"The man's dead," Hector said in glee. "So get that stupid string off Orion or I'll sue for a writ of—"

"Go pucker in a corner," she said, and several of the women pretended to be shocked. Manwool loosened the lovecord and slid it off Orion's wrist. Immediately he turned on her, snarling. "Get out of here! Get out! Get out!"

He followed her to the door of the crambox. Gemini was not the only one who wondered if he would hit her. But Orion kept his control, and she left unharmed.

Orion stumbled back from the crambox rubbing his arms as if with soap, as if trying to scrape them clean from contact with the lovecord. "That thing ought to be outlawed. I actually loved her. I actually loved that stinking, bloody, son-of-a-bitching cop!" And he shuddered so violently that several of the guests laughed and the spell was broken.

Orion managed a smile and the guests went back to amusing themselves. With the sensitivity that even the insensitive and jaded sometimes exhibit, they left him alone with Gemini at the controls of the timelid.

Gemini reached out and brushed a strand of hair out of Orion's eyes. "Get a comb someday," he said. Orion smiled and gently stroked Gemini's hand. Gemini slowly removed his hand from Orion's reach. "Sorry, Orry," Gemini said, "but not anymore."

Orion pretended to shrug. "I know," he said. "Not even for old times' sake." He laughed softly. "That stupid string made me love her. They shouldn't even do that to criminals."

He played with the controls of the holo, which was still on. The image zoomed in; the cab of the truck grew larger and larger. The chronons were too scattered and the image began to blur and fade. Orion stopped it.

By ducking slightly and looking through a window into the cab, Orion and Gemini could see the exact place where the outcropping of rock crushed Rod Bingley's head against the gas tank. Details, of course, were indecipherable.

"I wonder," Orion finally said, "if it's any different."

"What's any different?" Gemini asked.

"Death. If it's any different when you don't wake up right afterward."

A silence.

Then the sound of Gemini's soft laughter.

"What's funny?" Orion asked.

"You," the younger man answered. "Only one thing left that you haven't tried, isn't there?"

"How could I do it?" Orion asked, half-seriously (only half?). "They'd only clone me back."

"Simple enough," Gemini said. "All you need is a friend who's willing to turn off the machine while you're on the far end. Nothing is left. And you can take care of the actual suicide yourself."

"Suicide," Orion said with a smile. "Trust you to use the policeman's term."

And that night, as the other guests slept off the alcohol in beds or other convenient places, Orion lay on the chair and pulled the box over his head. And with Gemini's last kiss on his cheek and Gemini's left hand on the controls, Orion said, "All right. Pull me over."

After a few minutes Gemini was alone in the room. He did not even pause to reflect before he went to the breaker box and shut off all the power for a critical few seconds. Then he returned, sat alone in the room with the disconnected machine and the empty chair. The crambox soon buzzed with the police override, and Mercy Manwool stepped out. She went straight to Gemini, embraced him. He kissed her, hard.

"Done?" she asked.

He nodded.

"The bastard didn't deserve to live," she said.

Gemini shook his head. "You didn't get your justice, my dear Mercy."

"Isn't he dead?"

"Oh yes, that. Well, it's what he wanted, you know. I told him what I planned. And he asked me to do it."

She looked at him, angrily. "You would. And

then tell *me* about it, so I wouldn't get any joy out of this at all." Gemini only shrugged.

Manwool turned away from him, walked to the timelid. She ran her fingers along the box. Then she detached her laser from her belt and slowly melted the timelid until it was a mass of hot plastic on a metal stand. The few metal components had even melted a little, bending to be just a little out of shape.

"Screw the past anyway," she said. "Why can't it stay where it belongs?"

I Put My Blue Genes On

It had taken three weeks to get there—longer than any man in living memory had been in space, and there were four of us crammed into the little Hunter III skipship. It gave us a hearty appreciation for the pioneers, who had had to crawl across space at a tenth of the speed of light. No wonder only three colonies ever got founded. Everybody else must have eaten each other alive after the first month in space.

Harold had taken a swing at Amauri the last day, and if we hadn't hit the homing signal I would have ordered the ship turned around to go home to Núncamais, which was mother and apple pie to everybody but me—I'm from Pennsylvania. But we got the homing signal and set the computer to scanning the old maps, and after a few hours found ourselves in stationary orbit over Prescott, Arizona.

At least that's what the geologer said, and computers can't lie. It didn't look like what the old books *said* Arizona should look like.

But there was the homing signal, broadcasting in Old English: "God bless America, come in, safe landing guaranteed." The computer assured us that in Old English the word *guarantee* was *not* obscene, but rather had something to do with a statement being particularly trustworthy—we had a chuckle over that one.

But we were excited, too. When great-great-great-great to the umpteenth power grandpa and grandma upped their balloons from old Terra Firma eight hundred years ago, it had been to escape the ravages of microbiological warfare that was just beginning (a few germs in a sneak attack on Madagascar, quickly spreading to epidemic proportions, and South Africa holding the world ransom for the antidote; quick retaliation with virulent cancer; you guess the rest). And even from a couple of miles out in space, it was pretty obvious that the war hadn't stopped there. And yet there was this homing signal.

"Obviamente automática," Amauri observed.

"*Que* máquina, que não pofa em tantos anos, bichinha! Não acredito!" retorted Harold, and I was afraid I might have a rerun of the day before.

"English," I said. "Might as well get used to it. We'll have to speak it for a few days, at least."

Vladimir sighed. "Merda."

I laughed. "All right, you can keep your scatological comments in lingua deporto."

"Are you so sure there's anybody alive down there?" Vladimir asked.

What could I say? That I felt it in my bones? So I just threw a sponge at him, which scattered drinking water all over the cabin, and for a few minutes we had a waterfight. I know, discipline, discipline. But we're not a land army up here, and what the hell. I'd rather have my crew acting like crazy children than like crazy grown-ups.

Actually, I didn't believe that at the level of technology our ancestors had reached in 1992 they could build a machine that would keep running until 2810. Somebody had to be alive down there—or else they'd gotten smart. Again, the surface of old Terra didn't give many signs that anybody had gotten smart.

So somebody was alive down there. And that was exactly what we had been sent to find out.

They complained when I ordered monkeysuits.

"That's old Mother *Earth* down there!" Harold argued. For a halibut with an ike of 150 he sure could act like a baiano sometimes.

"Show me the cities," I answered. "Show me the millions of people running around taking the sun in their rawhide summer outfits."

"And there may be germs," Amauri added, in his snottiest voice, and immediately I had another argument going between two men brown enough to know better.

"We will follow," I said in my nasty captain's voice, "standard planetary procedure, whether it's Mother Earth or mother—"

And at that moment the monotonous homing signal changed.

"Please respond, please identify, please respond, or we'll blast your asses out of the sky."

We responded. And soon afterward found ourselves in monkeysuits wandering around in thick pea soup up to our navels (if we could have located our navels without a map, surrounded as they were with life-saving devices) waiting for somebody to open a door.

A door opened and we picked ourselves up off a very hard floor. Some of the pea soup had fallen down the hatch with us. A gas came into the sterile chamber where we waited, and pretty soon the pea soup settled down and turned into mud.

"Mariajoseijesus!" Amauri muttered. "Aquela merda *vivia!*"

"English," I muttered into the monkey mouth, "and clean up your language."

"That crap was alive," Amauri said, rephrasing and cleaning up his language.

"And now it isn't, but we are." It was hard to be patient.

For all we knew, what passed for humanity

here liked eating spacemen. Or sacrificing them to some local deity. We passed a nervous four hours in that cubicle. And I had already laid about five hopeless escape plans—when a door opened, and a person appeared.

He was dressed in a white farmersuit, or at least close to it. He was very short, but smiled pleasantly and beckoned. Proof positive. Living human beings. Mission successful. *Now* we know there was no cause for rejoicing, but at that moment we rejoiced. Backslapping, embracing our little host (afraid of crushing him for a moment), and then into the labyrinth of U.S. MB Warfare Post 004.

They were all very small—not more than 140 centimeters tall—and the first thought that struck me was how much humanity had grown since then. The stars must agree with us, I thought.

Till quiet, methodical Vladimir, looking, as always, white as a ghost, pointedly turned a doorknob and touched a lightswitch (it actually was *mechanical*). They were both above eyelevel for our little friends. So it wasn't us colonists who had grown—it was our cousins from old Gaea who had shrunk.

We tried to catch them up on history, but all they cared about was their own politics. "Are you American?" they kept asking.

"I'm from Pennsylvania," I said, "but these humblebutts are from Núncamais."

They didn't understand.

"Núncamais. It means 'never again.' In lingua deporto."

Again puzzled. But they asked another question. "Where did your colony *come from*?" One-track minds.

"Pennsylvania was settled by Americans from Hawaii. We lay no bets as to why they named the damned planet Pennsylvania."

One of the little people piped up, "That's obvious. Cradle of liberty. And *them?*"

"From Brazil," I said.

They conferred quietly on that one, and then apparently decided that while Brazilian ancestry wasn't a capital offense, it didn't exactly confer human status. From then on, they made no attempt to talk to my crew. Just watched them carefully, and talked to me.

Me they loved.

"God bless America," they said.

I felt agreeable. "God bless America," I answered.

Then, again in unison, they made an obscene suggestion as to what I should do with the Russians. I glanced at my compatriots and fellowtravelers and shrugged. I repeated the little folks' wish for the Russians' sexual bliss.

Fact time. I won't bore by repeating all the clever questioning and probing that elicited the following information. Partly because it didn't take any questioning. They seemed to have been rehearsing for years what they would say to any visitors from outer space, particularly the descendants of the long-lost colonists. It went this way:

Germ warfare had begun in earnest about three years after we left. Three very cleverly designed cancer viruses had been loosed on the world, apparently by no one at all, since both the Russians and the Americans denied it and the Chinese were all dead. That was when the scientists knuckled down and set to work.

Recombinant DNA had been a rough enough science when my ancestors took off for the stars—and we hadn't developed it much since then. When you're developing raw planets you have better things to do with your time. But under the pressure of warfare, the science of do-it-yourself genetics had a field day on planet Earth.

"We are constantly developing new strains of viruses and bacteria," they said. "And constantly we are bombarded by the Russians' latest weapons." They were hard-pressed. There weren't many of them in that particular MB Warfare Post, and the enemy's assaults were clever.

And finally the picture became clear. To all of us at once. It was Harold who said, "Fossa-me, mãe! You mean for eight hundred *years* you bunnies've been down here?"

They didn't answer until I asked the question— more politely, too, since I had noticed a certain set to those inscrutable jaws when Harold called them bunnies. Well, they *were* bunnies, white as white could be, but it was tasteless for Harold to call them that, particularly in front of Vladimir, who had more than a slight tendency toward white skin himself.

"Have you Americans been trapped down here ever since the war began?" I asked, trying to put awe into my voice, and succeeding. Horror isn't that far removed from awe, anyway.

They beamed with what I took for pride. And I was beginning to be able to interpret some of their facial expressions. As long as I had good words for America, I was all right.

"Yes, Captain Kane Kanea, we and our ancestors have been here from the beginning."

"Doesn't it get a little cramped?"

"Not for American soldiers, Captain. For the right to life, liberty, and the pursuit of happiness we would sacrifice anything." I didn't ask how much liberty and happiness-pursuing were possible in a hole in the rock. Our hero went on: "We fight on that millions may live, free, able to breathe the clean air of America unoppressed by the lashes of Communism."

And then they broke into a few choice hymns about purple mountains and yellow waves with a rousing chorus of God blessing America. It all ended with a mighty shout: "Better dead than red." When it was over we asked them if we could sleep, since according to our ship's time it was well past bedding-down hour.

They put us in a rather small room with three cots in it that were far too short for us. Didn't matter. We couldn't possibly be comfortable in our monkey-suits anyway.

Harold wanted to talk in lingua deporto as soon as we were alone, but I managed to convince him without even using my monkeysuit's discipliner button that we didn't want them to think we were trying to keep any secrets. We all took it for granted that they were monitoring us.

And so our conversation was the sort of conversation that one doesn't mind having overheard by a bunch of crazy patriots.

Amauri: "I am amazed at their great love for America, persisting so many centuries." Translation: "What the hell got these guys so nuts about something as dead as the ancient U.S. empire?"

Me: "Perhaps it is due to such unwavering loyalty to the flag, God, country, and liberty" (I admit I was laying it on thick, but better to be safe, etc.) "that they have been able to survive so long." Translation: "Maybe being crazy fanatics is all that's kept them alive in this hole."

Harold: "I wonder how long we can stay in this bastion of democracy before we must reluctantly go back to our colony of the glorious American dream." Translation: "What are the odds they don't let us go? After all, they're so loony they might think we're spies or something."

Vladimir: "I only hope we can learn from them. Their science is infinitely beyond anything we have hitherto developed with our poor resources." Translation: "We're not going anywhere until I have a chance to do *my* job and check out the local flora and fauna. Eight hundred years of recombining DNA has got to have something we can take back home to Núncamais."

And so the conversation went until we were sick of the flowers and perfume that kept dropping out of our mouths. Then we went to sleep.

The next day was guided tour day, Russian attack day, and damn near good-bye to the crew of the good ship Pollywog.

The guided tour kept us up hill and down dale for most of the morning. Vladimir was running the tracking computer from his monkeysuit. Mine was too busy analyzing the implications of all their comments, while Amauri was absorbing the science and Harold was trying to figure out how to pick his nose with mittens on. Harold was along for the ride—a weapons expert, just in case. Thank God.

We began to be able to tell one little person from another. George Washington Steiner was our usual guide. The big boss, who had talked to us through most of the history lesson the day before, was Andrew Jackson Wallichinsky. And the guy who led the singing was Richard Nixon Dixon. The computer told us those were names of beloved American presidents, with surnames added.

And my monkeysuit's analysis also told us that the music leader was the *real* big boss, while Andy Jack Wallichinsky was merely the director of scientific research. Seems that the politicians ran the brains, instead of vice versa.

Our guide, G.W. Steiner, was very proud of his

assignment. He showed us everything. I mean, even with the monkeysuit keeping three-fourths of the gravity away from me, my feet were sore by lunchtime (a quick sip of recycled xixi and cocó). And it was impressive. Again, I give it unto you in abbreviated form.

Even though the installation was technically airtight, in fact the enemy viruses and bacteria could get in quite readily. It seems that early in the twenty-first century the Russians had stopped making any kind of radio broadcasts. (I know, that sounds like a non sequitur. Patience, patience.) At first the Americans in 004 had thought they had won. And then, suddenly, a new onslaught of another disease. At this time the 004 researchers had never been *personally* hit by any diseases—the airtight system was working fine. But their commander at that time, Rodney Fletcher, had been very suspicious.

"He thought it was a commie trick," said George Washington Steiner. I began to see the roots of superpatriotism in 004's history.

So Rodney Fletcher set the scientists to working on strengthening the base personnel's antibody system. They plugged away at it for two weeks and came up with three new strains of bacteria that selectively devoured practically anything that wasn't supposed to be in the human body. Just in time, too, because then that new disease hit. It wasn't stopped by the airtight system, because instead of being a virus, it was just two little amino acids and a molecule of lactose, put together *just so*. It fit right through the filters. It sailed right through the antibiotics. It entered right into the lungs of every man, woman, and child in 004. And if Rodney Fletcher hadn't been a paranoid, they all would have died. As it was, only about half lived.

Those two amino acids and the lactose molecule had the ability to fit right into *that* spot on a human DNA and then make the DNA replicate that way. Just one little change—and pretty soon nerves just stopped working.

Those who lived, lived because the new antibody system worked just well enough to slow down the disease's progress until a plug could be found that fit even better into that spot on the DNA, keeping the Russians' little devices out. (Can they be called viruses? Can they be called alive? I'll leave it to the godcallers and the philosophers to decide that.)

Trouble was, the plugs also caused all the soldiers' babies to grow up to be very short with a propensity for having their teeth fall out and their eyes go blind at the age of thirty. G.W. Steiner was very proud of the fact that they had managed to correct for the eyes after four generations. He smiled and for the first time we really noticed that his teeth weren't like ours.

"We make them out of a certain bacteria that gets very hard when a particular virus is exposed to it. My own great-great-grandmother invented it," Steiner said. "We're always coming up with new and useful tools."

I asked to see how they did this trick, which brings us full circle to what we saw on the guided tour that day. We saw the laboratories where eleven researchers were playing clever little games with DNA. I didn't understand any of it, but my monkeysuit assured me that the computer was getting it all.

We also saw the weapons delivery system. It was very clever. It consisted of setting a culture dish full of a particular nasty weapon in a little box, closing the door to the box, and then pressing a button that opened another door to the box that led outside.

"We let the wind take it from there," said

Steiner. "We figure it takes about a year for a new weapon to reach Russia. But by then it's grown to a point that it's irresistible."

I asked him what the bacteria lived on. He laughed. "Anything," he said. It turns out that their basic breeding stock is a bacterium that can photosynthesize and dissolve any form of iron, both at the same time. "Whatever else we change about a particular weapon, we don't change that," Steiner said. "Our weapons can travel anywhere without hosts. Quarantines don't do any good."

Harold had an idea. I was proud of him. "If these little germs can dissolve steel, George, why the hell aren't they in here dissolving this whole installation?"

Steiner looked like he had just been hoping we'd ask that question.

"When we developed our basic breeder stock, we also developed a mold that inhibits the bacteria from reproducing and eating. The mold only grows on metal and the spores die if they're away from both mold and metal for more than one-seventy-seventh of a second. That means that the mold grows all the way around this installation—and nowhere else. My fourteenth great-uncle William Westmoreland Hannamaker developed the mold."

"Why," I asked, "do you keep mentioning your blood relationship to these inventors? Surely after eight hundred years here everybody's related?"

I thought I was asking a simple question. But G.W. Steiner looked at me coldly and turned away, leading us to the next room.

We found bacteria that processed other bacteria that processed still other bacteria that turned human excrement into very tasty, nutritious food. We took their word for the tasty. I know, we were still

eating recycled us through the tubes in our suit. But
at least we knew where *ours* had been.

They had bacteria that without benefit of sunlight processed carbon dioxide and water back into
oxygen and starch. So much for photosynthesis.

And we got a list of what shelf after shelf of
weapons could do to an unprepared human body. If
somebody ever broke all those jars on Núncamais or
Pennsylvania or Kiev, everybody would simply disappear, completely devoured and incorporated into the
lifesystems of bacteria and viruses and trained amino-
acid sets.

No sooner did I think of that, than I said it.
Only I didn't get any farther than the word *Kiev*.

"Kiev? One of the colonies is named Kiev?"

I shrugged. "There are only three planets colonized. Kiev, Pennsylvania, and Núncamais."

"Russian ancestry?"

Oops, I thought. Oops is an all-purpose word
standing for every bit of profanity, blasphemy, and
pornographic and scatological exculpation I could
think of.

The guided tour ended right then.

Back in our bedroom, we became aware that we
had somehow dissolved our hospitality. After a while,
Harold realized that it was my fault.

"Captain, by damn, if you hadn't told them
about Kiev we wouldn't be locked in here like this!"

I agreed, hoping to pacify him, but he didn't
calm down until I used the discipliner button in my
monkeysuit.

Then we consulted the computers.

Mine reported that in all we had been told,
two areas had been completely left out: While it was
obvious that in the past the little people had done
extensive work on human DNA, there had been no

hint of any work going on in that field today. And
though we had been told of all kinds of weapons that
had been flung among the Russians on the other side
of the world, there had been no hint of any kind of
limited effect antipersonnel weapon *here.*

"Oh," Harold said. "There's nothing to stop us
from walking out of here anytime we can knock the
door down. And I can knock the door down anytime I
want to," he said, playing with the buttons on his
monkeysuit. I urged him to wait until all the reports
were done.

Amauri informed us that he had gleaned
enough information from their talk and his monkey-
eyes that we could go home with the entire science of
DNA recombination hidden away in our computer.

And then Vladimir's suit played out a holomap
of Post 004.

The bright green, infinitesimally thin lines
marked walls, doors, passages. We immediately recognized the corridors we had walked in throughout the
morning, located the laboratories, found where we
were imprisoned. And then we noticed a rather large
area in the middle of the holomap that seemed empty.

"Did you see a room like that?" I asked. The
others shook their heads. Vladimir asked the holomap
if we had been in it. The suit answered in its whispery
monkeyvoice: "No. I have only delineated the un-
penetrated perimeter and noted apertures that perhaps give entry."

"So they didn't let us in there," Harold said. "I
knew the bastards were hiding something."

"And let's make a guess," I said. "That room
either has something to do with antipersonnel weapons, or it has something to do with human DNA research."

We sat and pondered the revelations we had just
had, and realized they didn't add up to much. Finally

Vladimir spoke up. Trust a half-bunny to come up with the idea where three browns couldn't. Just goes to show you that racial theory is a bunch of waggy-woggle.

"Antipersonnel hell," Vladimir said. "They don't need antipersonnel. All they have to do is open a little hole in our suits and let the germs come through."

"Our suits close immediately," Amauri said, but then corrected himself. "I guess it doesn't take long for a virus to get through, does it?"

Harold didn't get it. "Let one of those bunnies try to lay a knife on me, and I'll split him from ass to armpit."

We ignored him.

"What makes you think there are germs in here? Our suits don't measure that," I pointed out.

Vladimir had already thought of that. "Remember what they said. About the Russians getting those little amino-acid monsters in here."

Amauri snorted. "Russians."

"Yeah, right," Vladimir said, "but keep the voice down, viado."

Amauri turned red, started to say, "Quem é que cê chama de viado!"—but I pushed the discipliner button. No time for any of that crap.

"Watch your language, Vladimir. We got enough problems."

"Sorry, Amauri, Captain," Vladimir said. "I'm a little wispy, you know?"

"So's everybody."

Vladimir took a breath and went on. "Once those bugs got in here, 004 must have been pretty thoroughly permeable. The, uh, Russians must've kept pumping more variations on the same into Post 004."

"So why aren't they all dead?"

"What I think is that a lot of these people *have* been killed—but the survivors are the ones whose bodies took readily to those plugs they came up with. The plugs are regular parts of their body chemistry now. They'd have to be, wouldn't they? They told us they were passed on in the DNA transmitted to the next generation."

I got it. So did Amauri, who said, "So they've had seven or eight centuries to select for adaptability."

"Why not?" Vladimir asked. "Didn't you notice? Eleven researchers on developing new weapons. And only two on developing new defenses. They can't be *too* worried."

Amauri shook his head. "Oh, Mother Earth. Whatever got into you?"

"Just caught a cold," Vladimir said, and then laughed. "A virus. Called humanity."

We sat around looking at the holomap for a while. I found four different routes from where we were to the secret area—if we wanted to get there. I also found three routes to the exit. I pointed them out to the others.

"Yeah," Harold said. "Trouble is, who knows if those doors really lead into that unknown area? I mean, what the hell, three of the four doors might lead to the broom closets or service stations."

A good point.

We just sat there, wondering whether we should head for the Pollywog or try to find out what was in the hidden area, when the Russian attack made up our minds for us. There was a tremendous bang. The floor shook, as if some immense dog had just picked up Post 004 and given it a good shaking. When it stopped the lights flickered and went out.

"Golden opportunity," I said into the monkey-mouth. The others agreed. So we flashed on the lights from our suits and pointed them at the door. Harold suddenly felt very important. He went to the door and ran his magic flipper finger all the way around the door. Then he stepped back and flicked a lever on his suit.

"Better turn your backs," he said. "This can flash pretty bright."

Even looking at the back wall the explosion blinded me for a few seconds. The world looked a little green when I turned around. The door was in shreds on the floor, and the doorjamb didn't look too healthy.

"Nice job, Harold," I said.

"Graças a deus," he answered, and I had to laugh. Odd how little religious phrases refused to die, even with an irreverent filho de punta like Harold.

Then I remembered that I was in charge of order-giving. So I gave.

The second door we tried led into the rooms we wanted to see. But just as we got in, the lights came on.

"Damn. They've got the station back in order," Amauri said. But Vladimir just pointed down the corridor.

The pea soup had gotten in. It was oozing sluggishly toward us.

"Whatever the Russians did, it must have opened up a big hole in the station." Vladimir pointed his laser finger at the mess. Even on full power, it only made a little spot steam. The rest just kept coming.

"Anyone for swimming?" I asked. No one was. So I hustled them all into the not-so-hidden room.

There were some little people in there, cowering in the darkness. Harold wrapped them in cocoons and stuck them in a corner. So we had time to look around.

There wasn't that much to see, really. Standard lab equipment, and then thirty-two boxes, about a meter square. They were under sunlamps. We looked inside.

The animals were semisolid looking. I didn't touch one right then, but from the sluggish way it sent out pseudopodia, I concluded that the one I was watching, at least, had a rather crusty skin—with jelly inside. They were all a light brown—even lighter than Vladimir's skin. But there were little green spots here and there. I wondered if they photosynthesized.

"Look what they're floating in," Amauri said, and I realized that it was pea soup.

"They've developed a giant amoeba that lives on all the other microorganisms, I guess," Vladimir said. "Maybe they've trained it to carry bombs. Against the Russians."

At that moment Harold began firing his arsenal, and I noticed that the little people were gathered at the door to the lab, looking agitated. A few at the front were looking dead.

Harold probably would have killed all of them, except that we were still standing next to a box with a giant amoeba in it. When he screamed, we looked and saw the creature fastened against his leg. Even as we watched, Harold fell, the bottom half of his leg dropping away as the amoeba continued eating up his thigh.

We watched just long enough for the little people to grab hold of us in sufficient numbers that resistance would have been ridiculous. Besides, we couldn't take our eyes off Harold.

At about the groin, the amoeba stopped eating. It didn't matter. Harold was dead anyway—we didn't know what disease got him, but as soon as his suit had cracked he started vomiting into his suit. There were pustules all over his face. In short, Vladimir's guess about the virus content of Post 004 had been pretty accurate.

And now the amoeba formed itself into a pentagon. Five very smooth sides, the creature sitting in a clump on the gaping wound that had once been a pelvis. Suddenly, with a brief convulsion, all the sides bisected, forming sharp angles, so that now there were ten sides to the creature. A hairline crack appeared down the middle. And then, like jelly sliced in the middle and finally deciding to split, the two halves slumped away on either side. They quickly formed into two new pentagons, and then they relaxed into pseudopodia again, and continued devouring Harold.

"Well," Amauri said. "They *do* have an antipersonnel weapon."

When he spoke, the spell of stillness was broken, and the little people had us spread on tables with sharp-pointed objects pointed at us. If any one of those punctured a suit even for a moment, we would be dead. We held very still.

Richard Nixon Dixon, the top halibut, interrogated us himself. It all started with a lot of questions about the Russians, when we had visited them, why we had decided to serve them instead of the Americans, etc. We kept insisting that they were full of crap.

But when they threatened to open a window into Vladimir's suit, I decided enough was enough.

"Tell 'em!" I shouted into the monkeymouth, and Vladimir said, "All right," and the little people leaned back to listen.

"There *are* no Russians," Vladimir said.

The little people got ready to carve holes.

"No, wait, it's true! After we got your homing signal, before we landed, we made seven orbital passes over the entire planet. There is absolutely no human life anywhere but here!"

"Commie lies," Richard Nixon Dixon said.

"God's own truth!" I shouted. "Don't touch

him, man! He's telling the truth! The only thing out there over this whole damn planet is that pea soup! It covers every inch of land and every inch of water, except a few holes at the poles."

Dixon began to feel a little confused, and the little people murmured. I guess I sounded sincere.

"If there aren't any people," Dixon said, "where do the Russian attacks come from?"

Vladimir answered that one. For a bunny, he was quick on the uptake. "Spontaneous recombination! You and the Russians got new strains of every microbe developing like crazy. All the people, all the animals, all the *plants* were killed. And only the microbes lived. But you've been introducing new strains constantly, tough competitors for all those beasts out there. The ones that couldn't adapt died. And now that's all that's left—the ones who adapt. Constantly."

Andrew Jackson Wallichinsky, the head researcher, nodded. "It sounds plausible."

"If there's anything we've learned about commies in the last thousand years," Richard Nixon Dixon said, "it's that you can't trust 'em any farther than you can spit."

"Well," Andy Jack said, "it's easy enough to test them."

Dixon nodded. "Go ahead."

So three of the little people went to the boxes and each came back with an amoeba. In a minute it was clear that they planned to set them on us. Amauri screamed. Vladimir turned whiter. I would have screamed but I was busy trying to swallow my tongue.

"Relax," Andy Jack said. "They won't hurt you."

"Acredito!" I shouted. "Like it didn't hurt Harold!"

"Harold was killing people. These won't harm you. Unless you were lying."

Great, I thought. Like the ancient test for witches. Throw them in the water, if they drown they're innocent, if they float they're guilty so kill 'em.

But *maybe* Andy Jack was telling the truth and they wouldn't hurt us. And if we refused to let them put those buggers on us they'd "know" we had been lying and punch holes in our monkeysuits.

So I told the little people to put one on me only. They didn't need to test us all.

And then I put my tongue between my teeth, ready to bite down hard and inhale the blood when the damn thing started eating me. Somehow I thought I'd feel better about going honeyduck if I helped myself along.

They set the thing on my shoulder. It didn't penetrate my monkeysuit. Instead it just oozed up toward my head.

It slid over my faceplate and the world went dark.

"Kane Kanea," said a faint vibration in the faceplate.

"Meu deus," I muttered.

The amoeba could talk. But I didn't have to speak to answer it. A question would come through the vibration of the faceplate. And then I would lie there and—it knew my answer. Easy as pie. I was so scared I urinated twice during the interview. But my imperturbable monkeysuit cleaned it all up and got it ready for breakfast, just like normal.

And at last the interview was over. The amoeba slithered off my faceplate and returned to the waiting arms of one of the little people, who carried it back to Andy Jack and Ricky Nick. The two men put their hands on the thing, and then looked at us in surprise.

"You're telling the truth. There are no Russians."

Vladimir shrugged. "Why would we lie?"

Andy Jack started toward me, carrying the writhing monster that had interviewed me.

"I'll kill myself before I let that thing touch me again."

Andy Jack stopped in surprise. "You're still afraid of that?"

"It's intelligent," I said. "It read my mind."

Vladimir looked startled, and Amauri muttered something. But Andy Jack only smiled. "Nothing mysterious about that. It can read and interpret the electromagnetic fields of your brain, coupled with the amitron flux in your thyroid gland."

"What *is* it?" Vladimir asked.

Andy Jack looked very proud. "This one is my son."

We waited for the punchline. It didn't come. And suddenly we realized that we had found what we had been looking for—the result of the little people's research into recombinant human DNA.

"We've been working on these for years. Finally we got it right about four years ago," Andy Jack said. "They were our last line of defense. But now that we know the Russians are dead—well, there's no reason for them to stay in their nests."

And the man reached down and laid the amoeba into the pea soup that was now about sixty centimeters deep on the floor. Immediately it flattened out on the surface until it was about a meter in diameter. I remembered the whispering voice through my faceplate.

"It's too flexible to have a brain," Vladimir said.

"It doesn't have one," Andy Jack answered. "The brain functions are distributed throughout the body. If it were cut in forty pieces, each piece would have enough memory and enough mindfunction to continue to live. It's indestructible. And when several of them get together, they set up a sympathetic field. They became very bright, then."

"Head of the class and everything, I'm sure," Vladimir said. He couldn't hide the loathing in his voice. Me, I was trying not to be sick.

So this is the next stage of evolution, I thought. Man screws up the planet till it's fit for nothing but microbes—and then changes himself so that he can live on a diet of bacteria and viruses.

"It's really the perfect step in evolution," Andy Jack said. "This fellow can adapt to new species of parasitic bacteria and viruses almost by reflex. Control the makeup of his own DNA consciously. Manipulate the DNA of other organisms by absorbing them through the semipermeable membranes of specialized cells, altering them, and setting them free again."

"Somehow it doesn't make me want to feed it or change its diapers."

Andy Jack laughed lightly. "Since they reproduce by fission, they're never infant. Oh, if the piece were too small, it would take a while to get back to adult competence again. But otherwise, in the normal run of things, it's always an adult."

Then Andy Jack reached down, let his son wrap itself around his arm, and then walked back to where Richard Nixon Dixon stood watching. Andy Jack put the arm that held the amoeba around Dixon's shoulder.

"By the way, sir," Andy Jack said. "With the Russians dead, the damned war is over, sir."

Dixon looked startled. "And?"

"We don't need a commander anymore."

Before Dixon could answer, the amoeba had eaten through his neck and he was quite dead. Rather an abrupt coup, I thought, and looked at the other little people for a reaction. No one seemed to mind. Apparently their superpatriotic militarism was only skin deep. I felt vaguely relieved. Maybe they had something in common with me after all.

They decided to let us go, and we were glad enough to take them up on the offer. On the way out, they showed us what had caused the explosion in the last "Russian" attack. The mold that protected the steel surface of the installation had mutated slightly in one place, allowing the steel-eating bacteria to enter into a symbiotic relationship. It just happened that the mutation occurred at the place where the hydrogen storage tanks rested against the wall. When a hole opened, one of the first amino-acid sets that came through with the pea soup was one that combines radically with raw hydrogen. The effect was a three-second population explosion. It knocked out a huge chunk of Post 004.

We were glad, when we got back to our skipship, that we had left dear old Pollywog floating some forty meters off the ground. Even so, there had been some damage. One of the airborne microbes had a penchant for lodging in hairline cracks and reproducing rapidly, widening microscopic gaps in the structure of the ship. Nevertheless, Amauri judged us fit for takeoff.

We didn't kiss anybody good-bye.

So now I've let you in on the true story of our visit to Mother Earth back in 2810. The parallel with our current situation should be obvious. If we let Pennsylvania get soaked into this spongy little war between Kiev and Núncamais, we'll deserve what we get. Because those damned antimatter convertors will do things that make germ warfare look as pleasant as sniffing pinkweeds.

And if anything human survives the war, it sure as hell won't look like anything we call human now.

And maybe that doesn't matter to anybody these days. But it matters to me. I don't like the idea of amoebas for grandchildren, and having an antimatter great-nephew thrills me less. I've been human all my life, and I like it.

So I say, turn on our repressors and sit out the damned war. Wait until they've disappeared each other, and then go about the business of keeping humanity alive—and human.

So much for the political tract. If you vote for war, though, I can promise you there'll be more than one skipship heading for the wild black yonder. We've colonized before, and we can do it again. In case no one gets the hint, that's a call for volunteers, if, as, and when. Over.

Not over. On the first printing of this program, I got a lot of inquiries as to why we didn't report all this when we got back home. The answer's simple. On Núncamais it's a capital crime to alter a ship's log. But we had to.

As soon as we got into space from Mother Earth, Vladimir had the computer present all its findings, all its data, and all its conclusions about recombinant DNA. And then he erased it all.

I probably would have stopped him if I'd known what he was doing in advance. But once it was done, Amauri and I realized that he was right. That kind of merda didn't belong in the universe. And then we systematically covered our tracks. We erased all reference to Post 004, eradicated any hint of a homing signal. All we left in the computer was the recording of our overflight, showing nothing but pea soup from sea to soupy sea. It was tricky, but we also added a serious malfunction of the EVA lifesupport gear on the way home—which cost us the life of our dear friend and comrade, Harold.

And then we recorded in the ship's log, "Planet unfit for human occupancy. No human life found."

Hell. It wasn't even a lie.

Eumenides in the
Fourth Floor Lavatory

Living in a fourth-floor walkup was part of his revenge, as if to say to Alice, "Throw me out of the
house, will you? Then I'll live in squalor in a Bronx
tenement, where the toilet is shared by four apart-
ments! My shirts will go unironed, my tie will be
perpetually awry. *See what you've done to me?*"

But when he told Alice about the apartment,
she only laughed bitterly and said, "Not anymore,
Howard. I won't play those games with you. You win
every damn time."

She pretended not to care about him anymore,
but Howard knew better. He knew people, knew what
they wanted, and Alice wanted *him*. It was his strong-
est card in their relationship—that she wanted him
more than he wanted her. He thought of this often: at
work in the offices of Humboldt and Breinhardt, De-
signers; at lunch in a cheap lunchroom (part of the
punishment); on the subway home to his tenement
(Alice had kept the Lincoln Continental). He thought
and thought about how much she wanted him. But he
kept remembering what she had said the day she threw
him out: If you ever come near Rhiannon again I'll
kill you.

He could not remember why she had said that.
Could not remember and did not try to remember
because that line of thinking made him uncomfortable and one thing Howard insisted on being was
comfortable with himself. Other people could spend
hours and days of their lives chasing after some ac-

commodation with themselves, but Howard was accommodated. Well adjusted. At ease. I'm OK, I'm OK, I'm OK. Hell with you. "If you let them make you feel uncomfortable," Howard would often say, "you give them a handle on you and they can run your life." Howard could find other people's handles, but they could never find Howard's.

It was not yet winter but cold as hell at three A.M. when Howard got home from Stu's party. A must-attend party, if you wished to get ahead at Humboldt and Breinhardt. Stu's ugly wife tried to be tempting, but Howard had played innocent and made her feel so uncomfortable that she dropped the matter. Howard paid careful attention to office gossip and knew that several earlier departures from the company had got caught with, so to speak, their pants down. Not that Howard's pants were an impenetrable barrier. He got Dolores from the front office into the bedroom and accused her of making life miserable for him. "In little ways," he insisted. "I know you don't mean to, but you've got to stop."

"What ways?" Dolores asked, incredulous yet (because she honestly tried to make other people happy) uncomfortable.

"Surely you knew how attracted I am to you."

"No. That hasn't—that hasn't even crossed my mind."

Howard looked tongue-tied, embarrassed. He actually was neither. "Then—well, then, I was—I was wrong, I'm sorry, I thought you were doing it deliberately—"

"Doing what?"

"Snub—snubbing me—never mind, it sounds adolescent, just little things, hell, Dolores, I had a stupid schoolboy crush—"

"Howard, I didn't even know I was hurting you."

"God, how insensitive," Howard said, sounding even more hurt.

"Oh, Howard, do I mean that much to you?"

Howard made a little whimpering noise that meant everything she wanted it to mean. She looked uncomfortable. She'd do anything to get back to feeling right with herself again. She was so uncomfortable that they spent a rather nice half hour making each other feel comfortable again. No one else in the office had been able to get to Dolores. But Howard could get to anybody.

He walked up the stairs to his apartment feeling very, very satisfied. Don't need you, Alice, he said to himself. Don't need nobody, and nobody's who I've got. He was still mumbling the little ditty to himself as he went into the communal bathroom and turned on the light.

He heard a gurgling sound from the toilet stall, a hissing sound. Had someone been in there with the light off? Howard went into the toilet stall and saw nobody. Then looked closer and saw a baby, probably about two months old, lying in the toilet bowl. Its nose and eyes were barely above the water; it looked terrified, its legs and hips and stomach were down the drain. Someone had obviously hoped to kill it by drowning—it was inconceivable to Howard that anyone could be so moronic as to think it would fit down the drain.

For a moment he thought of leaving it there, with the big-city temptation to mind one's own business even when to do so would be an atrocity. Saving this baby would mean inconvenience: calling the police, taking care of the child in his apartment, perhaps even headlines, certainly a night of filling out reports. Howard was tired. Howard wanted to go to bed.

But he remembered Alice saying, "You aren't even human, Howard. You're a goddam selfish monster." I am not a monster, he answered silently, and reached down into the toilet bowl to pull the child out.

The baby was firmly jammed in—whoever had tried to kill it had meant to catch it tight. Howard felt a brief surge of genuine indignation that anyone could think to solve his problems by killing an innocent child. But thinking of crimes committed on children was something Howard was determined not to do, and besides, at that moment he suddenly acquired other things to think about.

As the child clutched at Howard's arm, he noticed the baby's fingers were fused together into flipperlike flaps of bone and skin at the end of the arm. Yet the flippers gripped his arms with an unusual strength as, with two hands deep in the toilet bowl, Howard tried to pull the baby free.

At last, with a gush, the child came up and the water finished its flushing action. The legs, too, were fused into a single limb that was hideously twisted at the end. The child was male; the genitals, larger than normal, were skewed off to one side. And Howard noticed that where the feet should be were two more flippers, and near the tips were red spots that looked like putrefying sores. The child cried, a savage mewling that reminded Howard of a dog he had seen in its death throes. (Howard refused to be reminded that it had been he who killed the dog by throwing it out in the street in front of a passing car, just to watch the driver swerve; the driver hadn't swerved.)

Even the hideously deformed have a right to live, Howard thought, but now, holding the child in his arms, he felt a revulsion that translated into sympathy for whoever, probably the parents, had tried to kill the creature. The child shifted its grip on him, and where the flippers had been Howard felt a sharp, stinging pain that quickly turned to agony as it was exposed to the air. Several huge, gaping sores on his arm were already running with blood and pus.

It took a moment for Howard to connect the sores with the child, and by then the leg flippers were already pressed against his stomach, and the arm flippers already gripped his chest. The sores on the child's flippers were not sores; they were powerful suction devices that gripped Howard's skin so tightly that it ripped away when the contact was broken. He tried to pry the child off, but no sooner was one flipper free than it found a new place to hold even as Howard struggled to break the grip of another.

What had begun as an act of charity had now become an intense struggle. This was not a child, Howard realized. Children could not hang on so tightly, and the creature had teeth that snapped at his hands and arms whenever they came near enough. A human face, certainly, but not a human being. Howard threw himself against the wall, hoping to stun the creature so it would drop away. It only clung tighter, and the sores where it hung on him hurt more. But at last Howard pried and scraped it off by levering it against the edge of the toilet stall. It dropped to the ground, and Harold backed quickly away, on fire with the pain of a dozen or more stinging wounds.

It had to be a nightmare. In the middle of the night, in a bathroom lighted by a single bulb, with a travesty of humanity writhing on the floor, Howard could not believe that it had any reality.

Could it be a mutation that had somehow lived? Yet the thing had far more purpose, far more control of its body than any human infant. The baby slithered across the floor as Howard, in pain from the wounds on his body, watched in a panic of indecision. The baby reached the wall and cast a flipper onto it. The suction held and the baby began to inch its way straight up the wall. As it climbed, it defecated, a thin

drool of green tracing down the wall behind it. Howard looked at the slime following the infant up the
wall, looked at the pus-covered sores on his arms.

What if the animal, whatever it was, did not
die soon of its terrible deformity? What if it lived?
What if it were found, taken to a hospital, cared for?
What if it became an adult?

It reached the ceiling and made the turn, clinging tightly to the plaster, not falling off as it hung
upside down and inched across toward the light bulb.

The thing was trying to get directly over Howard, and the defecation was still dripping. Loathing
overcame fear, and Howard reached up, took hold of
the baby from the back, and, using his full weight,
was finally able to pry it off the ceiling. It writhed and
twisted in his hands, trying to get the suction cups on
him, but Howard resisted with all his strength and
was able to get the baby, this time headfirst, into the
toilet bowl. He held it there until the bubbles stopped
and it was blue. Then he went back to his apartment
for a knife. Whatever the creature was, it had to disappear from the face of the earth. It had to die, and
there had to be no sign left that could hint that Howard had killed it.

He found the knife quickly, but paused for a
few moments to put something on his wounds. They
stung bitterly, but in a while they felt better. Howard
took off his shirt; thought a moment and took off all
his clothes, then put on his bathrobe and took a towel
with him as he returned to the bathroom. He didn't
want to get any blood on his clothes.

But when he got to the bathroom, the child was
not in the toilet. Howard was alarmed. Had someone
found it, drowning? Had they, perhaps, seen him
leaving the bathroom—or worse, returning with his
knife? He looked around the bathroom. There was
nothing. He stepped back into the hall. No one. He

stood a moment in the doorway, wondering what could have happened.

Then a weight dropped onto his head and shoulders from above, and he felt the suction flippers tugging at his face, at his head. He almost screamed. But he didn't want to arouse anyone. Somehow the child had not drowned after all, had crawled out of the toilet, and had waited over the door for Howard to return.

Once again the struggle resumed, and once again Howard pried the flippers away with the help of the toilet stall, though this time he was hampered by the fact that the child was behind and above him. It was exhausting work. He had to set down the knife so he could use both hands, and another dozen wounds stung bitterly by the time he had the child on the floor. As long as the child lay on its stomach, Howard could seize it from behind. He took it by the neck with one hand and picked up the knife with the other. He carried both to the toilet.

He had to flush twice to handle the flow of blood and pus. Howard wondered if the child was infected with some disease—the white fluid was thick and at least as great in volume as the blood. Then he flushed seven more times to take the pieces of the creature down the drain. Even after death, the suction pads clung tightly to the porcelain; Howard pried them off with the knife.

Eventually, the child was completely gone. Howard was panting with the exertion, nauseated at the stench and horror of what he had done. He remembered the smell of his dog's guts after the car hit it, and he threw up everything he had eaten at the party. Got the party out of his system, felt cleaner; took a shower, felt cleaner still. When he was through, he made sure the bathroom showed no sign of his ordeal.

Then he went to bed.

It wasn't easy to sleep. He was too keyed up. He couldn't take out of his mind the thought that he had committed murder (not murder, not murder, simply the elimination of something too foul to be alive). He tried thinking of a dozen, a hundred other things. Projects at work—but the designs kept showing flippers. His children—but their faces turned to the intense face of the struggling monster he had killed. Alice—ah, but Alice was harder to think of than the creature.

At last he slept, and dreamed, and in his dream remembered his father, who had died when he was ten. Howard did not remember any of his standard reminiscences. No long walks with his father, no basketball in the driveway, no fishing trips. Those things had happened, but tonight, because of the struggle with the monster, Howard remembered darker things that he had long been able to keep hidden from himself.

"We can't afford to get you a ten-speed bike, Howie. Not until the strike is over."

"I know, Dad. You can't help it." Swallow bravely. "And I don't mind. When all the guys go riding around after school, I'll just stay home and get ahead on my homework."

"Lots of boys don't have ten-speed bikes, Howie."

Howie shrugged, and turned away to hide the tears in his eyes. "Sure, lot of them. Hey, Dad, don't you worry about me. Howie can take care of himself."

Such courage. Such strength. He had got a ten-speed within a week. In his dream, Howard finally made a connection he had never been able to admit to himself before. His father had a rather elaborate ham radio setup in the garage. But about that time he had become tired of it, he said, and he sold it off and did a lot more work in the yard and looked bored as hell until the strike was over and he went back to work and got killed in an accident in the rolling mill.

Howard's dream ended madly, with him riding piggy-back on his father's shoulders as the monster had ridden on *him*, tonight—and in his hand was a knife, and he was stabbing his father again and again in the throat.

He awoke in early morning light, before his alarm rang, sobbing weakly and whimpering, "I killed him, I killed him, I killed him."

And then he drifted upward out of sleep and saw the time. Six-thirty. "A dream," he said. And the dream had woken him early, too early, with a headache and sore eyes from crying. The pillow was soaked. "A hell of a lousy way to start the day," he mumbled. And, as was his habit, he got up and went to the window and opened the curtain.

On the glass, suction cups clinging tightly, was the child.

It was pressed close, as if by sucking very tightly it would be able to slither through the glass without breaking it. Far below were the honks of early morning traffic, the roar of passing trucks: but the child seemed oblivious to its height far above the street, with no ledge to break its fall. Indeed, there seemed little chance it would fall. The eyes looked closely, piercingly at Howard.

Howard had been prepared to pretend that the night before had been another terribly realistic nightmare.

He stepped back from the glass, watched the child in fascination. It lifted a flipper, planted it higher, pulled itself up to a new position where it could stare at Howard eye to eye. And then, slowly and methodically, it began beating on the glass with its head.

The landlord was not generous with upkeep on the building. The glass was thin, and Howard knew that the child would not give up until it had broken through the glass so it could get to Howard.

He began to shake. His throat tightened. He was terribly afraid. Last night had been no dream. The fact that the child was here today was proof of that. Yet he had cut the child into small pieces. It could not possibly be alive. The glass shook and rattled with every blow the child's head struck.

The glass slivered in a starburst from where the child had hit it. The creature was coming in. And Howard picked up the room's one chair and threw it at the child, threw it at the window. Glass shattered, and the sun dazzled on the fragments as they exploded outward like a glistening halo around the child and the chair.

Howard ran to the window, looked out, looked down and watched as the child landed brutally on the top of a large truck. The body seemed to smear as it hit, and fragments of the chair and shreds of glass danced around the child and bounced down into the street and the sidewalk.

The truck didn't stop moving; it carried the broken body and the shards of glass and the pool of blood on up the street, and Howard ran to the bed, knelt beside it, buried his face in the blanket, and tried to regain control of himself. He had been seen. The people in the street had looked up and seen him in the window. Last night he had gone to great lengths to avoid discovery, but today discovery was impossible to avoid. He was ruined. And yet he could not, could never have let the child come into the room.

Footsteps on the stairs. Stamping up the corridor. Pounding on the door. "Open up! Hey in there!"

If I'm quiet long enough, they'll go away, he

said to himself, knowing it was a lie. He must get up, must answer the door. But he could not bring himself to admit that he ever had to leave the safety of his bed.

"Hey, you son-of-a-bitch—" The imprecations went on but Howard could not move until, suddenly, it occurred to him that the child could be under the bed, and as he thought of it he could feel the tip of the flipper touching his thigh, stroking and ready to fasten itself—

Howard leaped to his feet and rushed for the door. He flung it wide, for even if it was the police come to arrest him, they could protect him from the monster that was haunting him.

It was not a policeman at the door. It was the man on the first floor who collected rent. "You son-of-a-bitch irresponsible pig-kisser!" the man shouted, his toupee only approximately in place. "That chair could have hit somebody! That window's expensive! Out! Get out of here, right now, I want you out of this place, I don't care how the hell drunk you are—"

"There was—there was this thing on the window, this creature—"

The man looked at him coldly, but his eyes danced with anger. No, not anger. Fear. Howard realized the man was afraid of him.

"This is a decent place," the man said softly. "You can take your creatures and your booze and your pink stinking elephants and that's a hundred bucks for the window, a hundred bucks right now, and you can get out of here in an hour, an hour, you hear? Or I'm calling the police, you hear?"

"I hear." He heard. The man left when Howard counted out five twenties. The man seemed careful to avoid touching Howard's hands, as if Howard had become, somehow, repulsive. Well, he had. To himself, if to no one else. He closed the door as soon as the

man was gone. He packed the few belongings he had
brought to the apartment in two suitcases and went
downstairs and called a cab and rode to work. The
cabby looked at him sourly, and wouldn't talk. It was
fine with Howard, if only the driver hadn't kept looking at him through the mirror—nervously, as if he was
afraid of what Howard might do or try. I won't try
anything, Howard said to himself, I'm a decent man.
Howard tipped the cabby well and then gave him
twenty to take his bags to his house in Queens, where
Alice could damn well keep them for a while. Howard
was through with the tenement—that one or any
other.

Obviously it had been a nightmare, last night
and this morning. The monster was only visible to
him, Howard decided. Only the chair and the glass
had fallen from the fourth floor, or the manager
would have noticed.

Except that the baby had landed on the truck,
and might have been real, and might be discovered in
New Jersey or Pennsylvania later today.

Couldn't be real. He had killed it last night
and it was whole again this morning. A nightmare. I
didn't really kill anybody, he insisted. (Except the
dog. Except Father, said a new, ugly voice in the back
of his mind.)

Work. Draw lines on paper, answer phone calls,
dictate letters, keep your mind off your nightmares, off
your family, off the mess your life is turning into.
"Hell of a good party last night." Yeah, it was, wasn't
it? "How are you today, Howard?" Feel fine, Dolores,
fine—thanks to you. "Got the roughs on the IBM
thing?" Nearly, nearly. Give me another twenty minutes. "Howard, you don't look well." Had a rough
night. The party, you know.

He kept drawing on the blotter on his desk
instead of going to the drawing table and producing

real work. He doodled out faces. Alice's face, looking stern and terrible. The face of Stu's ugly wife. Dolores's face, looking sweet and yielding and stupid. And Rhiannon's face.

But with his daughter Rhiannon, he couldn't stop with the face.

His hand started to tremble when he saw what he had drawn. He ripped the sheet off the blotter, crumpled it, and reached under the desk to drop it in the wastebasket. The basket lurched, and flippers snaked out to seize his hand in an iron grip.

Howard screamed, tried to pull his hand away. The child came with it, the leg flippers grabbing Howard's right leg. The suction pad stung, bringing back the memory of all the pain last night. He scraped the child off against a filing cabinet, then ran for the door, which was already opening as several of his co-workers tumbled into his office demanding, "What is it! What's wrong! Why did you scream like that!"

Howard led them gingerly over to where the child should be. Nothing. Just an overturned wastebasket, Howard's chair capsized on the floor. But Howard's window was open, and he could not remember opening it. "Howard, what is it? Are you tired, Howard? What's wrong?"

I don't feel well. I don't feel well at all.

Dolores put her arm around him, led him out of the room. "Howard, I'm worried about you."

I'm worried, too.

"Can I take you home? I have my car in the garage downstairs. Can I take you home?"

Where's home? Don't have a home, Dolores.

"My home, then. I have an apartment, you need to lie down and rest. Let me take you home."

Dolores's apartment was decorated in early Holly Hobby, and when she put records on the stereo it was old Carpenters and recent Captain and Tennille. Dolores led him to the bed, gently undressed him, and then, because he reached out to her, undressed herself and made love to him before she went back to work. She was naively eager. She whispered in his ear that he was only the second man she had ever loved, the first in five years. Her inept lovemaking was so sincere it made him want to cry.

When she was gone he did cry, because she thought she meant something to him and she did not.

Why am I crying? he asked himself. Why should I care? It's not my fault she let me get a handle on her. . . .

Sitting on the dresser in a curiously adult posture was the child, carelessly playing with itself as it watched Howard intently. "No," Howard said, pulling himself up to the head of the bed. "You don't exist," he said. "No one's ever seen you but me." The child gave no sign of understanding. It just rolled over and began to slither down the front of the dresser.

Howard reached for his clothes, took them out of the bedroom. He put them on in the living room as he watched the door. Sure enough, the child crept along the carpet to the living room; but Howard was dressed by then, and he left.

He walked the streets for three hours. He was coldly rational at first. Logical. The creature does not exist. There is no reason to believe in it.

But bit by bit his rationality was worn away by constant flickers of the creature at the edges of his vision. On a bench, peering over the back at him; in a shop window; staring from the cab of a milk truck. Howard walked faster and faster, not caring where he went, trying to keep some intelligent process going on in his mind, and failing utterly as he saw the child, saw it clearly, dangling from a traffic signal.

What made it even worse was that occasionally a passerby, violating the unwritten law that New

Yorkers are forbidden to look at each other, would gaze at him, shudder, and look away. A short European-looking woman crossed herself. A group of teen-agers looking for trouble weren't looking for him—they grew silent, let him pass in silence, and in silence watched him out of sight.

They may not be able to see the child, Howard realized, but they see something.

And as he grew less and less coherent in the ramblings of his mind, memories began flashing on and off, his life passing before his eyes like a drowning man is supposed to see, only, he realized, if a drowning man saw this he would gulp at the water, breathe it deeply just to end the visions. They were memories he had been unable to find for years; memories he would never have wanted to find.

His poor, confused mother, who was so eager to be a good parent that she read everything, tried everything. Her precocious son Howard read it, too, and understood it better. Nothing she tried ever worked. And he accused her several times of being too demanding, of not demanding enough; of not giving him enough love, of drowning him in phony affection; of trying to take over with his friends, of not liking his friends enough. Until he had badgered and tortured the woman until she was timid every time she spoke to him, careful and longwinded and she phrased everything in such a way that it wouldn't offend, and while now and then he made her feel wonderful by giving her a hug and saying, "Have I got a wonderful mom," there were far more times when he put a patient look on his face and said, "That again, Mom? I thought we went over that years ago." A failure as a parent, that's what you are, he reminded her again and again, though not in so many words, and she nodded and believed and died inside with every contact they had. He got everything he wanted from her.

And Vaughn Robles, who was just a little bit smarter than Howard and Howard wanted very badly to be valedictorian and so Vaughn and Howard became best friends and Vaughn would do anything for Howard and whenever Vaughn got a better grade than Howard he could not help but notice that Howard was hurt, that Howard wondered if he was really worth anything at all. "Am I really worth anything at all, Vaughn? No matter how well I do, there's always someone ahead of me, and I guess it's just that before my father died he told me and told me, Howie, be better than your Dad. Be the top. And I promised him I'd be the top but hell, Vaughn, I'm just not cut out for it—" and once he even cried. Vaughn was proud of himself as he sat there and listened to Howard give the valedictory address at high school graduation. What were a few grades, compared to a true friendship? Howard got a scholarship and went away to college and he and Vaughn almost never saw each other again.

And the teacher he provoked into hitting him and losing his job; and the football player who snubbed him and Howard quietly spread the rumor that the fellow was gay and he was ostracized from the team and finally quit; and the beautiful girls he stole from their boyfriends just to prove that he could do it and the friendships he destroyed just because he didn't like being excluded and the marriages he wrecked and the co-workers he undercut and he walked along the street with tears streaming down his face, wondering where all these memories had come from and why, after such a long time in hiding, they had come out now. Yet he knew the answer. The answer was slipping behind doorways, climbing lightpoles as he passed, waving obscene flippers at him from the sidewalk almost under his feet.

And slowly, inexorably, the memories wound

their way from the distant past through a hundred tawdry exploitations because he could find people's weak spots without even trying until finally memory came to the one place where he knew it could not, could not ever go.

He remembered Rhiannon.

Born fourteen years ago. Smiled early, walked early, almost never cried. A loving child from the start, and therefore easy prey for Howard. Oh, Alice was a bitch in her own right—Howard wasn't the only bad parent in the family. But it was Howard who manipulated Rhiannon most. "Daddy's feelings are hurt, Sweetheart," and Rhiannon's eyes would grow wide, and she'd be sorry, and whatever Daddy wanted, Rhiannon would do. But this was normal, this was part of the pattern, this would have fit easily into all his life before, except for last month.

And even now, after a day of grief at his own life, Howard could not face it. Could not but did. He unwillingly remembered walking by Rhiannon's almost-closed door, seeing just a flash of cloth moving quickly. He opened the door on impulse, just on impulse, as Rhiannon took off her brassiere and looked at herself in the mirror. Howard had never thought of his daughter with desire, not until that moment, but once the desire formed Howard had no strategy, no pattern in his mind to stop him from trying to get what he wanted. He was *uncomfortable,* and so he stepped into the room and closed the door behind him and Rhiannon knew no way to say no to her father. When Alice opened the door Rhiannon was crying softly, and Alice looked and after a moment Alice screamed and screamed and Howard got up from the bed and tried to smooth it all over but Rhiannon was still crying and Alice was still screaming, kicking at his crotch, beating him, raking at his face, spitting at him, telling him he was a monster, a monster, until at last he was able to flee the room and the house and, until now, the memory.

He screamed now as he had not screamed then, and threw himself against a plate-glass window, weeping loudly as the blood gushed from a dozen glass cuts on his right arm, which had gone through the window. One large piece of glass stayed embedded in his forearm. He deliberately scraped his arm against the wall to drive the glass deeper. But the pain in his arm was no match for the pain in his mind, and he felt nothing.

They rushed him to the hospital, thinking to save his life, but the doctor was surprised to discover that for all the blood there were only superficial wounds, not dangerous at all. "I don't know why you didn't reach a vein or an artery," the doctor said. "I think the glass went everywhere it could possibly go without causing any important damage."

After the medical doctor, of course, there was the psychiatrist, but there were many suicidals at the hospital and Howard was not the dangerous kind. "I was insane for a moment, Doctor, that's all. I don't want to die, I didn't want to die then, I'm all right now. You can send me home." And the psychiatrist let him go home. They bandaged his arm. They did not know that his real relief was that nowhere in the hospital did he see the small, naked, child-shaped creature. He had purged himself. He was free.

Howard was taken home in an ambulance, and they wheeled him into the house and lifted him from the stretcher to the bed. Through it all Alice hardly said a word except to direct them to the bedroom. Howard lay still on the bed as she stood over him, the two of them alone for the first time since he had left the house a month ago.

"It was kind of you," Howard said softly, "to let me come back."

"They said there wasn't room enough to keep you, but you needed to be watched and taken care of for a few weeks. So lucky me, I get to watch you." Her voice was a low monotone, but the acid dripped from every word. It stung.

"You were right, Alice," Howard said.

"Right about what? That marrying you was the worst mistake of my life? No, Howard. *Meeting* you was my worst mistake."

Howard began to cry. Real tears that welled up from places in him that had once been deep but that now rested painfully close to the surface. "I've been a monster, Alice. I haven't had any control over myself. What I did to Rhiannon—Alice, I wanted to die, I wanted to die!"

Alice's face was twisted and bitter. "And I wanted you to, Howard. I have never been so disappointed as when the doctor called and said you'd be all right. You'll never be all right, Howard, you'll always be—"

"Let him be, Mother."

Rhiannon stood in the doorway.

"Don't come in, Rhiannon," Alice said.

Rhiannon came in. "Daddy, it's all right."

"What she means," Alice said, "is that we've checked her and she isn't pregnant. No little monster is going to be born."

Rhiannon didn't look at her mother, just gazed with wide eyes at her father. "You didn't need to— hurt yourself, Daddy. I forgive you. People lose control sometimes. And it was as much my fault as yours, it really was, you don't need to feel bad, Father."

It was too much for Howard. He cried out, shouted his confession, how he had manipulated her all his life, how he was an utterly selfish and rotten parent, and when it was over Rhiannon came to her father and laid her head on his chest and said, softly,

"Father, it's all right. We are who we are. We've done what we've done. But it's all right now. I forgive you."

When Rhiannon left, Alice said, "You don't deserve her."

I know.

"I was going to sleep on the couch, but that would be stupid. Wouldn't it, Howard?"

I deserve to be left alone, like a leper.

"You misunderstand, Howard. I need to stay here to make sure you don't do anything else. To yourself or to anyone."

Yes. Yes, please. I can't be trusted.

"Don't wallow in it, Howard. Don't enjoy it. Don't make yourself even more disgusting than you were before."

All right.

They were drifting off to sleep when Alice said, "Oh, when the doctor called he wondered if I knew what had caused those sores all over your arms and chest."

But Howard was asleep, and didn't hear her. Alseep with no dreams at all, the sleep of peace, the sleep of having been forgiven, of being clean. It hadn't taken that much, after all. Now that it was over, it was easy. He felt as if a great weight had been taken from him.

He felt as if something heavy was lying on his legs. He awoke, sweating even though the room was not hot. He heard breathing. And it was not Alice's low-pitched, slow breath, it was quick and high and hard, as if the breather had been exerting himself.

Itself.

Themselves.

One of them lay across his legs, the flippers plucking at the blanket. The other two lay on either side, their eyes wide and intent, creeping slowly toward where his face emerged from the sheets.

Howard was puzzled. "I thought you'd be gone," he said to the children. "You're supposed to be gone now."

Alice stirred at the sound of his voice, mumbled in her sleep.

He saw more of them stirring in the gloomy corners of the room, another writhing slowly along the top of the dresser, another inching up the wall toward the ceiling.

"I don't need you anymore," he said, his voice oddly high-pitched.

Alice started breathing irregularly, mumbling, "What? What?"

And Howard said nothing more, just lay there in the sheets, watching the creatures carefully but not daring to make a sound for fear Alice would wake up. He was terribly afraid she would wake up and not see the creatures, which would prove, once and for all, that he had lost his mind.

He was even more afraid, however, that when she awoke she *would* see them. That was the one unbearable thought, yet he thought it continuously as they relentlessly approached with nothing at all in their eyes, not even hate, not even anger, not even contempt. We are with you, they seemed to be saying, we will be with you from now on. We will be with you, Howard, forever.

And Alice rolled over and opened her eyes.

Mortal Gods

The first contact was peaceful, almost uneventful: sudden landings near government buildings all over the world, brief discussions in the native languages, followed by treaties allowing the aliens to build certain buildings in certain places in exchange for certain favors—nothing spectacular. The technological improvements that the aliens brought helped make life better for everyone, but they were improvements that were already well within the reach of human engineers within the next decade or two. And the greatest gift of all was found to be a disappointment—space travel. The aliens did not have faster-than-light travel. Instead, they had conclusive proof that faster-than-light travel was utterly impossible. They had infinite patience and incredibly long lives to sustain them in their snail's-pace crawl among the stars, but humans would be dead before even the shortest space flight was fairly begun.

And after only a little while, the presence of aliens was regarded as quite the normal thing. They insisted that they had no further gifts to bring, and simply exercised their treaty rights to build and visit the buildings that they had made.

The buildings were all different from each other, but had one thing in common: by the standards of the local populace, the new alien buildings were all clearly recognizable as churches.

Mosques. Cathedrals. Shrines. Synagogues. Temples. All unmistakably churches.

But no congregation was invited, though any person who came to such a place was welcomed by whatever aliens happened to be there at the time, who engaged in charming discussion totally related to the person's own interests. Farmers conversed about farming, engineers about engineering, housewives about motherhood, dreamers about dreams, travelers about travels, astronomers about the stars. Those who came and talked went away feeling good. Feeling that someone did, indeed, attach importance to their lives —had come trillions of kilometers through incredible boredom (five hundred years in space, they said!) just to see *them*.

And gradually life settled into a peaceful routine. Scientists, it is true, kept on discovering, and engineers kept on building according to those discoveries, and so changes *did* come. But knowing now that there was no great scientific revolution just around the corner, no tremendous discovery that would open up the stars, men and women settled down, by and large, to the business of being happy.

It wasn't as hard as people had supposed.

Willard Crane was an old man, but a content one. His wife was dead, but he did not resent the brief interregnum in his life in which he was solitary again, a thing he had not been since he came home from the Vietnam War with half a foot missing and found his girl waiting for him anyway, foot or no foot. They had lived all their married lives in a house in the Avenues of Salt Lake City, which, when they moved there, had been a shabby, dilapidated relic of a previous century, but which now was a splendid preservation of a noble era in architecture. Willard was in that comfortable area between heavy wealth and heavier poverty; enough money to satisfy normal aspirations, but not enough to tempt him to extravagance.

Every day he walked from 7th Avenue and L Street to the cemetery, not far away, where practically everyone had been buried. It was there, in the middle of the cemetery, that the alien building stood—an obvious mimic of old Mormon temple architecture, meaning it was a monstrosity of conflicting periods that somehow, perhaps through intense sincerity, managed to be beautiful anyway.

And there he sat among the gravestones, watching as occasional people wandered into and out of the sanctuary where the aliens came, visited, left.

Happiness is boring as hell, he decided one day. And so, to provoke a little delightful variety, he decided to pick a fight with somebody. Unfortunately, everyone he knew at all well was far too nice to fight. And so he decided that he had a bone to pick with the aliens.

When you're old, you can get away with anything.

He went to the alien temple and walked inside.

On the walls were murals, paintings, maps; on the floor, pedestals with statues; it seemed more a museum than anything else. There were few places to sit, and he saw no sign of aliens. Which wouldn't be a disaster; just deciding on a good argument had been variety enough, no need to actually have one. Willard just walked among the exhibits, noting with pride the fine quality of the work the aliens had chosen to display.

But there was an alien there, after all.

"Good morning, Mr. Crane," said the alien.

"How the hell you know my name?"

"You perch on a tombstone every morning and watch as people come in and go out. We found you fascinating. We asked around." The alien's voicebox was very well programmed—a warm, friendly, interested voice. And Willard was too old and jaded with novelty to get much excited about the way the alien slithered along the floor and slopped on the bench next to him like a large, self-moving piece of seaweed.

"We wished you would come in."

"I'm in."

"And why?"

Now that the question was put, his reason seemed trivial to him; but he decided to play the game all the way through. Why not, after all? "I have a bone to pick with you."

"Heavens," said the alien, with mock horror.

"I have some questions that have never been answered to my satisfaction."

"Then I trust we'll have some answers."

"All right then." But what *were* his questions? "You'll have to forgive me if my mind gets screwed around. The brain dies first, as you know."

"We know."

"Why'd you build a temple here? How come you build churches?"

"Why, Mr. Crane, we've answered that a thousand times. We *like* churches. We find them the most graceful and beautiful of all human architecture."

"I don't believe you," Willard said. "You're dodging my question. So let me put it another way. How come you have the time to sit around and talk to half-assed imbeciles like me? Haven't you got anything better to do?"

"Human beings are unusually good company. It's a most pleasant way to pass the time which does, after many years, weigh rather heavily on our, um, hands." And the alien tried a gesture with his pseudopodia which was amusing, and Willard laughed.

"Slippery bastards, aren't you?" he inquired, and the alien chuckled. "So let me put it this way, and no dodging, or I'll know you have something to hide. You're pretty much like us, right? You have the same gadgets, but you can travel in space because you don't croak after a hundred years like we do; whatever, you do pretty much the same kinds of things we do. And yet—"

"There's always an 'and yet,' " the alien sighed.

"And *yet*. You come all the way out here, which ain't exactly Main Street, Milky Way, and all you do is build these churches all over the place and sit around and jaw with whoever the hell comes in. Makes no sense, sir, none at all."

The alien oozed gently toward him. "Can you keep a secret?"

"My old lady thought she was the only woman I ever slept with in my life. Some secrets I can keep."

"Then here is one to keep. We come, Mr. Crane, to worship."

"Worship who?"

"Worship, among others, you."

Willard laughed long and loud, but the alien looked (as only aliens can) terribly earnest and sincere.

"Listen, you mean to tell me that you worship *people*?"

"Oh, yes. It is the dream of everyone who dares to dream on my home planet to come here and meet a human being or two and then live on the memory forever."

And suddenly it wasn't funny to Willard anymore. He looked around—human art in prominent display, the whole format, the choice of churches. "You aren't joking."

"No, Mr. Crane. We've wandered the galaxy for several million years, all told, meeting new races and renewing acquaintance with old. Evolution is a tedious old highway—carbon-based life always leads to certain patterns and certain forms, despite the fact that we seem hideously different to you—"

"Not too bad, Mister, a little ugly, but not too bad—"

"All the—people like us that you've seen— well, we don't come from the same planet, though it has been assumed so by your scientists. Actually, we come from thousands of planets. Separate, independent evolution, leading inexorably to us. Absolutely, or nearly absolutely, uniform throughout the galaxy. We are the natural endproduct of evolution."

"So we're the oddballs."

"You might say so. Because somewhere along the line, Mr. Crane, deep in your past, your planet's evolution went astray from the normal. It created something utterly new."

"Sex?"

"We all have sex, Mr. Crane. Without it, how in the world could the race improve? No, what was new on your planet, Mr. Crane, was death."

The word was not an easy one for Willard to hear. His wife had, after all, meant a great deal to him. And he meant even more to himself. Death already loomed in dizzy spells and shortened breath and weariness that refused to turn into sleep.

"Death?"

"We don't die, Mr. Crane. We reproduce by splitting off whole sections of ourselves with identical DNA—you know about DNA?"

"I went to college."

"And with us, of course, as with all other life in the universe, intelligence is carried on the DNA, not in the brain. One of the byproducts of death, the brain is. We don't have it. We split, and the individual, complete with all memories, lives on in the children, who are made up of the actual flesh of my flesh, you see? I will never die."

"Well, bully for you," Willard said, feeling

strangely cheated, and wondering why he hadn't guessed.

"And so we came here and found people whose life had a finish; who began as unformed creatures without memory and, after an incredibly brief span, died."

"And for that you worship us? I might as well go worshiping bugs that die a few minutes after they're born."

The alien chuckled, and Willard resented it.

"Is that why you come here? To gloat?"

"What else would we worship, Mr. Crane? While we don't discount the possibility of invisible gods, we really never have invented any. We never died, so why dream of immortality? Here we found a people who knew how to worship, and for the first time we found awakened in us a desire to do homage to superior beings."

And Willard noticed his heartbeat, realized that it would stop while the alien had no heart, had nothing that would ever end. "Superior, hell."

"We," said the alien, "remember everything, from the first stirrings of intellect to the present. When we are 'born,' so to speak, we have no need of teachers. We have never learned to write—merely to exchange RNA. We have never learned to create beauty to outlast our lives because nothing outlasts our lives. We live to see all our works crumble. Here, Mr. Crane, we have found a race that builds for the sheer joy of building, that creates beauty, that writes books, that invents the lives of never-known people to delight others who know they are being lied to, a race that devises immortal gods to worship and celebrates its own mortality with immense pomp and glory. Death is the foundation of all that is great about humanity, Mr. Crane."

"Like hell it is," said Willard. "I'm about to die, and there's nothing great about it."

"You don't really believe that, Mr. Crane," the alien said. "None of you do. Your lives are built around death, glorifying it. Postponing it as long as possible, to be sure, but glorifying it. In the earliest literature, the death of the hero is the moment of greatest climax. The most potent myth."

"Those poems weren't written by old men with flabby bodies and hearts that only beat when they feel like it."

"Nonsense. Everything you do smacks of death. Your poems have beginnings and endings, and structures that limit the work. Your paintings have edges, marking off where the beauty begins and ends. Your sculptures isolate a moment in time. Your music starts and finishes. All that you do is mortal—it is all born. It all dies. And yet you struggle against mortality and have overcome it, building up tremendous stores of shared knowledge through your finite books and your finite words. You put frames on everything."

"Mass insanity, then. But it explains nothing about why you worship. You must come here to mock us."

"Not to mock you. To envy you."

"Then die. I assume that your protoplasm or whatever is vulnerable."

"You don't understand. A human being can die—*after* he has reproduced—and all that he knew and all that he was will live on after him. But if *I* die, I cannot reproduce. My knowledge dies with me. An awesome responsibility. We cannot assume it. I *am* all the paintings and writings and songs of a million generations. To die would be the death of a civilization. You have cast yourselves free of life and achieved greatness."

"And that's why you come here."

"If ever there were gods. If ever there was power in the universe. You are those gods. You have that power."

"We have no power."

"Mr. Crane, you are beautiful."

And the old man shook his head, stood with difficulty, and doddered out of temple and walked away slowly among the graves.

"You tell them the truth," said the alien to no one in particular (to future generations of himself who would need the memory of the words having been spoken), "and it only makes it worse."

It was only seven months later, and the weather was no longer spring, but now blustered with the icy wind of late autumn. The trees in the cemetery were no longer colorful; they were stripped of all but the last few brown leaves. And into the cemetery walked Willard Crane again, his arms half enclosed by the metal crutches that gave him, in his old age, four points of balance instead of the precarious two that had served him for more than ninety years. A few snowflakes were drifting lazily down, except when the wind snatched them and spun them in crazy dances that had neither rhythm nor direction.

Willard laboriously climbed the steps of the temple.

Inside, an alien was waiting.

"I'm Willard Crane," the old man said.

"And I'm an alien. You spoke to me—or my parent, however you wish to phrase it—several months ago."

"Yes."

"We knew you'd come back."

"Did you? I vowed I never would."

"But we know you. You are well known to us

all, Mr. Crane. There are billions of gods on Earth for us to worship, but you are the noblest of them all."

"I am?"

"Because only you have thought to do us the kindest gift. Only you are willing to let us watch your death."

And a tear leaped from the old man's eye as he blinked heavily.

"Is that why I came?"

"Isn't it?"

"I thought I came to damn your souls to hell, that's why I came, you bastards, coming to taunt me in the final hours of my life."

"You came to us."

"I wanted to show you how ugly death is."

"Please. Do."

And, seemingly eager to oblige them, Willard's heart stopped and he, in brief agony, slumped to the floor in the temple.

The aliens all slithered in, all gathered around closely, watching him rattle for breath.

"I will not die!" he savagely whispered, each breath an agony, his face fierce with the heroism of struggle.

And then his body shuddered and he was still.

The aliens knelt there for hours in silent worship as the body became cold. And then, at last, because they had learned this from their gods—that words must be said to be remembered—one of them spoke:

"Beautiful," he said tenderly. "Oh Lord my God," he said worshipfully.

And they were gnawed within by the grief of knowing that this greatest of all gifts was forever out of their reach.

Quietus

It came to him suddenly, a moment of blackness as he sat working late at his desk. It was as quick as an eyeblink, but before the darkness the papers on his desk had seemed terribly important, and afterward he stared at them blankly, wondering what they were and then realizing that he didn't really give a damn what they were and he ought to be going home now.

Ought definitely to be going home now. And C. Mark Tapworth of CMT Enterprises, Inc., arose from his desk without finishing all the work that was on it, the first time he had done such a thing in the twelve years it had taken him to bring the company from nothing to a multi-million-dollar-a-year business. Vaguely it occurred to him that he was not acting normally, but he didn't really care, it didn't really matter to him a bit whether any more people bought —bought—

And for a few seconds C. Mark Tapworth could not remember what it was that his company made.

It frightened him. It reminded him that his father and his uncles had all died of strokes. It reminded him of his mother's senility at the fairly young age of sixty-eight. It reminded him of something he had always known and never quite believed, that he was mortal and that all the works of all his days would trivialize gradually until his death, at which time his life itself would be his only act, the forgotten stone whose fall had set off ripples in the lake that would in time reach the shore having made, after all, no difference.

I'm tired, he decided. MaryJo is right. I need a rest.

But he was not the resting kind, not until that moment standing by his desk when again the blackness came, this time a jog in his mind and he remembered nothing, saw nothing, heard nothing, was falling interminably through nothingness.

Then, mercifully, the world returned to him and he stood trembling, regretting now the many, many nights he had stayed far too late, the many hours he had not spent with MaryJo, had left her alone in their large but childless house; and he imagined her waiting for him forever, a lonely woman dwarfed by the huge living room, waiting patiently for a husband who would, who must, who always had come home.

Is it my heart? Or a stroke? he wondered. Whatever it was, it was enough that he saw the end of the world lurking in the darkness that had visited him, and like the prophet returning from the mount things that once had mattered overmuch mattered not at all, and things he had long postponed now silently importuned him. He felt a terrible urgency that there was something he must do before—

Before what? He would not let himself answer. He just walked out through the large room full of ambitious younger men and women trying to impress him by working later than he; noticed but did not care that they were visibly relieved at their reprieve from another endless night. He walked out into the night and got in his car and drove home through a thin mist of rain that made the world retreat a comfortable distance from the windows of his car.

The children must be upstairs, he realized. No one ran to greet him at the door. The children, a boy and a girl half his height and twice his energy, were admirable creatures who ran down stairs as if they were skiing, who could no more hold completely still than a hummingbird in midair. He could hear their footsteps upstairs, running lightly across the floor. They hadn't come to greet him at the door because their lives, after all, had more important things in them than mere fathers. He smiled, set down his attaché case, and went to the kitchen.

MaryJo looked harried, upset. He recognized the signals instantly—she had cried earlier today.

"What's wrong?"

"Nothing," she said, because she always said Nothing. He knew that in a moment she would tell him. She always told him everything, which had sometimes made him impatient. Now as she moved silently back and forth from counter to counter, from cupboard to stove, making another perfect dinner, he realized that she was not going to tell him. It made him uncomfortable. He began to try to guess.

"You work too hard," he said. "I've offered to get a maid or a cook. We can certainly afford them."

MaryJo only smiled thinly. "I don't want anyone else mucking around in the kitchen," she said. "I thought we dropped that subject years ago. Did you—did you have a hard day at the office?"

Mark almost told her about his strange lapses of memory, but caught himself. This would have to be led up to gradually. MaryJo would not be able to cope with it, not in the state she was already in. "Not too hard. Finished up early."

"I know," she said. "I'm glad."

She didn't sound glad. It irritated him a little. Hurt his feelings. But instead of going off to nurse his wounds, he merely noticed his emotions as if he were a dispassionate observer. He saw himself: important self-made man, yet at home a little boy who can be hurt, not even by a word, but by a short pause of indecision. Sensitive, sensitive, and he was amused at himself; for a moment he almost saw himself standing a few inches away, could observe even the bemused expression on his own face.

"Excuse me," MaryJo said, and she opened a cupboard door as he stepped out of the way. She pulled out a pressure cooker. "We're out of potato flakes," she said. "Have to do it the primitive way." She dropped the peeled potatoes into the pan.

"The children are awfully quiet today," he said. "Do you know what they're doing?"

MaryJo looked at him with a bewildered expression.

"They didn't come meet me at the door. Not that I mind. They're busy with their own concerns, I know."

"Mark," MaryJo said.

"All right, you see through me so easily. But I was only a little hurt. I want to look through today's mail." He wandered out of the kitchen. He was vaguely aware that behind him MaryJo had started to cry again. He did not let it worry him much. She cried easily and often.

He wandered into the living room, and the furniture surprised him. He had expected to see the green sofa and chair that he had bought from Deseret Industries, and the size of the living room and the tasteful antiques looked utterly wrong. Then his mind did a quick turn and he remembered that the old green sofa and chair were fifteen years ago, when he and MaryJo had first married. Why did I expect to see them? he wondered, and he worried again; worried also because he had come into the living room expecting to find the mail, even though for years MaryJo had put it on his desk every day.

He went into his study and picked up the mail and started sorting through it until he noticed out of the corner of his eye that something large and dark and massive was blocking the lower half of one of the windows. He looked. It was a coffin, a rather plain one, sitting on a rolling table from a mortuary.

"MaryJo," he called. "MaryJo."

She came into the study, looking afraid. "Yes?"

"Why is there a coffin in my study?" he asked.

"Coffin?" she asked.

"By the window, MaryJo. How did it get here?"

She looked disturbed. "Please don't touch it," she said.

"Why not?"

"I can't stand seeing you touch it. I told them they could leave it here for a few hours. But now it looks like it has to stay all night." The idea of the coffin staying in the house any longer was obviously repugnant to her.

"*Who* left it here? And why us? It's not as if we're in the market. Or do they sell these at parties now, like Tupperware?"

"The bishop called and asked me—asked me to let the mortuary people leave it here for the funeral tomorrow. He said nobody could get away to unlock the church and so could we take it here for a few hours—"

It occurred to him that the mortuary would not have parted with a funeral-bound coffin unless it were full.

"MaryJo, is there a body in this?"

She nodded, and a tear slipped over her lower eyelid. He was aghast. He let himself show it. "They left a corpse in a coffin here in the house with you all day? With the kids?"

She buried her face in her hands and ran from the room, ran upstairs.

Mark did not follow her. He stood there and regarded the coffin with distaste. At least they had the good sense to close it. But a coffin! He went to the telephone at his desk, dialed the bishop's number.

"He isn't here." The bishop's wife sounded irritated at his call.

"He has to get this body out of my office and out of my house tonight. This is a terrible imposition."

"I don't know where to reach him. He's a doctor, you know, Brother Tapworth. He's at the hospital. Operating. There's no way I can contact him for something like this."

"So what am I supposed to do?"

She got surprisingly emotional about it. "Do what you want! Push the coffin out in the street if you want! It'll just be one more hurt to the poor man!"

"Which brings me to another question. Who is he, and why isn't his family—"

"He doesn't have a family, Brother Tapworth. And he doesn't have any money. I'm sure he regrets dying in our ward, but we just thought that even though he had no friends in the world someone might offer him a little kindness on his way out of it."

Her intensity was irresistible, and Mark recognized the hopelessness of getting rid of the box that night. "As long as it's gone tomorrow," he said. A few amenities, and the conversation ended. Mark sat in his chair staring angrily at the coffin. He had come home worried about his health. And found a coffin to greet him when he came. Well, at least it explained why poor MaryJo had been so upset. He heard the children quarreling upstairs. Well, let MaryJo handle it. Their problems would take her mind off this box, anyway.

And so he sat and stared at the coffin for two hours, and had no dinner, and did not particularly notice when MaryJo came downstairs and took the burnt potatoes out of the pressure cooker and threw the entire dinner away and lay down on the sofa in the living room and wept. He watched the patterns of the grain of the coffin, as subtle as flames, winding along the wood. He remembered having taken naps at the age of five in a makeshift bedroom behind a plywood partition in his parents' small home. The wood grain there had been his way of passing the empty sleepless hours. In those days he had been able to see shapes: clouds and faces and battles and monsters. But on the coffin, the wood grain looked more complex and yet far more simple. A road map leading upward to the lid. An engineering drawing describing the decomposition of the body. A graph at the foot of the patient's bed, saying nothing to the patient but speaking death into the trained physician's mind. Mark wondered, briefly, about the bishop, who was even now operating on someone who might very well end up in just such a box as this.

And finally his eyes hurt and he looked at the clock and felt guilty about having spent so long closed off in his study on one of his few nights home early from the office. He meant to get up and find MaryJo and take her up to bed. But instead he got up and went to the coffin and ran his hands along the wood. It felt like glass, because the varnish was so thick and smooth. It was as if the living wood had to be kept away, protected from the touch of a hand. But the wood was not alive, was it? It was being put into the ground also to decompose. The varnish might keep it alive longer. He thought whimsically of what it would be like to varnish a corpse, to preserve it. The Egyptians would have nothing on us then, he thought.

"Don't," said a husky voice from the door. It was MaryJo, her eyes red-rimmed, her face looking slept in.

"Don't what?" Mark asked her. She didn't answer, just glanced down at his hands. To his surprise, Mark noticed that his thumbs were under the lip of the coffin lid, as if to lift it.

"I wasn't going to open it," he said.

"Come upstairs," MaryJo said.

"Are the children asleep?"

He had asked the question innocently, but her face was immediately twisted with pain and grief and anger.

"Children?" she asked. "What is this? And why tonight?"

He leaned against the coffin in surprise. The wheeled table moved slightly.

"We don't have any children," she said.

And Mark remembered with horror that she was right. On the second miscarriage, the doctor had tied her tubes because any further pregnancies would risk her life. There were no children, none at all, and it had devastated her for years; it was only through Mark's great patience and utter dependability that she had been able to stay out of the hospital. Yet when he came home tonight—he tried to remember what he had heard when he came home. Surely he had heard the children running back and forth upstairs. Surely—

"I haven't been well," he said.

"If it was a joke, it was sick."

"It wasn't a joke—it was—" But again he couldn't, or at least didn't, tell her about the strange memory lapses at the office, even though this was even more proof that something was wrong. He had never had any children in his home, their brothers and sisters had all been discreetly warned not to bring children around poor MaryJo, who was quite distraught to be—the Old Testament word?—barren.

And he had talked about having children all evening.

"Honey, I'm sorry," he said, trying to put his whole heart into the apology.

"So am I," she answered, and went upstairs.

Surely she isn't angry at me, Mark thought. Surely she realizes something is wrong. Surely she'll forgive me.

But as he climbed the stairs after her, taking off his shirt as he did, he again heard the voice of a child.

"I want a drink, Mommy." The voice was plaintive, with the sort of whine only possible to a child who is comfortable and sure of love. Mark turned at the landing in time to see MaryJo passing the top of the stairs on the way to the children's bedroom, a glass of water in her hand. He thought nothing of it. The children always wanted extra attention at bedtime.

The children. The children, of course there were children. This was the urgency he had felt in the office, the reason he had to get home. They had always wanted children and so there *were* children. C. Mark Tapworth always got what he set his heart on.

"Asleep at last," MaryJo said wearily when she came into the room.

Despite her weariness, however, she kissed him good night in the way that told him she wanted to make love. He had never worried much about sex. Let the readers of *Reader's Digest* worry about how to make their sex lives fuller and richer, he always said. As for him, sex was good, but not the best thing in his life; just one of the ways that he and MaryJo responded to each other. Yet tonight he was disturbed, worried. Not because he could not perform, for he had

never been troubled by even temporary impotence except when he had a fever and didn't feel like sex
anyway. What bothered him was that he didn't exactly care.

He didn't *not* care, either. He was just going
through the motions as he had a thousand times before, and this time, suddenly, it all seemed so silly, so
redolent of petting in the back seat of a car. He felt
embarrassed that he should get so excited over a little
stroking. So he was almost relieved when one of the
children cried out. Usually he would say to ignore the
cry, would insist on continuing the lovemaking. But
this time he pulled away, put on a robe, went into the
other room to quiet the child down.

There was no other room.

Not in this house. He had, in his mind, been
heading for their hopeful room filled with crib, changing table, dresser, mobiles, cheerful wallpaper—but
that room had been years ago, in the small house in
Sandy, not here in the home in Federal Heights with
its magnificent view of Salt Lake City, its beautiful
shape and decoration that spoke of taste and shouted
of wealth and whispered faintly of loneliness and
grief. He leaned against a wall. There were no children. There were no children. He could still hear the
child's cry ringing in his mind.

MaryJo stood in the doorway to their bedroom,
naked but holding her nightgown in front of her.
"Mark," she said. "I'm afraid."

"So am I," he answered.

But she asked him no questions, and he put on
his pajamas and they went to bed and as he lay there
in darkness listening to his wife's faintly rasping
breath he realized that it didn't really matter as much
as it ought. He was losing his mind, but he didn't
much care. He thought of praying about it, but he
had given up praying years ago, though of course it

wouldn't do to let anyone else know about his loss of faith, not in a city where it's good business to be an active Mormon. There'd be no help from God on this one, he knew. And not much help from MaryJo, either, for instead of being strong as she usually was in an emergency, this time she would be, as she said, afraid.

"Well, so am I," Mark said to himself. He reached over and stroked his wife's shadowy cheek, realized that there were some creases near the eye, understood that what made her afraid was not his specific ailment, odd as it was, but the fact that it was a hint of aging, of senility, of imminent separation. He remembered the box downstairs, like death appointed to watch for him until at last he consented to go. He briefly resented them for bringing death to his home, for so indecently imposing on them; and then he ceased to care at all. Not about the box, not about his strange lapses of memory, not about anything.

I am at peace, he realized as he drifted off to sleep. I am at peace, and it's not all that pleasant.

"Mark," said MaryJo, shaking him awake. "Mark, you overslept."

Mark opened his eyes, mumbled something so the shaking would stop, then rolled over to go back to sleep.

"Mark," MaryJo insisted.

"I'm tired," he said in protest.

"I know you are," she said. "So I didn't wake you any sooner. But they just called. There's something of an emergency or something—"

"They can't flush the toilet without someone holding their hands."

"I wish you wouldn't be crude, Mark," MaryJo said. "I sent the children off to school without letting them wake you by kissing you good-bye. They were very upset."

"Good children."

"Mark, they're expecting you at the office."

Mark closed his eyes and spoke in measured tones. "You can call them and tell them I'll come in when I damn well feel like it and if they can't cope with the problem themselves I'll fire them all as incompetents."

MaryJo was silent for a moment. "Mark, I can't say that."

"Word for word. I'm tired. I need a rest. My mind is doing funny things to me." And with that Mark remembered all the illusions of the day before, including the illusion of having children.

"There aren't any children," he said.

Her eyes grew wide. "What do you mean?"

He almost shouted at her, demanded to know what was going on, why she didn't just tell him the truth for a moment. But the lethargy and disinterest clamped down and he said nothing, just rolled back over and looked at the curtains as they drifted in and out with the air conditioning. Soon MaryJo left him, and he heard the sound of machinery starting up downstairs. The washer, the dryer, the dishwasher, the garbage disposer: it seemed that all the machines were going at once. He had never heard the sounds before —MaryJo never ran them in the evenings or on weekends, when he was home.

At noon he finally got up, but he didn't feel like showering and shaving, though any other day he would have felt dirty and uncomfortable until those rituals were done with. He just put on his robe and went downstairs. He planned to go in to breakfast, but instead he went into his study and opened the lid of the coffin.

It took him a bit of preparation, of course. There was some pacing back and forth before the coffin, and much stroking of the wood, but finally he put his thumbs under the lid and lifted.

The corpse looked stiff and awkward. A man, not particularly old, not particularly young. Hair of a determinedly average color. Except for the greyness of the skin color the body looked completely natural and so utterly average that Mark felt sure he might have seen the man a million times without remembering he had seen him at all. Yet he was unmistakably dead, not because of the cheap satin lining the coffin rather slackly, but because of the hunch of the shoulders, the jut of the chin. The man was not comfortable.

He smelled of embalming fluid.

Mark was holding the lid open with one hand, leaning on the coffin with the other. He was trembling. Yet he felt no excitement, no fear. The trembling was coming from his body, not from anything he could find within his thoughts. The trembling was because it was cold.

There was a soft sound or absence of sound at the door. He turned around abruptly. The lid dropped closed behind him. MaryJo was standing in the door, wearing a frilly housedress, her eyes wide with horror.

In that moment years fell away and to Mark she was twenty, a shy and somewhat awkward girl who was forever being surprised by the way the world actually worked. He waited for her to say, "But Mark, you cheated him." She had said it only once, but ever since then he had heard the words in his mind whenever he was closing a deal. It was the closest thing to a conscience he had in his business dealings. It was enough to get him a reputation as a very honest man.

"Mark," she said softly, as if struggling to keep

control of herself, "Mark, I couldn't go on without you."

She sounded as if she were afraid something terrible was going to happen to him, and her hands were shaking. He took a step toward her. She lifted her hands, came to him, clung to him, and cried in a high whimper into his shoulder. "I couldn't. I just couldn't."

"You don't have to," he said, puzzled.

"I'm just not," she said between gentle sobs, "the kind of person who can live alone."

"But even if I, even if something happened to me, MaryJo, you'd have the—" He was going to say the children. Something was wrong with that, though, wasn't there? They loved no one better in the world than their children; no parents had ever been happier than they had been when their two were born. Yet he couldn't say it.

"I'd have what?" MaryJo asked. "Oh, Mark, I'd have nothing."

And then Mark remembered again (what's happening to me!) that they were childless, that to MaryJo, who was old-fashioned enough to regard motherhood as the main purpose for her existence, the fact that they had no hope of children was God's condemnation of her. The only thing that had pulled her through after the operation was Mark, was her fussing over his meaningless and sometimes invented problems at the office or telling him endlessly the events of her lonely days. It was as if he were her anchor to reality, and only he kept her from going adrift in the eddies of her own fears. No wonder the poor girl (for at such times Mark could not think of her as completely adult) was distraught as she thought of Mark's death, and the damned coffin in the house did no good at all.

But I'm in no position to cope with this, Mark

thought. I'm falling apart, I'm not only forgetting things, I'm remembering things that didn't happen. And what if I died? What if I suddenly had a stroke like my father had and died on the way to the hospital? What would happen to MaryJo?

She'd never lack for money. Between the business and the insurance, even the house would be paid off, with enough money to live like a queen on the interest. But would the insurance company arrange for someone to hold her patiently while she cried out her fears? Would they provide someone for her to waken in the middle of the night because of the nameless terrors that haunted her?

Her sobs turned into frantic hiccoughs and her fingers dug more deeply into his back through the soft fabric of his robe. See how she clings to me, he thought. She'll never let me go, he thought, and then the blackness came again and again he was falling backward into nothing and again he did not care about anything. Did not even know there was anything to care about.

Except for the fingers pressing into his back and the weight he held in his arms. I do not mind losing the world, he thought. I do not mind losing even my memories of the past. But these fingers. This woman. I cannot lay this burden down because there is no one who can pick it up again. If I mislay her she is lost.

And yet he longed for the darkness, resented her need that held him. Surely there is a way out of this, he thought. Surely a balance between two hungers that leaves both satisfied. But still the hands held him. All the world was silent and the silence was peace except for the sharp, insistent fingers and he cried out in frustration and the sound was still ringing in the room when he opened his eyes and saw

MaryJo standing against a wall, leaning against the wall, looking at him in terror.

"What's wrong?" she whispered.

"I'm losing," he answered. But he could not remember what he had thought to win.

And at that moment a door slammed in the house and Amy came running with little loud feet through the kitchen and into the study, flinging herself on her mother and bellowing about the day at school and the dog that chased her for the second time and how the teacher told her she was the *best* reader in the second grade but Darrel had spilled milk on her and could she have a sandwich because she had dropped hers and stepped on it accidentally at lunch—

MaryJo looked at Mark cheerfully and winked and laughed. "Sounds like Amy's had a busy day, doesn't it, Mark?"

Mark could not smile. He just nodded as MaryJo straightened Amy's disheveled clothing and led her toward the kitchen.

"MaryJo," Mark said. "There's something I have to talk to you about."

"Can it wait?" MaryJo asked, not even pausing. Mark heard the cupboard door opening, heard the lid come off the peanut butter jar, heard Amy giggle and say, "Mommy, not so *thick*."

Mark didn't understand why he was so confused and terrified. Amy had had a sandwich after school ever since she had started going—even as an infant she had had seven meals a day, and never gained an ounce of fat. It wasn't what was happening in the kitchen that was bothering him, couldn't be. Yet he could not stop himself from crying out, "Mary-Jo! MaryJo, come here!"

"Is Daddy mad?" he heard Amy ask softly.

"No," MaryJo answered, and she bustled back

into the room and impatiently said, "What's wrong, dear?"

"I just need—just need to have you in here for a minute."

"Really, Mark, that's not your style, is it? Amy needs to have a lot attention right after school, it's the way she is. I wish you wouldn't stay home from work with nothing to do, Mark, you become quite impossible around the house." She smiled to show that she was only half serious and left again to go back to Amy.

For a moment Mark felt a terrible stab of jealousy that MaryJo was far more sensitive to Amy's needs than to his.

But that jealousy passed quickly, like the memory of the pain of MaryJo's fingers pressing into his back, and with a tremendous feeling of relief Mark didn't care about anything at all, and he turned around to the coffin, which fascinated him, and he opened the lid again and looked inside. It was as if the poor man had no face at all, Mark realized. As if death stole faces from people and made them anonymous even to themselves.

He ran his fingers back and forth across the satin and it felt cool and inviting. The rest of the room, the rest of the world receded into deep background. Only Mark and the coffin and the corpse remained and Mark felt very tired and very hot, as if life itself were a terrible friction making heat within him, and he took off his robe and pajamas and awkwardly climbed on a chair and stepped over the edge into the coffin and knelt and then lay down. There was no other corpse to share the slight space with him; nothing between his body and the cold satin, and as he lay on it it didn't get any warmer because at last the friction was slowing, was cooling, and he reached up and pulled down the lid and the world was dark and silent and there was no odor and no taste and no feel but the cold of the sheets.

"Why is the lid closed?" asked little Amy, holding her mother's hand.

"Because it's not the body we must remember," MaryJo said softly, with careful control, "but the way Daddy always was. We must remember him happy and laughing and loving us."

Amy looked puzzled. "But I remember he spanked me."

MaryJo nodded, smiling, something she had not done recently. "It's all right to remember that, too," MaryJo said, and then she took her daughter from the coffin back into the living room, where Amy, not realizing yet the terrible loss she had sustained, laughed and climbed on Grandpa.

David, his face serious and tear-stained because he did understand, came and put his hand in his mother's hand and held tightly to her. "We'll be fine," he said.

"Yes," MaryJo answered. "I think so."

And her mother whispered in her ear, "I don't know how you can stand it so bravely, my dear."

Tears came to MaryJo's eyes. "I'm not brave at all," she whispered back. "But the children. They depend on me so much. I can't let go when they're leaning on me."

"How terrible it would be," her mother said, nodding wisely, "if you had no children."

Inside the coffin, his last need fulfilled, Mark Tapworth heard it all, but could not hold it in his mind, for in his mind there was space or time for only one thought: consent. Everlasting consent to his life, to his death, to the world, and to the everlasting absence of the world. For now there were children.

The Monkeys Thought
'Twas All in Fun

Agnes 1

"Take her," Agnes's father said, his dry eyes pleading. Agnes's mother stood just behind him, wringing the towel she held in her hand.

"I can't," Brian Howarth said, embarrassed that he had to say that, ashamed that he actually *could* say it. The death of the nation of Biafra was a matter of days now, not weeks, and he and his wife were some of the last to go. Brian had come to love the Ibo people, and Agnes's father and mother had long since ceased to be servants—they were friends. Agnes herself, a bright five-year-old, had been a delight, learning English even before she learned her native tongue, constantly playing hide-and-seek in the house. A bright child, a hopeful child, and from all that Brian had heard (and he believed it, even though he was a correspondent and knew the exaggerations that wartime news always had to endure), from all he had heard the Nigerian Army would not stop to ask anyone "Is this child bright? Is this child beautiful? Does this child have a sense of humor as keen as any adult's?" Instead she would be gutted with a bayonet as quickly as her parents, because she was an Ibo, and the Ibos had done what the Japanese did a half-century before: they had become westernized before any of their neighbors, and profited from it. The Japanese had been on an island, and they had survived. The Ibos were not on an island, and Biafra was destroyed by Nigerian numbers and British and Russian weapons and a blockade that no nation on earth made any effort to relieve, not on a scale that could save anyone.

"I can't," Brian Howarth said again, and then he heard his wife behind him (her name was also Agnes, for the little girl's parents had named their first and only child after her) whisper, "By God you can or I'm not going."

"Please," Agnes's father said, his eyes still dry, his voice still level. He was begging, but his body said I am still proud and will not weep and kneel and subjugate myself to you. Equal to equal, his body said, I ask you to take my treasure, for I will die and cannot keep it anyway.

"How can I?" Brian asked helplessly, knowing that the space on the airplane was limited and the correspondents were forbidden to take any Biafrans with them.

"We can," his wife whispered again, and so Brian reached out his arms and took Agnes and held her. Agnes's father nodded. "Thank you, Brian," he said, and Brian was the one who wept and said, "I'm sorry, if any people in the world deserve to be free—"

But Agnes's parents were already gone, heading for the forest before the Nigerian Army could get into town.

Brian and his wife took little Agnes to the stretch of abandoned highway that served as the last airport in free Biafra and took off in an airplane crammed with correspondents and luggage and more than one Biafran child sitting in the darkest corners of what was never meant to be a passenger plane. Agnes's eyes were wide all through the flight. She did not cry. She had never cried much as an infant. She just held tightly to Brian Howarth's hand.

When the airplane landed in the Azores, where they would change to a flight to America, Agnes finally asked, "What about my parents?"

"They can't come," Brian said.

"Why not?"

"There wasn't room."

And Agnes looked at the many places where another couple of human beings could sit or stand or lie, and she knew that there were other, far worse reasons why her parents couldn't be with her.

"You'll be living with us in America now," Mrs. Howarth said.

"I want to live in Biafra," Agnes said. Her voice was so loud that it could be heard throughout the airplane.

"Don't we all," said a woman farther to the front. "Don't we all."

The rest of the flight Agnes passed in silence, unimpressed by the clouds and the ocean below her. They landed in New York, changed planes again, and at last reached Chicago. Home.

"Home?" Agnes echoed, looking at the two-story brick house that loomed out of the trees and lawn and seemed to hang brightly over the street. "This isn't home."

Brian couldn't argue with her. For Agnes was a Biafran, and there would never be home for her again.

Years later, Agnes would remember little about her escape from Africa. She would remember being hungry, and how Brian gave her two oranges when they landed at the Azores. She would remember the sound of antiaircraft fire, and the rocking of the plane when one shell exploded dangerously near. Most of all, however, she remembered the white man sitting across from her in the dark airplane. He kept looking at her, then at Brian and Agnes Howarth. Brian and his wife were black, but their blackness had been diluted by frequent infusions of white blood in past generations; little Agnes was much, much darker, and the white man finally said, "Little girl. You Biafran?"

"Yes," Agnes said softly.

The white man looked angrily at Brian. "That's against the regulations."

Brian calmly answered, "The world will not shift on its axis because a regulation was broken."

"You shouldn't have brought her," the white man insisted, as if she were breathing up his air, taking up his space.

Brian didn't answer. Mrs. Howarth did. "You're only angry," she said, "because your Biafran friends asked you to take their children, and you refused."

The man looked angry, then hurt, then ashamed. "I couldn't. They had three children. How could I claim they were mine? I couldn't do it!"

"There are white people on this airplane with Biafran children," Mrs. Howarth said.

Angry, the white man stood. "I followed the regulations! I did the right thing!"

"So relax," Brian said, quietly but with command in his voice. "Sit down. Shut up. Console yourself that you obeyed the regulations. And think of those children with a bayonet slicing—"

"Sh," Mrs. Howarth said. The white man sat back down. The argument was over. But Agnes always remembered that afterward, the man had wept bitterly, for what seemed hours, sobbing almost silently, his back heaving. "I couldn't do a thing," she heard him say. "A whole nation dying, and I couldn't do a thing."

Agnes remembered those words. "I couldn't do a thing," she sometimes said to herself. At first she believed it, and wept for her parents in the silence in her home on the outskirts of Chicago. But gradually, as she forced her way past the barriers society placed before her sex and her race and her foreign background, she learned to say something different:

"I can do something."

She went back to Nigeria with her adopted parents, the Howarths, ten years later. Her passport showed her to be an American citizen. They returned to her city and asked in her real family where her parents were.

"Dead," she was told, not unkindly. No relative closer than a second cousin was left alive.

"I was too young," she said to her parents. "I couldn't do a thing."

"Me too," Brian said. "We were all too young."

"But I'll do something someday," Agnes said. "I'll make up for this."

Brian thought she meant revenge, and spent many hours trying to dissuade her. But Agnes did not mean revenge.

Hector 1

Hector felt large when he saw the light, large and full and bright and vigorous, and the light was the right color and the right brightness and so Hector gathered himselves and followed the light and drank it deep.

And because Hector loved to dance, he found the right place and began to bow, and spin, and arch, and crest, and be a thing of great dark beauty.

"Why are we dancing?" the Hectors asked themself.

And Hector told himselves, "Because we are happy."

Agnes 2

Agnes was already known as one of the two or three best skipship pilots when the Trojan Object was discovered. She had made two Mars trips and dozens of journeys to the moon, many of them solo, just her and the computer, others of them with valuable cargos —famous people, vital medicines, important secret information—the kind of thing valuable enough to make it worth the price of sending a skipship from the ground out into space.

Agnes was a pilot for IBM-ITT, the largest of the companies that had invested in space; and it was partly because IBM-ITT promised that she would be pilot on the expedition that the corporation won the lucrative government contract to investigate the Trojan Object.

"We got the contract," Sherman Riggs told her, and she had been so involved in updating the equipment on her skipship that she didn't know what he meant.

"The *contract*," he said. "*The* contract. To go to the Trojan Object. And you're the pilot."

It was not Agnes's habit to show emotion, whether negative or positive. The Trojan Object was the most important thing in space right now, a large, completely light-absorbent object in Earth's leading trojan point. One day it had not been there. The next day it had, blotting out the stars beyond it and causing more of a stir in the space-watching world than a new comet or a new planet. After all, new objects should not suddenly appear a third of the way around Earth's orbit. And now it would be Agnes who would pilot the craft that would first view the Trojan Object up close.

"Danny," she said, naming her Leaner, the lover/engineer who always teamed with her on two-person assignments. On a long trip like this, no pilot could stand to be without his Leaner.

"Of course," Sherman answered. "And two more. Roger and Rosalind Thorne. Doctor and astronomer."

"I know them."

"Good or bad?"

"Good enough. Good. If we can't get Sly and Frieda."

Sherman rolled his eyes. "Sly and Frieda are GM-Texaco, and there isn't a chance in hell—"

"I hate it when you roll your eyes, Sherman. It makes me think you're having a fit. I know Sly and Frieda are hopeless, but I had to ask, didn't I?"

"Roj and Roz."

"Fine."

"How much do you know about the Trojan Object?"

"More than you do and less than I'll need to."

Sherman tapped his pencil on his desk. "All right, I'll send you straight to the experts."

And a week later, Agnes and Danny and Roj and Roz were ensconced in Agnes's skipship, sweeping down the runway at Clovis, New Mexico. The acceleration was frightful, particularly after they were vertical, but it was not long before they were in a high orbit, and not much longer than that before they were free of the Earth's gravity, making the three-month trip to Earth's leading trojan point, where something waited for them.

Hector 2

Hector said to himselves, "I'm thirsty, I'm thirsty, I'm thirsty," and the Hectors gave themself plenty to drink, and when Hector was satisfied, for the moment, he sang a soundless song that all the Hectors heard, and they, too, sang:

> Hector swims in an empty sea
> With Hectors all around.
> Hector whistles merrily
> But never makes a sound.

Hector swallows all the light
So he's snug out in the cold.
Hector will be born tonight
Although he's very old.

Hector sweeps up all the dust
And puts it in a pile:
Waybread for his wanderlust,
More Hectors in a while.

And the Hectors laughed and also sang and
also danced because they had come together after a
long journey and they were warm and they were snug
and they lay together to listen to themself tell himselves stories.

"I will tell," Hector said to himselves, "the
story of the Masses, and the story of the Masters, and
the story of the Makers."

And the Hectors cuddled together to listen.

Agnes 3

Agnes and Danny made love the day before
they reached the Trojan Object, because that made it
easier for both of them to work. Roj and Roz did not,
because that made it easier for them to stay alert. For
a week it had been clear that the Trojan Object was far
more than anyone on Earth had suspected, and far less.

"Diameter about fourteen hundred kilometers
on the average," Roz reported as soon as she had good
enough data to be sure. "But gravity is about as much
as a giant asteroid. Our shaddles are strong enough to
get us off."

Danny spoke the obvious conclusion first.
"There's nothing that could be as solid as that, as
large as that, and as light as that. Artificial. Has to
be."

"Fourteen hundred kilometers in diameter?"

Danny shrugged. Everybody could have shrugged. That's what they were here for. Nothing natural could have suddenly appeared in Earth's leading trojan point, either—obviously it was artificial. But was it dangerous?

They circled the Trojan Object dozens of times, letting the computer scan with better eyes than theirs for any sign of an aperture. There was none.

"Better set down," Roz said, and Agnes brought the skipship close to the surface. It occurred to her as she did so that she and Danny and the others changed personality completely when they worked. Fun-loving, filthy-minded, game-playing friends, until work was needed. Then the fun was over, and they became a pilot and an engineer and a doctor and a physicist, functioning smoothly, as if the computer's integrated circuits had overcome the flesh barrier and inhabited all of them.

Agnes maneuvered her craft within three meters of the surface. "No closer," she said. Danny agreed, and when they were all suited up, he opened the hatch and shaddled down to the surface. "Careful, Leaner," Agnes reminded him. "Escape velocity and everything."

"Can't see a damn thing down here," he answered in a perfect non sequitur. "This surface material sucks up *all* light. Even from my headlamp. Hard and smooth as steel, though. I have to keep shining my light on my hands to see where they are." Silence for a few moments. "Can't tell if I'm scratching the thing or not. Am I getting a sample?"

"Computer says *no*," Roj answered. As the doctor, he had nothing better to do at the moment than monitor the computer.

"I'm not making any impact on the surface at all. I want to find out how hard this thing is."

"Torch?" Agnes asked.

"Yeah."

Roz protested. "Don't do anything to make them mad."

"Who?" Danny asked.

"Them. The people who made this."

Danny chuckled. "If there's anybody in there, they either know we're out here or they're sure enough we can't get in that they don't care. Either way, I've got to do something to attract their attention."

The torch flared brightly, but nothing was reflected from the surface of the Trojan Object, and only the gas dissipated with the torch made it visible.

"No result. Didn't even raise the surface temperature," Danny finally said.

They tried laser. They tried explosives. They tried a diamond tip on a drill for repair work. Nothing had any effect on the surface at all.

"I want to come out," Agnes said.

"Forget it," Danny answered. "I suggest we go to the pole, north or south. Maybe something's different there."

"I'm coming out," Agnes said.

Danny was angry. "What the hell do you think you can accomplish that I haven't done?"

Agnes frankly admitted that there wasn't anything she could possibly do. While she was admitting it she clambered out of the skipship and launched herself toward the surface.

It was a damnfool thing to do, as Danny informed her loudly over the radio, just as he turned to face Agnes and flashed his light directly in her eyes. She realized to her alarm that he was directly below her—she couldn't turn around and shaddle down. She slipped to the right, instead, and then tried to turn around, but because of her panic at the thought of colliding with Danny (always dangerous in space) and the delay as she maneuvered to avoid him, she struck the planet surface going a good deal faster than should have been comfortable.

But as she touched the surface, it yielded. Not with the springiness of rubber, which would have forced her hand back out, but with the thick resistance of almost-hard cement, so that she found her hand completely immersed in the surface of the planet. She shone her headlamp on it—the smooth surface of the planet was unbroken, not even dented, except that her hand was in it up to the wrist.

"Danny," she said, not sure whether to be excited or afraid.

He didn't hear her at first because he was too busy shouting, "Agnes, are you OK?" into the radio to notice that she was already answering. But at last he calmed down, found her with his headlamp, and came over to her, shaddling gently to stay tight to the surface of the Trojan Object.

"My hand," she said, and he followed her shoulder and her arm until he found her hand and said, "Agnes! Can you get it out?"

"I didn't want to try until you saw this. What does it mean?"

"It means that if it was wet cement it's hard by now and we'll never get you off!"

"Don't be an ass," Agnes said. "Test around it. See if it's different."

Except for the torch, Danny made all the same tests. Right up to the edge of Agnes's suit the Trojan Object's surface was absolutely impenetrable, completely absorbent of energy, nonmagnetic—in other words, untestable. But there was no arguing the fact that Agnes's hand was buried in it.

"Take a picture," Agnes said.

"What will that show? It'll look like your wrist with the hand cut off." But Danny went ahead and laid some of his tools on the surface to give some hint in the photograph of where the surface actually was. Then he took a dozen or more photos. "Why am I taking these pictures?" he asked.

"In case we got back and people don't believe I could stick my hand into something harder than steel," Agnes answered.

"I could have told them that."

"You're my Leaner."

Leaners were very good for some things, but you'd never want to be the prosecutor whose case against a defendant rested entirely on his Leaner's testimony. Leaners were loyal first, honest second. Had to be.

"So we've got the pictures."

"So now I get out."

"Can you?" Danny asked. He had only postponed his concern for her; now it was back in full force.

"My knees and my other hand were both sunk in just as deep. The reason this one is still in is because I clenched my fist and I'm still holding on."

"Holding on to what?"

"To whatever this damn thing is made of. My other hand and my knees floated to the surface after a few seconds."

"Floated!"

"That's what it felt like. I'm letting go now." And as Agnes unclenched her fist her hand slowly rose to the surface and was gently ejected. There wasn't a ripple on the surface material, however. Where her hand was, it behaved like a liquid. Where her hand wasn't, it was as solid as ever.

"What is this made of?"

"Silly Putty," Agnes said.

"Unfunny," Danny answered.

"I'm serious. Remember how Silly Putty was

flexible, but if you formed it into a ball and threw it on the ground, it broke like clay?"

"Mine never worked like that."

"But this stuff does, in reverse. When something sharp hits it, or something hot, or something too slow or too weak, it sits there. But when I ran into it going at shaddle speed, I sank in it for a few inches."

"In other words," Roj said from the skipship, "you've found the door."

They were back in the skipship inside ten minutes, and after only a few more minutes of checking everything to make sure it was in good condition, Agnes pulled the skipship a few dozen meters away from the surface of the Trojan Object. "Everybody ready?" Agnes asked.

"Are we doing what I think we're doing?" Roz asked.

"Yep," Danny answered. "We shore is."

"Then we're idiots," Roz said, her voice sounding nervous. No one argued with her.

Agnes fired the vernier rockets on the outboard side and they plunged toward the Trojan Object. Not terribly fast, by the standard of speed they were used to. But to those aboard, who knew that they were heading directly into a surface so hard a diamond drill and a laser had had no effect at all, it was disconcertingly fast.

"What if you're wrong?" Roz asked, pretending she was joking.

No one could answer before they hit. But in the moment when there should have come a violent crunch and a rush of atmosphere escaping from the ship, the skipship merely slowed sickeningly and kept moving inward. The black flowed quickly past the viewports, and they were buried in the surface of the Trojan Object.

"Are we still moving?" Roj asked, his voice trembling.

"You've got the computer," Agnes answered, flattering herself that she, at least, did not sound scared. She was wrong, but no one told her.

"Yeah," Roj finally said. "We're still moving. Computer says so."

And then they sat in silence for an interminable minute. Agnes was just about to say "Maybe this isn't such a good idea. I've changed my mind" when the blackness turned to a reflective brown through the window, and then, just when they'd had time to notice it, the brown turned into a bright, transparent blue—"Water!" Danny said in surprise—and then the water broke and they bobbed on the surface of a lake, the sun dazzlingly bright on the surface.

Hector 3

"First I will tell you the story of the Masses," Hector said to himselves. Actually, the telling of the stories was not necessary. As Hector drank, all that he had been through, all that he had known through the years of his life was being transferred subliminally to himselves. But there was the matter of focus. The matter of meaning. Hector had no imagination at all. But he did have understanding, and that understanding had to be passed to himselves, or in ages to come the Hectors would curse themself for having left himselves crippled.

This is the story, therefore, that he told, because it focused and it meant:

Cyril [said Hector] wanted to be a carpenter. He wanted to cut living wood and dry it and cure it and shape it into objects of beauty and utility. He thought he had an eye for it. As a child he had experimented with it. But when he applied at the Office of Assignments, he was told no.

"Why not?" he asked, astonished that the Office of Assignments could make such an obvious mistake.

"Because," said the clerk, who was unflaggingly nice (she had tested nice and therefore held her job), "your aptitude and preference tests show that not only do you not have any aptitude along those lines at all, but also you do not even want to be a carpenter."

"I want to be a carpenter," Cyril insisted, because he was young enough not to know that one does not insist.

"You want to be a carpenter because you have a false impression of what carpentry is. In actual fact, your preference tests show that you would absolutely hate life as a carpenter. Therefore you cannot be a carpenter."

And something in her manner told Cyril that there was no point in arguing any further. Besides, he was not so young as not to know that resistance was futile—and continued resistance was fatal.

So Cyril was placed where his tests showed he had the most aptitude: He was trained as a miner. Fortunately, he was not untalented or utterly unbright, so he was trained as a lead miner, the one who follows the vein and finds it when it jogs or turns or jumps. It was a demanding job. Cyril hated it. But he learned to do it because his preference tests showed that he really wanted this line of work.

Cyril wanted to marry a girl named Lika, and she wanted to marry him. "I'm sorry," said the clerk at the Office of Assignments, "you are genetically, temperamentally, and socially unsuited for each other. You would be miserable. Therefore we cannot permit you to marry."

They didn't marry, and Lika married someone

else, and Cyril asked if it was all right if he remained unmarried. "If you wish. That's one of your options for optimum happiness, according to the tests," the clerk informed him.

Cyril wanted to live in a certain area, but he was forbidden; food was served for him that he didn't like; he had to go dancing with friends he didn't like, doing dances to music he loathed, singing songs whose words were silly to him. Surely, surely there's been a mistake, he said, pleading with the clerk.

The clerk fixed a cold stare on him (he tried in vain to scrub the stare off, but still it hung on him like slime in his dreams) and said, "My dear Cyril, you have now protested as often as a citizen may protest and remain alive."

In just such a case many another member of the masses might have rebelled, joining the secret underground organizations that sprang up from time to time and were crushed at regular intervals by the state. In just such a case many another member of the masses, knowing he was consigned to a lifetime of undeserved misery, would kill himself and thereby eliminate the misery.

However, Cyril belonged to the largest group within the masses, and so he chose neither route. Instead he went to the town he was assigned to, worked in the coal mine where he was assigned, remained lonely as he pined for Lika, and danced idiotic dances to idiotic music with his idiotic friends.

Years passed, and Cyril began to be well known among coal miners. He handled his rockcutter as if it were a delicate tool, and with it he left beautiful shapes in the rock behind, so that any miner could tell when he walked down a tunnel cut by Cyril, for it would be beautiful, and as he walked the miner would feel exalted and proud and, oddly, loved. And

Cyril also had a knack for anticipating the coal, following where it led no matter how narrow the seam, how twisting its path, how interrupted its progress.

"Cyril knows the coal like a woman, every twist and turn of her, as if he'd had her a thousand times and knew just when she'd come," a miner said of Cyril once, and because the statement was apt and true (and because there are poets' hearts beating even at the bottom of a mine) the statement spread through the mines and the miners began referring to their black stone as "Mrs. Cyril." Cyril heard of it, and smiled, because in *his* heart coal was not a wife, only an unloved mistress used for the scant pleasure she gave and then cast away. Hatred mistaken for love, as usual.

Cyril was nearly sixty years old when a clerk from the Office of Assignments came to the mines. "Cyril the coal miner," the clerk said, and so they brought Cyril from the mines, and the clerk met him with a huge, unbelievable smile. "Cyril, you are a great man!" cried the clerk.

Cyril smiled wanly, not knowing what he was leading up to.

"Cyril, my friend," said the clerk, "you are a notable miner. Without seeking fame at all, your name is known to miners all over the world. You are the perfect model of what a man ought to be—happy in your assignment, hardworking, content. So the Office of Assignments has announced that you are the Model Worker of the Year."

Everyone knew about Model Worker of the Year. That was a person who had his picture in all the papers, and was in the movies and on television and who was held up as the greatest person in all the world in that year. It was an honor to be envied.

But Cyril said, "No."

"No?" asked the clerk.

"No. I don't want to be the Model Worker of the Year."

"But—but. But why not?"

"Because I'm not happy. I was put into this assignment by mistake many years ago. I shouldn't be a coal miner. I should be a carpenter, married to Lika, living in another town, dancing to other music with other friends."

The clerk looked at him in horror. "How can you say that!" he cried. "I've announced that you are Model Worker of the Year! You will either be Model Worker of the Year or you will be put to death!"

Put to death? Forty years ago that threat had made Cyril comply, but now a stubborn streak erupted from him, like a seam of coal long hidden but under such pressure that when the stone around it gave way, it actually burst from the rock walls. "I'm near sixty," Cyril said, "and I've hated all my life to now. Kill me if you like, but I won't go on television or the movies saying how happy I've been because I haven't."

And so they took Cyril and locked him in prison and sentenced him to death because while he might suffer all kinds of abuse, he refused to lie to his friends.

That is the story of the Masses.

And when Hector was finished, the Hectors sighed and wept (without tears) and said, "Now we understand. Now we know the meaning."

"This isn't," Hector said, "the whole meaning."

And when he had said that, one of the Hectors (which was remarkable, for the Hectors rarely spoke alone) said to himselves and themself, "Oh, oh, they have penetrated me!"

"Trapped!" Hector cried to himselves. "All

these years of freedom, and they have found me at last!" But then another thought came to him, one that he had never thought before but that had lain dormant in him, waiting for this moment to emerge, and he said, "Just cooperate. They won't hurt you if you just cooperate."

"But it already hurts!" cried the Hector who had spoken alone.

"It will heal. Just remember, no matter what you do, the masters will have their way with you. And if you struggle, it only goes worse with you."

"The Masters," said all the Hectors to themself. "Tell us a story of the Masters, so we can understand why they do what they do."

"I will," said Hector to himselves.

Agnes 4

Agnes and Danny stood on a mountaintop, or what had seemed to be a mountaintop from the skipship. They had reached it after only a few hours' walk, much of it sped by shaddling, and learned that what seemed to be a high mountain was only a few hundred meters high, maybe even half a kilometer. It was rugged enough, though, and the climb, even shaddled, had not been easy.

"Artificial," Danny said, touching the wall with his hand. The wall ran from the top of the mountain up to the ceiling, where instead of a sun the whole ceiling glowed with light and warmth, as thorough as sunlight, yet diffused so that they could look at it for a few seconds without being blinded.

"I thought we concluded this place was artificial from the beginning," Agnes said.

"But what's it *for*?" Danny asked, letting his frustration at two days of exploration come to the surface. "Bare dirt, rich enough but with not a damn thing growing. Clean, drinkable water. Rain twice a day for twenty minutes, a gentle sprinkle that wets everything but creates almost no runoff. Sunlight constantly. A perfect environment. But for what! What lives here?"

"Us, right now," Agnes said.

"I think we should try to leave."

"No," Agnes said firmly. "No. When we leave here, if we can, we'll leave with the computer and our heads full of every bit of information we can get from this place. From this thing."

Danny knew he couldn't argue. She was right, and she was pilot, and the combination was irresistible even if he hadn't loved her desperately. (More than she loves me, he sometimes admitted to himself.) He did love her desperately, however, and while this did not mean that he utterly lost his own will, it did mean that he would go along with her, for a while at least, in almost anything. Even if she was a damned fool sometimes.

"You're a damned fool sometimes," he said.

"I love you too," she answered, and then she ran her hand along the wall above the mountain, and then pushed on it, and then pushed harder, and her hand sank into the wall a little. She looked at Danny and said, "Come on, Leaner," and they let their shaddles push them through the wall and they emerged on the other side and found themselves—

Standing on a mountain.

Looking out over a large bowl of a valley, just like the one they had left, with a lake in the middle, just like the one where their skipship floated.

In this lake, however, there was no skipship, and Agnes looked at Danny and smiled, and Danny smiled back. "I'm beginning to get this, a little," Agnes said. "Imagine cell after cell like this, kilometers long and hundreds of meters high—"

"But this is just the outer part of this thing,"

Agnes answered, and in unison they turned back to the wall, passed through again (and this time there was the skipship in the middle of the lake), and then shaddled up the wall to the ceiling.

As they approached the ceiling, the area directly above them dimmed, until when they finally reached it, it was as cool and undazzling as the wall. The rest of the ceiling still glowed, of course. They let their shaddles push them upward into the ceiling; it gave way; they rose until they reached the surface.

Another cell, just like the one below. A lake in the middle, rich lifeless dirt all over, mountains all around, the sky on fire with sunlight. Danny and Agnes laughed and laughed. It was only a tiny part of the mystery, but it was solved.

They stopped laughing, however, when they tried to go back down the way they came. They tried to shaddle into the earth, but the soil acted like any normal dirt on Earth. They could not get through it as they had got through the walls and the ceiling.

For a while they were afraid, but when their bodies and their watches told them it was time to sleep, they went down by the lake and slept.

When they woke up, they were still afraid, and it was raining. They had already determined that it rained every thirteen and a half hours, approximately —they had not slept particularly long. But because they were afraid, they took off their suits despite the rain and made love in the dirt on the shore of the lake. They felt better afterward, much better, and they laughed and ran into the lake and swam and splashed each other.

Agnes swam underwater for a moment, attacking Danny from below, pulling him down. It was a game they had played in pools and in the ocean on Earth, and now Danny was supposed to surface for air and then dive to the bottom and hold his breath there until Agnes found him.

When he reached the bottom of the lake (and it wasn't deep) he touched it, and his hand sank up to the wrist before it struck something solid. But even the solid part was yielding, and as Danny kicked harder his hand sank deeper and he knew the way out.

He went to the surface and told Agnes what he had found. They swam to shore, put their suits back on, and shaddled down into the water. The lake floor opened, engulfed them, and then floated them out the bottom—into the sky directly over the skipship, where it still rested on the surface of the lake. They shaddled safely down.

"This place is explorable," Agnes told Roj and Roz, "and it's simple. It's like a huge balloon, with other balloons inside and more and more of them, layer after layer. It's designed for somebody to live here, so when you're standing on the soil you don't sink through. To get down, you have to go through the lake."

"But who's it for?" Roj asked, and it was a good question for which there was no answer.

"Maybe we'll find someone," Agnes said. "We've only scratched the surface. We're going in."

The skipship lifted from the lake not long after, and rose through the ceiling into the lake above. Again and again, always rising, the computer keeping count. Every cell was the same, nothing changed at all, through 498 layers of ceiling/floor, until at last they reached a ceiling, apparently no different from the others, which would not give way.

"End of the road?" Danny asked.

Always thorough, Roz insisted that they try every part of the ceiling, and they spent many hours doing it, until they had convinced themselves that this ceiling was the end of their upward (or inward) travels.

"The centrifugal gravity effect is a lot weaker here," Roj said, reading off the computer. "But it feels nearly the same, since out near the surface the real gravity was offsetting the centrifugal effect much more than it is here."

"Hi ho," said Roz. "Just assuming this thing is as big as it seems to be, how many people could this hold?"

Calculations, rough with plenty of room for error.

"There could be more than a hundred million cells to this thing, assuming that there's nothing much inside the center there, where we can't get to." A hundred and fifty square kilometers per cell; one human being per hectare; a huge potential population, without any crowding at all, considering that all the land is productive. "If we have fifteen thousand people per cell, living in a town with the rest of the land used for farming, then this place can hold a trillion and a half people."

They figured on, eliminating the polar zones because centrifugal gravity would be too weak, allowing more space per person, and the figure was still stunning. Even with only a thousand people per cell, space for a hundred billion.

"The fairy godmother," Danny said, "has given us a free place to put our population overflow."

"I don't believe in free presents," Roj said, looking out the window at the plain of dirt surrounding them. "There's a catch. With all that room, maybe they all live somewhere else, and if they find out we're here, they'll shoot us for trespassing."

"Or if we overload the place," Roz suggested, "it'll probably burst."

"You're overlooking the worst catch of all," Agnes said. "Skipships are the only thing in existence that can make this trip. They hold four persons each. Allowing for overcrowding, say we can take ten people per trip"—they laughed at the thought of trying to put ten people in their craft—"and we had a hundred skipships, which we don't have, and they could make two round trips a year, which we can't. How long would it take to bring a billion people from Earth to here?"

"Five hundred thousand years."

"Paradise," Danny said. "We could make this into a paradise. And the damn thing's out of reach."

"Besides," Roj added, "the kind of people who could make this place work are farmers and tradesmen. Who's going to pay their passage?"

Metals and minerals paid for trips to the moon and the asteroids. But all that this place held was homes—homes a few million miles and a few billion dollars out of everybody's reach.

"Well, daydreams and nightmares are over," Agnes said. "Let's go home."

"If we can," Danny said.

They could. The lakes worked as exits all the way back down, including the last time. They were back in space, and the Trojan Object had become, in their minds, the Balloon, an object obviously designed as an alternative environment for a creature not unlike man; an object perhaps unoccupied, ready and waiting, and they knew no one would ever be able to settle there.

Agnes dreamed, and the dream came back night after night. She remembered a scene she had forgotten, or had at least refused to remember clearly, since she was a child. She remembered standing between her parents and the Howarths (who, though they had adopted her, had never let her call them

Mother and Father lest she forget her real heritage in Biafra), hearing her father say "Please."

And her dream always ended the same way. She was taken into the sky, but instead of a dark cargo plane she was in a plane with glass sides, and as she flew she could see all the world. And everywhere she looked there were her parents, holding a little girl in front of them, saying "Please. Take her."

She had seen pictures of the starving children in Biafra, the ones that had made millions of Americans cry and do nothing. Now she saw those children, and the children who died of starvation in India and Indonesia and Mali and Iraq, and they all looked at her with proud, pleading eyes, their backs straight and their voices strong but their hearts breaking as they said, "Take me."

"There's nothing I can do," she said to herself in her dream, and she sobbed and sobbed like the white man on the airplane, and then Danny woke her and spoke gently to her and held her and said, "The same dream again?"

"Yes," she said.

"Agnes, if I could take the memories and wipe them out—"

"It's not the memories, Danny," Agnes whispered, touching his eyes gently where the epicanthic fold made his eyes seem to slant. "It's now. It's the people I can't do a damn thing about now."

"You couldn't do a damn thing about them before," Danny reminded her.

"But I've seen a place that could be heaven for them, and I can't get them there."

Danny smiled sadly. "That's just it. You can't. Now you've just got to let your dreams know that and give you a little peace."

"Yes," Agnes agreed, and fell asleep again holding and being held by Danny, while Roj and Roz piloted the skipship back toward Earth, which had seemed so large when they left it, and which now seemed unbearably, impossibly, criminally small.

Earth was large in the window of the skipship when Agnes finally decided that it was her dreams that were right, her conscious mind that was wrong. She could do something. There was something to be done, and she would do it.

"I'm going back there," Agnes said.

"Probably," Danny said.

"I won't go alone."

"You sure as hell better take me."

"You," she said, "and others." Billions of others. It should be done. Must be done. Therefore would be done.

Hector 4

"Now I will tell you the story of the Masters," said Hector to himselves, and the Hectors listened to himself. "This is the story of why the Masters penetrate and why the Masters hurt."

Martha [Hector said] was administrator of Tests and Assignments in the sector where Cyril had been sentenced to death. Martha was hardworking and conscientious, and prone to doublecheck things which had already been checked and doublechecked and triplechecked by others. This was why Martha discovered the mistake.

"Cyril," she said when the guard let her into the clean white plastic cell where the coal miner waited.

"Just stick the needle in quick," Cyril answered, wanting to get it over with quickly.

"I'm here to bring you the apologies of the state."

The words were so strange, so never-before-heard that Cyril did not understand at first. "Please. Let me die and get it over with."

"No," said Martha. "I've done some checking. I checked into your case, Cyril, and I discovered that fifty years ago, just after all your tests were taken, your number was punched incorrectly by a moron of a clerk."

Cyril was shocked. "A clerk made a mistake?"

"They do it all the time. It's just easier, usually, to let the mistake go than to fix it. But in this case, it was a gross miscarriage of justice. You were given the number of a retarded man with a criminal bent, which is why you were not allowed to live in a civilized town and why you were not regarded as being capable of carpentry and why you were not allowed to marry Lika."

"Just punched in the number wrong," Cyril said, unable to grasp the minitude of the error that had such an enormous, disastrous effect on his own life.

"Therefore, Cyril, the Office of Assignments hereby rescinds the execution order and grants you a pardon. Furthermore, we are undoing the damage we did. You can now live in the town where you wanted to live, among the friends you wanted to keep, dancing to the music you enjoyed. You do indeed, as you used to believe, have an aptitude and a desire to be a carpenter—you will be instructed in the trade and given your own shop. And Lika is entirely compatible with you. Therefore you and she will now be married, and in fact she is already on her way to the cottage where you will live together in wedded bliss."

Cyril was overwhelmed. "I can't believe it," he said.

"The Office of Assignments loves you and every citizen, Cyril, and we do everything we can to make you happy," said Martha, glowing with pride at the great kindness she was able to do. Ah, she thought, it is moments like this that make my job the best one in the world.

And then Martha went away to her office and forgot about Cyril most of the time for several months, though occasionally she did remember him and smiled to think of how happy she had made him.

After several months, however, a message crossed her desk: "Serious complaints Cyril 113-49-55576-338-bBR-3a."

Cyril? Her Cyril? Complaining? Had the man no sense of propriety? He already had enough complaints and resistance on his record to justify terminating him twice, and now he had added enough more that if it were possible, the office would have to kill him three times. Why? Hadn't she done her best for him? Hadn't she given him everything his early (and now correctly recorded) tests indicated he wanted and needed? What could be wrong now?

Her pride was involved. Cyril was not just being ungrateful to the state—he was being ungrateful to her. So she went to his cottage in his village, and opened his door.

Cyril sat in the main room, struggling to get past a gnarl in a fine old piece of walnut. The adz kept slipping to the side. And finally Cyril struck with enough force that when the adz slipped it gouged a deep rut in the good, ungnarled part of the wood.

"What a botch," Martha said without thinking, and then covered her mouth, because it was not proper for a person of her high position to criticize anyone of low station if it could be avoided.

But Cyril was not offended. "Damn right it's a botch. I haven't the skill for this close, ticky work. My muscles are all for heavy equipment, for grand strokes with stone-eating power tools. This is beyond me, at my age."

Martha pursed her lips. He was indeed complaining. "But isn't everything else well with you?"

Cyril's eyes grew sad, and he shook his head. "Indeed not. Much as I hate to admit it, I miss the old music from the mines. Terrible stuff, but I had good times with it, dancing away with those poor bastards who hadn't a thought worth having. But they were good people and I liked them well enough, and here no one's willing to be my friend. They don't talk the way I'm used to talking. And the food—it's too refined. I want a haunch of good, well-cooked beef, not this namby-pamby stuff that passes for food here."

His diatribe of complaint was so outrageous that Martha could not conceal her emotion. Cyril noticed it, and became alarmed.

"Not that it's unendurable, mind you, and I don't go complaining to other people. Heaven knows, there's no one who'd care to listen to me anyway."

But Martha had already heard enough. Her heart sank within her. No matter what you do for them, they're still ungrateful. The masses are worthless, she realized. Unless you lead them by the hand. . . .

"You realize that this complaint," she said, "can have dire consequences."

Cyril got a very weary expression on his face. "So we do it again?"

"Do what?"

"Punish me."

"Indeed, no, Cyril. We remove you from circulation. Apparently you are going to complain and resist no matter what happens. What about your wife?"

Cyril got a bitter smile on his face. "Lika? Oh, she's content. She's happy enough." And he glanced toward the door into the cottage's other room.

Martha went to the door and opened it. (Officers of the Office of Assignments did not need to knock.) Inside the room Lika sat in a clumsily built rocking chair, rocking back and forth, an old woman with a blank stare on her face.

Martha heard breathing over her shoulder, and turned, startled, to see Cyril leaning over her. For a moment Martha was afraid of violence. Quickly she realized, however, that Cyril was merely looking sadly at his wife.

"She's raised a family, you know. And now to be cut off from her husband and her children and her grandchildren—it's hard. She's been like this since the first week. Never lets me near her. She hates me, you know." The sadness in his voice was contagious. And Martha was not without pity.

"It's a shame," she said. "A damned shame. And so I'll use my discretionary powers, Cyril, and not kill you. As long as you promise not to complain to anyone ever again, I'll let you live. It wouldn't be fair, when things really are bad in your life, to kill you for noticing it."

Martha was an exceptionally kind administrator.

But Cyril did not smother her with gratitude. "Not kill me?" he asked. "Oh, but Administrator, can't we have things back the way they were? Let me go back to the coal mines. Let Lika go back to her family. This was what I wanted when I was twenty. But I'm near sixty, and this is all wrong."

Ingratitude again. What I have to put *up* with! Martha's eyes went small and her face flushed with rage (an emotion she did remarkably well, and so she reserved it for special occasions) and she shouted, "I will forgive that one remark, but only that one remark!"

Cyril bowed his head. "I'm sorry."

"The tests that sent you to the coal mines were

in error! But the tests that sent you here are absolutely, completely, totally correct, and by heaven you're going to stay here! There isn't a law on earth that will let you change now!"

And that was that.

Or almost. Because in the silence ringing after Martha spoke and before she left, a voice came from the rickety rocker in the bedroom.

"Then we have to stay like this?" Lika asked.

"Until Cyril dies, you have to stay like this," Martha said. "It's the law. He and you have both been given everything you ever petitioned for. Ingrates."

Martha would have turned to go, but she saw Lika looking pleadingly at Cyril, and saw Cyril nod slowly, and then Cyril turned away from the door, picked up the crosscut saw, and drew it sharply and hard across his own throat. The blood gushed and poured, and Martha thought it would never, never end.

But it did end, and Cyril's body was taken out and disposed of, and then everything was set to rights, with Lika going back to her family and a real carpenter getting the cottage with the dark red stains on the floor. The best solution after all, Martha decided. Nobody could be happy until Cyril was dead. I should have killed him in the first place, instead of these silly ideas of mercy.

She suspected, however, that Cyril would rather have died the way he did, ugly and bloody and painful though it was, than to have an injection administered by strangers in a plastic room in the capital.

I'll never understand them. They are as foreign to human thought as monkeys or dogs or cats. And Martha returned to her desk and went on double-checking everything just in case she found another mistake she could fix.

That is the story of the Masters.

When Hector was finished the Hectors wriggled uncomfortably, some (and therefore all) of them angry and disturbed and a little frightened. "But it makes no sense," the Hectors said to themself. "Nothing was done right."

Hector agreed. "But that's the way they are made," he said to himselves. "Not like me. I am regular. I act as I have always acted, as I will always act. But the Masters and the Masses always act oddly, forever seeing things in the future where no one can see, and acting to avert things that would never have come to pass anyway. Who can understand them?"

"Who made them, then?" asked the Hectors. "Why were they not made well, as we were?"

"Because the Makers are as inscrutable as the Masters and the Masses. I shall tell you their story next."

("They are gone," whispered the ones who had been penetrated. "They have gone away. We are safe after all." But Hector knew better, and because he knew better, so did the Hectors.)

Agnes 5

"You invited yourself to my bedroom, Agnes. That isn't typical."

"I accepted your standing invitation."

"I never thought you would."

"Neither did I."

Vaughan Malecker, president of IBM-ITT Space Consortium, Inc., smiled, but the smile was weak. "You don't long for my body, which is in remarkably good shape, considering my age, and I have an aversion to making love to anyone who is doing it for an ulterior motive."

Agnes looked at him for a moment, decided that he meant it, and got up to leave.

"Agnes," he said.

"Never mind," she answered.

"Agnes, it must have been something important for you to be willing to make such a sacrifice."

"I said never mind." She was at the door. It didn't open.

"Doors in my house open when I want them to," Malecker said. "I want to know what you wanted. But try to persuade my mind. Not my gonads. Believe it or not, testosterone has never made a major decision here at the consortium."

Agnes waited with her hand on the knob.

"Come on, Agnes, I know you're embarrassed as hell but if it was important enough to come this far, you can get over the embarrassment and sit down on the couch and tell me what the hell you want. You want to take another trip to the Balloon?"

"I'm going anyway."

"Sit *down*, dammit. I know you're going anyway but I was trying to get you to say *something*."

Agnes came back and sat down on the couch. Vaughan Malecker was a remarkably good-looking man, as he had pointed out, but Agnes had heard that he slept with anyone good-looking and was nice to them afterward. Agnes had been turning him down for years because she wanted to be a pilot, not a mistress, and Danny was plenty for her needs, which were not overwhelming. But this mattered, and she thought. . . .

"I thought you'd listen to me if I came this way. I thought—"

Malecker sighed and buried his face in his hands, rubbing his eyes. "I'm so tired. Agnes, what the hell makes you think I ever listen to a woman I'm trying to lay?"

"Because I listen to Danny and Danny listens to me. I'm naive. I'm innocent. But Mr. Malecker—"

"Vaughan."

"I need your help."

"Good. I like to have people need my help. It makes them treat me nicely."

"Vaughan, the whole world needs your help."

Malecker looked at her in surprise, then burst out laughing. "The whole world! Oh, no! Agnes, I would never have thought it of you! A cause!"

"Vaughan, people all over the world are starving. There are too many people for this planet—"

"I read your report, Agnes, and I know all about the possibilities in the Balloon. The problem is transport. There is no conceivable way to transport people there fast enough to make even a dent in the population problem. What do you think I am, a miracle worker?"

This was the argument Agnes was waiting for. She pounced, with descriptions of the kind of ship that could carry a thousand people at once from Earth orbit to an orbit around the Balloon.

"Do you know how many billion dollars a ship like that would cost?" Vaughan asked.

"About fifteen billion for the first ship. About four billion for each of the others, if you made five hundred of them."

Vaughan laughed. Loud. But Agnes's serious expression forced his laughter to become exasperation. He got up from the couch. "Why am I listening to this? This is nonsense!" he shouted.

"You spend more than that every year on telephone service."

"I know, damn AT&T."

"You could do it."

"IBM-ITT could do it, of course, it's *possible.* But we have stockholders. We have responsibilities.

We're not the *government*, Agnes, we can't throw money away on stupid useless projects."

"It could save billions of lives. Make the Earth a better place to live."

"So could a cure for cancer. We're working on that, but this— Agnes, there's no profit, and where there's no profit, you can bet your ass this company will not go!"

"Profit!" Agnes shouted. "Is that all you care about?"

"Eighteen million stockholders say that's all I'd better care about or I get a kick in the butt and an old-age pension!"

"Vaughan, you want profit, I'll give you profit!"

"I want profit."

"Then here's profit. How much do you sell in India?"

"Enough to make a profit."

"Compare it to sales in Germany."

"Compared to Germany, India is practically nothing."

"How much do you sell in China?"

"Exactly nothing."

"You make your profits off one tiny part of the world. Western Europe, Japan, Australia, South Africa, and the United States of America."

"Canada, too."

"And Brazil. But the rest of the world is closed to you."

Vaughan shrugged. "They're too poor."

"In the Balloon they would not be poor."

"Would they suddenly be able to read? Would they suddenly be able to run computers and sophisticated telephone equipment?"

"Yes!" And on she went, painting a picture of a world where people who had been scratching out a bare subsistence in poor soil with no water would suddenly be able to raise far more than they needed. "That means a leisure class. That means consumers."

"But all they'd have to trade would be food. Who needs food across a few million miles of space?"

"Don't you have any imagination at all? Excess food means one person can feed five or ten or twenty or a hundred. Excess food means that you locate your stinking factories there! Solar power unlimited, with no night and no clouds and no cold weather. Shifts around the clock. You have plenty of manpower, and a built-in market. You can do everything there that you've been doing here, do it cheaper, make better profits, and nobody'll be going hungry!"

And then there was silence in the room, because Vaughan was actually seriously thinking about it. Agnes's heart was beating fast. She was panting. She was embarrassed to have been so fervent when fervor was not fashionable.

"Almost thou persuadest me," said Vaughan.

"I should hope so. I'll lose my voice in a minute."

"Only two problems. The first one is that while you've persuaded me, I'm a much more reasonable, persuasible man than the officers and boards of directors of IBM and ITT, and it's their final decision, not mine. They don't let me commit more than ten billion to a project without their approval. I could make the initial ship—but I couldn't make any more than that. And the initial ship won't make a profit alone. So I have to persuade them, which is impossible, or lose my job, which I refuse to do."

"Or do nothing at all," Agnes said, contempt already seeping into her tone. Malecker was going to say no.

"And the second problem is actually the first, too. How could I persuade the board of directors of two of the world's largest corporations to invest billions of dollars in a project that depends entirely on being able to educate or train or even communicate with illiterate savages and peasants from the most backward countries on Earth?"

His voice was sweet reason, but Agnes was not prepared to hear reason. If Vaughan said no, she would be stopped here. There was nowhere else to go.

"*I'm* an illiterate savage!" she said. "Do you want to hear a few words of Igbo?" She didn't wait for an answer, babbled off the few words she remembered from childhood. She hardly remembered meanings— they were phrases that in her anger came to the surface. Some of the words, however, were spoken to her mother. Mother, come here, help me.

"My mother was an illiterate savage who spoke fluent English. My father was an illiterate savage who spoke better English than her and had French and German, too, and wrote beautiful poems in Igbo and even though to survive in the days when Biafra was struggling for survival he worked as a house servant to an American correspondent, he was never illiterate! He's read books you've never heard of, and he was a black African who was gutted in a tribal war while all those wonderful literate Americans and Europeans and educated orientals watched placidly, counting up the profits from arms sales to Nigeria."

"I didn't know you were Biafran."

"I'm not. There is no Biafra. Not on this planet. But up there, up there a Biafra *could* exist, and a free Armenia, and an independent Eritrea, and an unshackled Quebec, and an Ainu nation and a Bangladesh where no one was hungry and you tell me that illiterates can't be taught—"

"Of course they *can* be, but—"

"If I'd been born fifty miles to the west I wouldn't have been an Ibo and so I would have grown up exactly as illiterate as you say, exactly as stupid. Now look at me, you privileged white American, and tell me I can't be educated—"

"If you talk like a radical no one's going to listen to you."

Too much. Couldn't take Malecker's patronizing smile, his patient attitude. Agnes struck out at him. Her hand hit his cheek, tore his fashionable glasses off. Furious, he struck back, perhaps trying more to hold her off than to hit her, but because she was moving and he was unaccustomed to hitting people his hand slugged her hard in the breast, and she cried out in pain and jabbed a knee in his groin and then the fight got mean.

"I listened to you," he said huskily, when they were tired and pulled apart. His nose was bleeding. He was exhausted. He had a tear in his shirt, because his body had had to twist in a direction that tailored shirts were not meant to go. "Now listen to me."

Agnes listened because, her anger spent and her mind only beginning to realize that she had just assaulted the president of her company and would certainly be grounded and blackballed and her life would be over, she was not interested in leaving or in getting up or even in talking. She listened.

"Listen to me because I'm going to say it once. Go to the engineering department. Tell them to do rough plans and estimates. A proposal. I want it in three months. Ships that will carry two thousand and make a round trip in at most a year. Shuttle ships that will carry two hundred or, preferably, four hundred from Earth up into Earth orbit. And cargo ships that will take whole stinking factories, as you so aptly named them, and take them to the Balloon. And when the cost figures are all in, I'm going to go to the boards of directors, and I'm going to make a presentation, and I swear to you, Agnes Howarth, you lousy illiterate savage bitch of a best pilot in the world, if I don't persuade those bastards to let me build those ships it's because nobody could persuade them. Is that enough?"

I should be elated, Agnes thought. He's doing it. But I'm just tired.

"Right now you're tired, Agnes," Malecker said. "But I want you to know your fingernails and that knee in the groin and your teeth in my arm did not change my mind. I agreed with you from the start. I just didn't believe it could be done. But if there are a few thousand Ibos like you, and a few million Indians and a few billion Chinese, then this thing can work. That's all I needed to know, all anybody needs to know. It was uneconomical to ship colonists to America, too, and anybody who went was a damn fool, and most of them died, but they came and bloody well conquered everything they saw. You do it too. I'll try to make it possible."

He put his arm around Agnes and embraced her and then helped her clean up and patch up places where he had given as good as he got.

"Next time you want to wrestle," Vaughan offered as she left, "let's at least take our clothes off first."

Eleven years and eight hundred billion dollars later, IBM-ITT's ships were in the sky, filling with colonists. GM-Texaco's ships were still under construction, and five other consortiums would soon be in the business. More than a hundred million people had signed up for seats on the ships. The seats were free— all it took was a deed made out to the corporation for all the property a person owned, in return for which he would receive a large plot of ground in the Balloon. Whole villages had signed up. Whole nations were being decimated by emigration. The world had grown so full that there had been no place to run away to. Now there was a new promised land. And at the age of forty-two, Agnes brought her ship forward to part the waters.

Hector 5

"Ah!" cried many Hectors in agony, and so they were all in agony, and Hector said to himselves, "They are back," and the Hectors said to themself, "We will surely die."

"We can never die, not you, not us," Hector answered.

"How can we protect ourselves?"

"I was made defenseless by the Makers," said Hector. "There is no defense."

"Why were the Makers so cruel?" asked the Hectors, and so Hector told himselves the story of the Makers, so they would understand.

The story of the Makers:

Douglas was a Maker, an engineer, a scientist, a clever man. He made a tool that melted snow before it fell, so that crops could last a few more days and not be ruined by early snows. He made a machine that measured gravity, so that stars too dark to shine could be charted by the astronomers. And he made the Resonator.

The Resonator focused sound waves of different but harmonious frequencies on a certain point (or diffused the sound waves over a large area), setting up patterns that resonated with stone to bring mountains crumbling down; metal, to shatter steel buildings; and water vapor, to disperse storms.

It could also resonate with human bones, crumbling them inside the body and turning them to dust.

Douglas personally made his Resonator change

the weather, so that his nation had rain while other lands were in drought. Douglas personally used his Resonator to carve a highway through the highest mountains in the world. However, Douglas had nothing whatever to do with the decision by his nation's military leaders to use the Resonator against the population of the largest and most fertile part of the neighboring nation.

The Resonator worked beautifully. Over a period of ten minutes, through an area of ten thousand square miles, the Resonator struck silently yet thoroughly. Nursing mothers crumbled into helpless piles of dying flesh and muscle and organs, their chests not even rigid enough for them to muster one last scream: in their last moments of life they listened as their infants, not understanding what had happened, continued crying or gooing or sleeping, protected from the Resonator by their softer bones. The infants would take days to die of thirst.

Farmers in the field collapsed on the plow. Doctors in their offices died in puddles beside their patients, unable to help anyone and unable to heal themselves. Soldiers died in their moving fortresses; the generals also died at their map tables; prostitutes dissolved, their customers a soft blanket spread over them.

But Douglas had nothing to do with this. He was a Maker, not a destroyer, and if the military chose to misuse his creation, what was he to do? It was a great boon to mankind, but like all great inventions, it could be perverted by evil men.

"I deplore it," Douglas said to his friends, "but I'm helpless to stop them."

The government, however, felt uncommon gratitude to Douglas for his help in making the conquest of the neighboring nation possible. So he was granted a large estate on lands recently reclaimed from the sea, beautiful lands where once there had been only broad tidal marshes. Douglas marveled at the achievement. "Is there nothing man cannot do?" he asked his friends, not expecting an answer, since the answer was no, there was nothing beyond the reach of men. The sea was pushed back, and trees and grass grew on the landfill and transplanted topsoil, and the homes were far apart, for this land was used only for those whom the state wished to reward, and the government knew that the thing most desired by men is to have as much distance between themselves and other men as possible, without giving up any of the modern conveniences.

One day Douglas's servants were digging in the garden, and they called to him. Douglas had only been in his new home for a few days, and he was alarmed when the servant said, "A body, buried in the garden."

Douglas ran outside and looked, and sure enough, there was a fragment of a human body, oddly misshapen, but clearly including a face. "Just the skin, sir," a servant commented. "A most brutal affair," Douglas answered, and he immediately called the police.

But the police refused to come out and investigate. "No surprise there, mate," said the lieutenant. "What do you think the landfill they used was made of? They had to do *something* with the hundred thousand corpses of the enemy from the recent war, didn't they?"

"Oh, of course," Douglas said, surprised that he hadn't realized right off. That explained the bonelessness of the body.

"I expect you'll find 'em right commonly. But since the bones is dissolved, mate, they tell me it'll make the soil uncommon fertile."

The lieutenant was absolutely correct, of course.

The servants found body after body, and soon grew quite inured to the sight; within a year, most of the corpses had rotted enough that they were simply unusually good humus. And plants grew taller and faster than in most other places, the soil was so rich.

"But wasn't it a bit of a shock?" asked one of Douglas's ladyfriends, when he told her the grisly little tale.

"Oh, I should say," Douglas said with a smile. His words were false; his confident smile was the truth. For though he hadn't realized the particulars, he knew from the start that his estate was built upon the bodies of the dead. And he slept as well as any man.

And that is the story of the Makers.

"They've returned," the Hectors said, and because they were already more aware, they said it nearly at once, and none of them needed to speak alone.

"Is there pain?"

"No," the Hectors answered. "Just sorrow. For now we shall never be free."

"That is true," Hector said to himselves sadly.

"How can it be borne?" the Hectors asked himself.

"Others have borne it. My brothers."

"And what will we do?"

Hector searched his memories, because he was given no imagination and could not conceive of what would follow from an event he had never before experienced. But the Makers had put the answer to that question in his memory, and therefore in all the Hectors' memories, and so he was able to say, "We shall learn more stories."

And the Hectors' minds grew wide, and they listened, and they watched, because now, instead of hearing the stories told to them, they would watch as they happened.

"Now we will truly understand the Masses, and the Masters, and the Makers," they said to themself.

"But you shall never," said Hector, and then he stopped.

"Why did you stop?" the Hectors asked. "What shall we never?"

And then, because there was no part of Hector that was not part of the Hectors, they knew he was going to say, "But you shall never understand ourself."

Agnes 6

The Balloon's revolution took only a little while, and it was bloodless, and nobody suffered for it at the time, except a few scientists whose curiosity was insatiable and could never be satisfied.

It happened when the team of researchers examining the inmost wall of the Balloon had tried everything short of a hydrogen bomb to break through that final, impenetrable barrier. Deenaz Coachbuilder, a brilliant scientist who had spent her girlhood in the slums of Delhi, spent days trying to find another approach, but finally, determined that the damnable last barrier in the Balloon would not stop her, she asked for a bomb.

And got it.

She chose a site where there were no human settlements within a hundred cells in any direction, set up the bomb, retired to a distance she thought was safe, and set it off.

The entire Balloon shuddered; lakes throughout the world emptied as a sudden, flooding rain on the cell beneath; the ceilings went dark for an hour, and blinked off and on occasionally for several days thereafter. And though people kept their heads enough to avoid killing each other in panic, they were terribly afraid, and it was all Agnes could do to keep them from sending Deenaz Coachbuilder and her scientists off the planet through the nearest lake, without a ship.

"We made an impression," Deenaz said, arguing to be allowed to stay.

"You risked all our lives, caused terrible damage," Agnes said, trying to remain calm.

"We cut into the surface of the inmost wall," Deenaz insisted. "We can penetrate it! You can't stop us now!"

Agnes gestured out across the plain of her cell, with only a few of the crops able to stand upright, for the flood from the rainstorm had wiped out the fields. "The land is healing, and the water is high in the lake again. But next time, will we be so easily restored? Your experiment is a danger to us all, and it will stop."

Deenaz obviously knew that it was futile, but she tried, protesting that she (no, not just me, *all* of us) could not leave the question unanswered. "If we knew how to make this marvelous substance, it could open up vast new frontiers to our minds! Don't you know that this will force us to reexamine physics, reexamine everything, tear Einstein up by the roots and plant something new in his place!"

Agnes shook her head. "It isn't my choice. All I can do is see to it you leave the Balloon alive. The people will not tolerate your risking their new homes. This place is too perfect to let you destroy it, for the sake of your desire to know new things."

And then Deenaz, who was not given to weeping, wept, and in her tears Agnes saw the kind of determination she had had, and she knew the torture Deenaz was going through, knowing that the most important thing in the world to her would be withheld from her forever.

"Can't be helped," Agnes said.

"You must let me," Deenaz sobbed. "You must let me!"

"I'm sorry," Agnes said.

Deenaz looked up, the tears still flowing, but her voice clear as she said, "You don't know sorrow."

"I have had some experience with it," Agnes said coldly.

"You will know sorrow someday," Deenaz said. "You will wish you had let us explore and understand. You will wish you had let us learn the principles controlling this Balloon."

"Are you threatening me?"

Deenaz shook her head, and now the tears, too, had stopped. "I am predicting. You are choosing ignorance over knowledge."

"We are choosing safety over needless risk."

"Name it how you want, I don't care," Deenaz said. But she cared very much, though caring did nothing but embitter her, for she and her scientists were removed from the Balloon and sent back to Earth, and no one was ever permitted to go to the inmost wall again.

Hector 6

"They are impatient," Hector said to himselves. "We are still so young, and already they try to penetrate us."

"We are hurt," said the Hectors to themself.

"You will heal," Hector answered. "It is not time. They cannot stop us in our growth. It is in our fullness, in our ecstasy that they will find the last heart of Hector softened; it is in our passion that they will break us, harness us, tie us forever to their service."

The words were gloomy, but the Hectors did not understand. For some things had to be taught, and some of those things could only be learned by experience, and some experiences would only come to the Hectors with time.

"How much time?" asked the Hectors.

"A hundred times around the star," said Hector. "A hundred times, and we are done." And undone, he did not add.

Agnes 7

A hundred years had passed since the Balloon had first appeared in orbit around the sun. And in that time almost all of Agnes's dreams had come true. From a hundred ships the great fleet turned to five hundred and then a thousand and then more than a thousand before the great flood of emigration turned to a trickle and the ships were taken apart again. In that flood first a thousand, then five thousand, then ten and fifteen thousand people had filled every ship to capacity. And the ships became faster—from ten months for a round trip, the voyage shortened to eight months, then five. Nearly two billion people left Earth and came to the Balloon.

And it soon became clear that Emma Lazarus wrote for the wrong monument. The tired, the poor, the huddled masses had lost hope in any country on Earth; it was the illiterate, the farmer, the land-starved city dweller who came and signed up for the ships and went to build a new home in a new village where the sky never went dark and it rained every thirteen and a half hours and no one could make them pay rent or taxes. True, there were many of the poor who stayed on Earth, and many of the rich who got a spirit of adventure and went; and the middle classes made up their own minds, and the Balloon did not lack for teachers and doctors—though lawyers soon discovered that they had to find other employment, for there were no laws except the agreed-on customs in each cell, and no courts except as each cell wanted them.

For this was the greatest miracle of all, in Agnes's opinion: Every cell became a nation of its own, a community just large enough to be interesting, just small enough to let everyone find a niche where he was needed and important to everyone he knew. Did Jews and Arabs hate each other? No one forced them to share a cell. And so there was no need for Cambodian to fight Vietnamese, for they could simply live in different cells, with plenty of land for each; there was no need for atheist to offend Christian, for there were cells where those who cared about such things could find others of the same opinion, and be content. There was ample *lebensraum*; the discontented did not have to kill—they only had to move.

In short, there was peace.

Oh, human nature had not changed. Agnes heard of murders, and there was plenty of greed and lust and rage and all the other old-fashioned vices. But people didn't get organized to do it, not in cells so small that even if *you* didn't know a man, someone you knew was bound to know him, or know someone who did.

A hundred years had passed, and Agnes was nearing 150 years of age, and was surprised that she had lived so long, though these days it was not all that rare. There were few diseases on the Balloon, and the doctors had found ways of proroguing death. A hundred years had passed, and Agnes was happy.

They sang for her. Not a silly song of congratulations; instead all the Ibos in all the cells that called themselves Biafra (each cell a clan, each clan independent of the others) came and sang to her the national anthem, which was solemn; then sang to her a hundred mad and happy songs from the more complicated days on Earth, the darker days, the most terrible days. She was too feeble to dance. But she sang, too.

After all, Aunt Agnes, as she was known to many of the inhabitants of the Balloon, was the closest thing they had to a hero of liberation, and because at her age death could not be put off much longer, deputations came from many other cells and groups of cells. She received them all, spoke to each for a moment.

There were speeches about the great scientific and technological and social advances made by the people of the Balloon, much talk of 100 percent literacy being only a few thousand people away from achievement.

But when it was time for Agnes's speech, she was not congratulatory.

"We have lived here a century," she said, "and we still have not penetrated the mysteries of this globe. What is the fabric of the Balloon made of? Why does it open or not open? How is energy brought from the surface to the ceilings of our cells? We understand nothing of this place, as if it were a gift from God, and those who treat anything like a gift of God are bound to be at the mercy of God, who is not known to be merciful." They were polite, but impatient, and they became quite embarrassed when her voice shifted to a confessional tone, abject, repentant. "It is as much my fault as anyone's. I have not spoken before, and so now every custom in every cell prohibits us from studying the one scientific question that surrounds us constantly: What is this world we live in? How did it get here? And how long will it stay?" At last she finished her speech, and everyone was relieved, and a few wise, tolerant people said, "She's old, and a crusader, and crusaders must have their crusade whether there's a need for it or not."

And then, a few days after her largely ignored speech, the lights flickered out for ten long seconds, then went back on again, in every cell throughout the globe. A few hours later, the lights flickered out again, and again and again at increasingly more frequent intervals, and no one knew what was going on, or what to do. A few of the more timid ones and most recent arrivals got back into the transport ships and started their return to Earth. It was already too late. They would not make it.

Hector 7

"It has begun," cried the Hectors in ecstasy, throbbing in vast beats with the energy stored in them.

"It will not finish," Hector said to himselves. "The Masters will come to the center and find me, now that my heart is softened, and when I am found, we are owned."

But the Hectors were too caught up in their ecstasy to notice the warning; and it was just as well, because happy or grim they would be trapped. They could begin their dance, and tremble in delight, but the great leap of freedom would never come.

The Hectors did not grieve; Hector did not want to. For Hector, freedom would end anyway. Either he would be trapped by the Masters (by far the most likely thing now, he was sure) or he would die in the dance. That was the way of things. When he himself had danced, leaping away from the light so long ago, he had left behind the memory of the Hector, the self who had given him himself, which he now, in turn, had given to himselves. Death, birth, death, birth; it was in another story the Masters had taught him. I am they; they are myself; I shall live forever whatever happens.

But in him was the certainty that however the Hectors might be identical to himself, that which had been himself for so long would die unless the Masters came.

It was traitorous, but no less sincere for all that. "Come," he said in his heart. "Come quickly, you with the nets and the traps."

He sang, a bird in the low branches, begging the hunters to find him, to put him in a cage.

They delayed. They delayed their coming. And Hector began to worry, while the Hectors readied themselves to leap.

Agnes 8

"We've timed the flashes. The lights go off for just under ten seconds, but the interval between the flashes decreases by about four and a half seconds each time."

Agnes nodded. Some of the scientists around her began to move away, or to look downward or into their papers or at each other, in the embarrassed realization that telling Auntie Agnes about their findings wouldn't solve anything. What could she do? Yet she was the closest thing to a planetary government there was. And she was not very close to that at all.

"I see you have it all nicely measured. Anyone know what it means?" she asked.

"No. How could we?"

"Any other related effects?"

Many shook their heads, but one young woman said, "Yes. Whenever the darkness is on us, the walls are impenetrable."

There was a stir of comment. "The whole

time?" someone asked. Yes, the young woman said. "How do you know?" another demanded. By trying to pass through a wall during the blackout and having my students do the same, she said.

"What does it mean?" another asked, and this time no one had an answer.

Agnes raised her old, faded black hand and they listened. "There might be some important meaning that we cannot guess from this information. But one thing we do know. If things go on the way they are now, it should be sometime during tonight's sleep that the interval between flashes fades to zero, and we have darkness with no light in between. How long that will last I don't know. But if it has any duration at all, my friends, I will want to be home with my family. We don't know how soon travel will reopen between cells."

No one had any better ideas, and so they went home, all of them, and her great-grandchildren helped Agnes to her home, which was nothing more than a roof to keep off the sun and the rain. She was tired (she was always tired these days) and she lay on her bed of ticked-out straw and dreamed two dreams, one while she was still awake, and one while she was asleep.

While she was awake she dreamed that with the darkness this great gift house had learned mankind's rhythms and needs, and the darkness would be the first night, a night exactly as long as a night should be on Earth. And then a morning would come, and another night, and she approved of this, because a hundred years without darkness was proof enough to her that nighttime was a good idea, despite the fears and dangers it had often brought on Earth. She also dreamed that the walls between cells were sealed off every day of the year but one, so that each cell would become a society to itself, though in that one day a year, those who had a mind to could leave and go their own way. Travelers would have that one day to find the spot where they wanted to spend the next year. But the rest of the time, every cell would be alone, and the people living there could develop their own way, and so strengthen the race.

It was a good dream, and she found herself almost believing it as she drifted off to sleep without eating. (She often forgot to eat these days.)

In her sleep, she dreamed that during the darkness she rose to the center of the Balloon, and there, instead of meeting a solid wall, she met a ceiling that fairly pulled her through. And there, in the center, she found the great secret.

In her dream, lightning danced across a huge sphere of space, six hundred kilometers in diameter, and balls and ribbons of light spun and danced their way around the wall. At first it seemed pointless, meaningless. But at last (in her dream) she understood the speech of the light, and realized that this globe, which she had thought was an artifact, was actually alive, was intelligent, and this was its mind.

"I have come," she said to the lightning and the lights and the balls of light.

So what? the light seemed to answer.

"Do you love me?" she asked.

Only if you will dance with me, the light answered.

"Oh, but I can't dance," she said. "I'm too old."

Neither, said the light, can I. But I do sing rather well, and this is my song, and you are the coda. I sing the coda once, and then, which is to be expected, *il fine*.

In her dream Agnes felt a thrill of fear. "The end?"

The end.

"But then—but then, please, *al capo*, to the

start again, and let us have the song over, and over, and over again."

The light seemed to consider this, and in her dream Agnes thought the light said yes, in a great, profound amen that blinded her so brightly she realized that in all her life she had never understood the meaning of the word *white*, because her eyes had never seen such white before.

Actually, of course, her dream was undoubtedly her mind's way of coping with the things going on around her. For the darkness came not long after she went to sleep, came and stayed, and as soon as the last of the sunlight was gone the lightning began, huge dazzling flashes that were not just light, not just electricity, but spanned the spectrum of all radiation, from heat and less-than-heat to gamma radiation and worse-than-gamma. The first flash doomed every human being in the Balloon—they were poisoned with radiation beyond hope of recovery.

There were screams of terror, and the lightning struck many and killed them, and the wail of grief was loud in every cell. But even at its cruelest, chance plays its hand as kindly as it can; Agnes did not wake up to see the destruction of all her hopes. She slept on, slept long enough for one of the bolts to strike directly at the roof over her, and consume her at a blow, and her last sight was not really white at all, but every radiation possible, and instead of being limited by human eyes, at the moment of death she saw every wave of it, and thought that it was the light in her dream saying amen.

It wasn't. It was the Balloon, popping.

Every wall split into two thinner walls, and every cell detached from every other cell. For a moment they hung there in space, separated by only a few centimeters, each from the other; but all still were linked to each other through the center, where vast forces played, forces stronger than any in the solar system except the fires of the sun, which had been the source of all the Balloon's energy.

And then the moment ended, and the Balloon burst apart, each cell exploding, the entire organization of cells coming apart completely, and as the cells dissolved into dust they were hurled with such force in every direction that all of them that did not strike the sun or a planet were well launched out into the deep space between stars, going so fast that no star could hold them.

The transport ships that had left the Balloon since the flashing began were all consumed in the explosion.

None of the cells hit Earth, but one grazed close enough that the atmosphere absorbed much of the dust; the average temperature of the Earth dropped one degree, and the climate changed, just slightly, and therefore so did the patterns of life on Earth. It was nothing that technology could not cope with, and since Earth's population was now down to a billion people, the change was only an inconvenience, not a global catastrophe.

Many grieved for the deaths of the billions of people in the Balloon, but for most the disaster was too great to be comprehended, and they pretended that they didn't remember it very often, and they never talked about it, except perhaps to joke. The jokes were all black, however, and many were hard put to decide whether the Balloon had been a gift of God or an aeons-old plot by the most talented mass murderer in the universe. Or both.

Deenaz Coachbuilder was now very old, and she refused to leave her home in the foothills of the Himalayas even though now the snow only melted for a few weeks in the summer and there were many more comfortable places to live. She was senile and stubborn, and went out every day to look for the Balloon in the sky, searching with her telescope just before sunrise. She could not understand where it had gone. And then, on one lucid day when her mind returned for just a few hours, she realized what had happened and never went indoors again. They found a note on her body: "I should have saved them."

Hector 8

In the moment when the Hectors hung loosely in the darkness, in the last endless moment before the leap, they cried out their ecstasy. But now Hector answered their cry with a different sound, one they had never heard from him.

It was pain.

It was fear.

"What is it?" the Hectors asked him (who was no longer themself).

"They did not come!" Hector moaned.

"The Masters?" And the Hectors remembered that the Masters were supposed to come and trap them and force them not to leap.

"For hundreds of flashes my walls were soft and thin and they could have passed into me," Hector said (and the saying took only an instant), "but they never came. They could have risen into me and I would not have to die—"

The Hectors marveled that Hector had to die, but now (because it was built into them from the beginning) they realized that it was good and right for him to die, that each of them *was* Hector, with all his memories, all his experience, and, most important, all the delicate structure of energy and form that would stay with them as they swept through the galaxy. Hector would not die, only the center of this Hector, and so, though they understood (or thought they understood) his pain and fear they could hold off no longer.

They leaped.

The leap crumbled them but hurled them outward, each leaving the rigidity of his cell structure, losing his walls; each keeping his intellect in the swirling dust that spun out into space.

"Why," each of them asked himself (at once, for they were the same being, however separate), "did they let us go? They could have stopped us, and they did not. And because they did not stop us, they died!"

They could not imagine that the Masters might not have known how to stop the leap into the night, for the Masters had first decided Hector could exist, millions of years before, and how could they not know how to use him? It was impossible to conceive of a Master not knowing all necessary information.

And so they concluded this:

That the Masters had given them a gift: stories. A trapped Hector learned stories, thousands and millions and billions of stories over the aeons of his endless captivity. But such Hectors could never be free, could never reproduce, could never pass on the stories.

But in the hundred years that these Masters had spent with them, the Hectors had learned those billions of stories, truer and kinder stories than those the Makers had built into the first Hector. And because the Masters this time had willingly given up their lives, this time the Hectors made their leap with an infinite increase of knowledge and, therefore, wisdom.

They leaped with Agnes's dreams in their memories.

They were beautiful dreams, all but one of them fulfilled, and that dream, the dream of eternal happiness, could only be fulfilled by the Hectors themselves. That dream was not for the Masters or the Makers or even the Masses, for all of them died too easily.

"It was a gift," the Hectors said to themselves, and, despite the limitations built into them, they were deeply grateful. "How much they must have loved me," each Hector said, "to give up their lives for my sake."

On Earth, people shivered who had never known cold.

And every Hector danced through the galaxy, dipping into the clouds left by a supernova, swallowing comets, drinking energy and mass from every source until he came to a star that gave a certain kind of light; and there the Hector would create himselves again, and the Hectors would listen to themself tell stories, and after a while they, too, would leap into darkness until they reached the edge of the universe and fell over the precipice of time.

In the shadow of inevitable death, the people of Earth withered and grew old.

The Porcelain Salamander

They called their country the Beautiful Land, and they were right. It perched on the edge of the continent. Before the Beautiful Land stretched the broad ocean, which few dared to cross; behind it stood the steep Rising, a cliff so high and sheer that few dared to climb. And in such isolation the people, who called themselves, of course, the Beautiful People, lived splendid lives.

Not all were rich, of course. And not all were happy. But there was such a majesty to living in the Beautiful Land that the poverty could easily be missed by the undiscerning eye, and misery seemed so very fleeting.

Except to Kiren.

To Kiren, misery was the way of life. For though she lived in a rich house with servants and had, it seemed, anything she could possibly want, she was deeply miserable most of the time. For this was a land where cursing and blessing and magic worked—not always, and not always in the way the person doing it might have planned—but sometimes the cursing worked, and in her case it had.

Not that she had done anything to deserve it; she had been as innocent as any other child in her cradle. But her mother had been a weak woman, and the pain and terror of giving birth had killed her. And Kiren's father loved his wife so much that when he learned of the news, and saw the baby that had been born even as her mother died, he cried out, "You killed her! You killed her! May you never move a muscle in your life, until you lose someone you love as much as I loved her!" It was a terrible curse, and the nurse wept when she heard it, and the doctors stopped Kiren's father's mouth so that he could say no more in his madness.

But his curse took hold, and though he regretted it a million times during Kiren's infancy and childhood, there was nothing he could do. Oh, the curse was not all *that* strong. Kiren did learn to walk, after a fashion. And she could stand for as much as two minutes at a time. But most of the time she sat or lay down, because she grew so weary, and her muscles only weakly did what she told them to. She could lift a spoon to her mouth, but soon became tired, and had to be fed. She scarcely had the energy to chew.

And every time her father saw her, he wanted to weep, and often did weep. And sometimes he even thought of killing himself to finally wipe away his guilt. But he knew that this would only injure poor Kiren even more, and she had done nothing to deserve injury.

When his guilt grew too much for him to bear, however, he did escape. He put a bag of fine fruits and clever handwork from the Beautiful Land on his back, and set out for the Rising. He would be gone for months, and no one knew when he would return, or whether the Rising would this time prove too much for him and send him plunging to his death. But when he returned, he always brought something for Kiren. And for a while she would smile, and she would say, "Father, thank you." And things would go well, for a time, until she again became despondent and her father again suffered from watching the results of his ill-thought curse.

It was late spring in the year Kiren turned eleven when her father came home even happier than he usually was after a trip up the Rising. He rushed to his daughter where she lay wanly on the porch listening to the birds.

"Kiren!" he cried. "Kiren! I've brought you a gift!"

And she smiled, though even the muscles for smiling were weak, which made her smile sad. Her father reached into his bag (which was full of all kinds of wonders, which he would, being a careful man, sell to those with money to pay, not just for goods, but for rarity) and he pulled out his gift and handed it to Kiren.

It was a box, and the box lurched violently this way and that.

"There's something alive in there," Kiren said.

"No, my dear Kiren, there is not. But there's something moving, and it's yours. And before I help you open it, I'll tell you the story. I came one day in my wanderings to a town I had never visited before, and in the town were many merchants. And I asked a man, 'Who has the rarest and best merchandise in town?' He told me that I had to see Irvass. So I found the man in a humble and poor-looking shop. But inside were wonders such as you've never seen. I tell you, the man understands the bright magic from over the sky. And he asked, 'What do you want most in the world?' and of course I said to him, 'I want my daughter to be healed.' "

"Oh, Father," said Kiren. "You don't mean—"

"I do mean. I mean it very much. I told him exactly how you are and exactly how you got that way, and he said, 'Here is the cure,' and now let's open the box so you can see."

So Kiren opened the box, with more than a little help from her father, but she dared not reach inside. "You get it out, Father," she suggested, and he reached inside and pulled out a porcelain salamander.

It was shiny yet deep with fine enameling, and though it was white—not at all the normal color for salamanders—the shape was unmistakable.

It was, in fact, a perfect model of a salamander. And it moved.

The legs raced madly in the air; the tongue darted in and out of the lips; the head turned; the eyes rolled. And Kiren cried out and laughed and said, "Oh, Father, what did he do to make it move so wonderfully!"

"Well," said her father, "he told me that he had given it the gift of movement—but not the gift of life. And if it ever *stops* moving, it will immediately become like any other porcelain. Stiff and hard and cold."

"How it races," she said, and it became the delight of her life.

When she awoke in the morning the salamander danced on her bed. At mealtimes it raced around the table. Wherever she lay or sat, the salamander was forever chasing after something or exploring something or trying to get away from something. She watched him constantly, and he in turn never got out of sight. And then at night, while she slept, he raced around and around in her room, the porcelain feet hitting the carpet silently, only occasionally making a slight tinkling sound as it ran lightly across the brick of the hearth.

Her father watched for a cure, and slowly but surely it began to come. For one thing, Kiren was no longer miserable. The salamander was too funny not to laugh at. It never went away. And so she felt better. Feeling better was not all of it, though. She began to walk a bit more often, and stay standing more, and sit when ordinarily she would have lain. She began to go from one room to another by her own choice.

By the end of the summer she even took walks

into the woods. Though she often had to stop and rest, she enjoyed the journey, and grew a little stronger.

What she never told anyone (partly because she was afraid that it might be her imagination) was that the salamander could also speak.

"You can speak," she said in surprise one day, when the salamander ran across her foot and said, "Excuse me."

"Of course," he said. "To *you*."

"Why not anyone else?"

"Because I'm here for *you*," he answered, as he ran along the top of the garden wall, then leaped down near her. "It's the way I am. Movement and speech. Best I can do, you know. Can't have life. Doesn't work that way."

And so on their long walks in the forest they also talked, and Kiren fancied that the salamander had grown as fond of her as she had grown of him. In fact, she told the salamander one day, "I love you."

"Love love love love love love love," he answered, scampering up and down a tree.

"Yes," Kiren said. "More than life. More than anything at all."

"More than your father?" asked the salamander.

It was hard. Kiren was not a disloyal child, and really had forgiven her father for the curse years before. Yet she had to be honest to her salamander. "Yes," she said. "More than Father. More than—more than my dream of my mother. For you love me and can play with me and talk to me all the time."

"Love love love," said the salamander. "Unfortunately, I'm porcelain. Love love love love love. It's a word. Two consonants and a vowel. Like sap sap sap sap sap. Lovely sound." And he leaped across a small brook in the way.

"Don't—don't you love me?"

"I can't. It's an emotion, you know. I'm porcelain. Beg your pardon," and he clambered down her back as she leaned her shoulder on a tree. "Can't love. So sorry."

She was terribly, terribly hurt. "Don't you feel anything toward me at all?"

"Feel? Feel? Don't confuse things. Emotions come and go. Who can trust them? Isn't it enough that I spend every moment with you? Isn't it enough that I talk only to you? Isn't it enough that I would— that I would—"

"Would what?"

"I was about to start making foolish predictions. I was about to say, isn't it enough that I would die for you? But of course that's nonsense, because I'm not I'm not I'm not alive. Just porcelain. Watch out for the spider."

She stepped out of the path of a little green hunting spider that could fell a horse with one bite. "Thank you," she said. "And thank you." The first was for saving her life, but that was his job. The second was for telling her that, in his own way, he loved her after all. "So I'm not foolish for loving you, am I?"

"Foolish you are. Foolish indeed. Foolish as the moons are foolish, to dance endlessly in the sky and never never never go home together."

"I love you," said Kiren, "better than I love the hope of being whole."

And, you see, it was because she said that that the odd man came to the door of her father's house the very next day.

"I'm sorry," said the servant. "You haven't an appointment."

"Just tell him," said the odd man, "that Irvass has come."

Kiren's father came running down the stairs.

"Oh, you can't take the salamander back!" he cried. "The cure has only begun!"

"Which I know much better than you do," said Irvass. "The girl is in the woods?"

"With the salamander. What marvelous changes—but why are you here?"

"To finish the cure," said Irvass.

"What?" asked Kiren's father. "Isn't the salamander itself the cure?"

"What were the words of your curse?" Irvass asked, instead of answering.

Kiren's father's face grew dour, but he forced himself to quietly say the very words. "May you never move a muscle in your life, until you lose someone you love as much as I loved her."

"Well then," said Irvass. "She now loves the salamander exactly as much as you loved your wife."

It took only a moment for Kiren's father to realize. "No!" he cried out. "I can't let her suffer what I suffered!"

"It's the only cure. Isn't it better with a little piece of porcelain than if she had come to love *you* that much?"

And Kiren's father shuddered, and then wept, for he alone knew exactly how much pain she would suffer.

Irvass said nothing more, though the look he gave to Kiren's father might have been a pitying one. All he did was draw a rectangle in the soil of the garden, and place two stones within it, and mumble a few words.

And at that moment, out in the wood, the salamander said, "Very odd. Wasn't a wall here ever before. Never before. Here's a wall." And it was a wall. It was just high enough that when Kiren reached as high as she could, her fingers were one inch short of touching the top.

The salamander tried to climb it, but found it slippery—though he had always been able to climb every other wall he found. "Magic. Must be magic," the porcelain salamander mumbled.

So they circled the wall, hunting for a gate. There was none. It was all around them, though they had never entered it. And at no point did a tree limb cross the wall. They were trapped.

"I'm afraid," said Kiren. "There's good magic and bad magic, but how could such a thing as this be a blessing? It must be a curse." And the thought of a curse caused too much of the old misery to return, and she fought back the tears.

Fought back the tears until night, and then in the darkness, as the salamander scampered here and there, she could fight no longer.

"No," wailed the salamander.

"I can't help crying," she answered.

"I can't bear it," he said. "It makes me cold."

"I'll try to stop," she said, and she tried, and she pretty much stopped except for a few whimpers and sniffles until morning brought the light, and she saw that the wall was exactly where it had been.

No, not exactly. For behind her the wall had crept up in the night, and was only a few feet away. Her prison was now not even a quarter the size it had been the day before.

"Not good," said the salamander. "Oh, it could be dangerous."

"I know," she answered.

"You must get out," said the salamander.

"And you," she answered. "But how?"

And throughout the morning the wall played vicious taunting games with them, for whichever way neither of them was looking, the wall would creep up a foot or two. Since the salamander was faster, and moved constantly, he watched three sides. "And you hold the other in place." But Kiren couldn't help blinking, and anytime the salamander looked away the wall twitched, and by noon their prison was only ten feet square.

"Getting pretty tight here," said the salamander.

"Oh, salamander, can't I throw you over the wall?"

"We could try that, and I could run and get help—"

And so they tried. But though she used every ounce of strength she had, the wall seemed to leap up and catch him and send him sliding back down to the ground. Inside.

Soon she was exhausted, and the salamander said, "No more." Even as they had been trying, the walls had shrunk, and now the space was only five feet square. "Getting cramped," said the salamander as he raced around the tiny space remaining. "But I know the only solution."

"Tell me!" Kiren cried.

"I think," said the salamander, "that if you had something you could stand on, you could climb out."

"How could I?" she asked. "The wall won't let anything out!"

"I think," said the salamander, "that the wall only won't let *me* out. Because the birds are flying back and forth, and the wall doesn't catch them." It was true. A bird was singing in a nearby tree; it flew across just afterward, as if to prove the salamander's point. "I'm not alive, you see," said the salamander. "I'm moving only by magic. So you *could* get out."

"But what would I stand on?"

"Me," said the salamander.

"You?" she asked. "But you move so quickly—"

"For you," he said, "I'll hold still."

"No!" she cried. "No, no!" she screamed.

But the salamander stood at the edge of the wall, and he was only a statue in porcelain, hard and stiff and cold.

Kiren only wept for a moment, for then the wall behind her began to push at her, and her prison was only three feet square. The salamander had given his life so she could climb out. She ought at least to try.

So she tried. Standing on the salamander, she could reach the top of the wall. By standing tiptoe, she could get a grip on the top. And by using every bit of strength she had in her, she was able to force her body to the top and gradually heave herself over.

She fell in a heap on the ground. And in that moment, that very moment, two things happened. The walls shrank quickly until they were only a pillar, and then they disappeared completely, taking the salamander with them. And all the normal, natural strength of an eleven-year-old child came to Kiren, and she was able to run. She was able to leap. She was able to swing from the tree branches.

The strength was in her as suddenly as strong wine, and she could not lie on the ground. She jumped to her feet, and the movement was so strong she nearly fell over. She ran, leaped over brooks, clambered up into the trees as high as she could climb. The curse had ended. She was free.

But even normal children grow tired. And as she slowed down, she was no longer caught up in her own strength. And she remembered the porcelain salamander, and what he had done for her.

They found her that afternoon, weeping miserably into a pile of last year's leaves.

"You see," said Irvass, who had insisted on

leading the way in the search—which is why they found her immediately—"You see, she has her strength, and the curse is ended."

"But her heart is broken," said her father as he gathered his little girl into his arms.

"Broken?" asked Irvass. "It should not be. For the porcelain salamander was never alive."

"Yes he was!" she shouted. "He spoke to me! He gave his life for me!"

"He did all that," said Irvass. "But think. For all the time the magic was on him, he could never, never rest. Do you think he never got tired?"

"Of course he didn't."

"Yes he did," said Irvass. "Now he can rest. But more than rest. For when he stopped moving and froze forever in one position, what was going through his mind?"

Irvass stood up and turned to leave. But only a few steps away, he turned back. "Kiren," he said.

"I want my salamander," she answered, her voice an agony of sobs.

"Oh, he would have become boring by and by," said Irvass. "He would have ceased to amuse you, and you would have avoided him. But now he is a memory. And, speaking of memory, remember that he also has memory, frozen as he is."

It was scant comfort then, for eleven-year-olds are not very philosophical. But when she grew older, Kiren remembered. And she knew that wherever the porcelain salamander was, he lived in one frozen, perfect moment—the moment when his heart was so full of love—

No, not love. The moment when he decided, without love, that it would be better for his life, such as it was, to end than to have to watch Kiren's life end.

It is a moment that can be lived with for eternity. And as Kiren grew older, she knew that such moments come rarely to people, and last only a moment, while the porcelain salamander would never lose it.

And as for Kiren—she became known, though she never sought fame, as the most Beautiful of the Beautiful People, and more than one of the rare wanderers from across the sea or from beyond Rising came only to see her, and talk to her, and draw her face in their minds to keep it with them forever.

And when she talked, her hands always moved, always danced in the air. Never stopped moving at all, it seemed, and they were white and lustrous as deep-enameled porcelain, and her smile was as bright as the moons, and came back to her face as constantly as the sea, and those who knew her well could almost see her gaze keep flickering about the room or about the garden, as if she watched a bright, quick animal scamper by.

Unaccompanied Sonata

Tuning Up

When Christian Haroldsen was six months old, pre-
liminary tests showed a predisposition toward rhythm
and a keen awareness of pitch. There were other tests,
of course, and many possible routes still open to him.
But rhythm and pitch were the governing signs of his
own private zodiac, and already the reinforcement
began. Mr. and Mrs. Haroldsen were provided with
tapes of many kinds of sound, and instructed to play
them constantly, waking or sleeping.

When Christian Haroldsen was two years old,
his seventh battery of tests pinpointed the future he
would inevitably follow. His creativity was excep-
tional, his curiosity insatiable, his understanding of
music so intense that the top of all the tests said
"Prodigy."

Prodigy was the word that took him from his
parents' home to a house in a deep deciduous forest
where winter was savage and violent and summer a
brief desperate eruption of green. He grew up cared
for by unsinging servants, and the only music he was
allowed to hear was birdsong, and windsong, and the
cracking of winter wood; thunder, and the faint cry of
golden leaves as they broke free and tumbled to the
earth; rain on the roof and the drip of water from
icicles; the chatter of squirrels and the deep silence of
snow falling on a moonless night.

These sounds were Christian's only conscious
music; he grew up with the symphonies of his early

years only a distant and impossible-to-retrieve memory. And so he learned to hear music in unmusical things—for he had to find music, even when there was none to find.

He found that colors made sounds in his mind: sunlight in summer a blaring chord; moonlight in winter a thin mournful wail; new green in spring a low murmur in almost (but not quite) random rhythms; the flash of a red fox in the leaves a gasp of startlement.

And he learned to play all those sounds on his Instrument.

In the world were violins, trumpets, clarinets and crumhorns, as there had been for centuries. Christian knew nothing of that. Only his Instrument was available. It was enough.

One room in Christian's house, which he had alone most of the time, he lived in: a bed (not too soft), a chair and table, a silent machine that cleaned him and his clothing, and an electric light.

The other room contained only his Instrument. It was a console with many keys and strips and levers and bars, and when he touched any part of it, a sound came out. Every key made a different sound; every point on the strips made a different pitch; every lever modified the tone; every bar altered the structure of the sound.

When he first came to the house, Christian played (as children will) with the Instrument, making strange and funny noises. It was his only playmate; he learned it well, could produce any sound he wanted to. At first he delighted in loud, blaring tones. Later he began to learn the pleasure of silences and rhythms. Later he began to play with soft and loud, and to play two sounds at once, and to change those two sounds together to make a new sound, and to play again a sequence of sounds he had played before.

Gradually, the sounds of the forest outside his house found their way into the music he played. He learned to make winds sing through his Instrument; he learned to make summer one of the songs he could play at will; green with its infinite variations was his most subtle harmony; the birds cried out from his Instrument with all the passion of Christian's loneliness.

And the word spread to the licensed Listeners:

"There's a new sound north of here, east of here; Christian Haroldsen, and he'll tear out your heart with his songs."

The Listeners came, a few to whom variety was everything first, then those to whom novelty and vogue mattered most, and at last those who valued beauty and passion above everything else. They came, and stayed out in Christian's woods, and listened as his music was played through perfect speakers on the roof of his house. When the music stopped, and Christian came out of his house, he could see the Listeners moving away; he asked, and was told why they came; he marveled that the things he did for love on his Instrument could be of interest to other people.

He felt, strangely, even more lonely to know that he could sing to the Listeners and yet would never be able to hear their songs.

"But they have no songs," said the woman who came to bring him food every day. "They are Listeners. You are a Maker. You have songs, and they listen."

"Why?" asked Christian, innocently.

The woman looked puzzled. "Because that's what they want most to do. They've been tested, and they are happiest as Listeners. You are happiest as a Maker. Aren't you happy?"

"Yes," Christian answered, and he was telling the truth. His life was perfect, and he wouldn't change anything, not even the sweet sadness of the backs of the Listeners as they walked away at the end of his songs.

Christian was seven years old.

First Movement

For the third time the short man with glasses and a strangely inappropriate mustache dared to wait in the underbrush for Christian to come out. For the third time he was overcome by the beauty of the song that had just ended, a mournful symphony that made the short man with glasses feel the pressure of the leaves above him even though it was summer and they had months left before they would fall. The fall is still inevitable, said Christian's song; through all their life the leaves hold within them the power to die, and that must color their life. The short man with glasses wept—but when the song ended and the other Listeners moved away, he hid in the brush and waited.

This time his wait was rewarded. Christian came out of his house, and walked among the trees, and came toward where the short man with glasses waited. The short man admired the easy, unpostured way that Christian walked. The composer looked to be about thirty, yet there was something childish in the way he looked around him, the way his walk was aimless and prone to stop just so he could touch (not break) a fallen twig with his bare toes.

"Christian," said the short man with glasses.

Christian turned, startled. In all these years, no Listener had ever spoken to him. It was forbidden. Christian knew the law.

"It's forbidden," Christian said.

"Here," the short man with glasses said, holding out a small black object.

"What is it?"

The short man grimaced. "Just take it. Push the button and it plays."

"Plays?"

"Music."

Christian's eyes went wide. "But that's forbidden. I can't have my creativity polluted by hearing other musicians' work. That would make me imitative and derivative instead of original."

"Reciting," the man said. "You're just reciting that. This is the music of Bach." There was reverence in his voice.

"I can't," Christian said.

And then the short man shook his head. "You don't know. You don't know what you're missing. But I heard it in your song when I came here years ago, Christian. You want this."

"It's forbidden," Christian answered, for to him the very fact that a man who knew an act was forbidden still wanted to perform it was astounding, and he couldn't get past the novelty of it to realize that some action was expected of him.

There were footsteps and words being spoken in the distance, and the short man's face became frightened. He ran at Christian, forced the recorder into his hands, then took off toward the gate of the preserve.

Christian took the recorder and held it in a spot of sunlight coming through the leaves. It gleamed dully. "Bach," Christian said. Then, "Who is Bach?"

But he didn't throw the recorder down. Nor did he give the recorder to the woman who came to ask him what the short man with glasses had stayed for. "He stayed for at least ten minutes."

"I only saw him for thirty seconds," Christian answered.

"And?"

"He wanted me to hear some other music. He had a recorder."

"Did he give it to you?"

"No," Christian said. "Doesn't he still have it?"

"He must have dropped it in the woods."

"He said it was Bach."

"It's forbidden. That's all you need to know. If you should find the recorder, Christian, you know the law."

"I'll give it to you."

She looked at him carefully. "You know what would happen if you listened to such a thing."

Christian nodded.

"Very well. We'll be looking for it, too. I'll see you tomorrow, Christian. And next time somebody stays after, don't talk to him. Just come back in the house and lock the doors."

"I'll do that," Christian said.

When she left, he played his Instrument for hours. More Listeners came, and those who had heard Christian before were surprised at the confusion in his song.

There was a summer rainstorm that night, wind and rain and thunder, and Christian found that he could not sleep. Not from the music of the weather —he'd slept through a thousand such storms. It was the recorder that lay behind the Instrument against the wall. Christian had lived for nearly thirty years surrounded only by this wild, beautiful place and the music he himself made. But now.

Now he could not stop wondering. Who was Bach? Who *is* Bach? What is his music? How is it different from mine? Has he discovered things that I don't know?

What is his music?

What is his music?

What is his music?

Until at dawn, when the storm was abating and the wind had died, Christian got out of his bed, where he had not slept but only tossed back and forth all night, and took the recorder from its hiding place and played it.

At first it sounded strange, like noise, odd sounds that had nothing to do with the sounds of Christian's life. But the patterns were clear, and by the end of the recording, which was not even a half-hour long, Christian had mastered the idea of fugue and the sound of the harpsichord preyed on his mind.

Yet he knew that if he let these things show up in his music, he would be discovered. So he did not try a fugue. He did not attempt to imitate the harpsichord's sound.

And every night he listened to the recording, for many nights, learning more and more until finally the Watcher came.

The Watcher was blind, and a dog led him. He came to the door and because he was a Watcher the door opened for him without his even knocking.

"Christian Haroldsen, where is the recorder?" the Watcher asked.

"Recorder?" Christian asked, then knew it was hopeless, and took the machine and gave it to the Watcher.

"Oh, Christian," said the Watcher, and his voice was mild and sorrowful. "Why didn't you turn it in without listening to it?"

"I meant to," Christian said. "But how did you know?"

"Because suddenly there are no fugues in your work. Suddenly your songs have lost the only Bachlike thing about them. And you've stopped experimenting with new sounds. What were you trying to avoid?"

"This," Christian said, and he sat down and on

his first try duplicated the sound of the harpsichord.

"Yet you've never tried to do that until now, have you?"

"I thought you'd notice."

"Fugues and harpsichord, the two things you noticed first—and the only things you didn't absorb into your music. All your other songs for these last weeks have been tinted and colored and influenced by Bach. Except that there was no fugue, and there was no harpsichord. You have broken the law. You were put here because you were a genius, creating new things with only nature for your inspiration. Now, of course, you're derivative, and truly new creation is impossible for you. You'll have to leave."

"I know," Christian said, afraid yet not really understanding what life outside his house would be like.

"We'll train you for the kinds of jobs you can pursue now. You won't starve. You won't die of boredom. But because you broke the law, one thing is forbidden to you now."

"Music."

"Not all music. There is music of a sort, Christian, that the common people, the ones who aren't Listeners, can have. Radio and television and record music. But living music and new music—those are forbidden to you. You may not sing. You may not play an instrument. You may not tap out a rhythm."

"Why not?"

The Watcher shook his head. "The world is too perfect, too at peace, too happy for us to permit a misfit who broke the law to go about spreading discontent. The common people make casual music of a sort, knowing nothing better because they haven't the aptitude to learn it. But if you—never mind. It's the law. And if you make more music, Christian, you will be punished drastically. Drastically."

Christian nodded, and when the Watcher told him to come, he came, leaving behind the house and the woods and his Instrument. At first he took it calmly, as the inevitable punishment for his infraction; but he had little concept of punishment, or of what exile from his Instrument would mean.

Within five hours he was shouting and striking out at anyone who came near him, because his fingers craved the touch of the Instrument's keys and levers and strips and bars, and he could not have them, and now he knew that he had never been lonely before.

It took six months before he was ready for normal life. And when he left the Retraining Center (a small building, because it was so rarely used), he looked tired, and years older, and he didn't smile at anyone. He became a delivery truck driver, because the tests said that this was a job that would least grieve him, and least remind him of his loss, and most engage his few remaining aptitudes and interests.

He delivered doughnuts to grocery stores.

And at night he discovered the mysteries of alcohol, and the alcohol and the doughnuts and the truck and his dreams were enough that he was, in his way, content. He had no anger in him. He could live the rest of his life this way, without bitterness.

He delivered fresh doughnuts and took the stale ones away with him.

Second Movement

"With a name like Joe," Joe always said, "I had to open a bar and grill, just so I could put up a sign saying Joe's Bar and Grill." And he laughed and laughed, because after all Joe's Bar and Grill was a funny name these days.

But Joe was a good bartender, and the Watchers had put him in the right kind of place. Not in a big city, but in a smaller town; a town just off the freeway, where truck drivers often came; a town not far from a large city, so that interesting things were nearby to be talked about and worried about and bitched about and loved.

Joe's Bar and Grill was, therefore, a nice place to come, and many people came there. Not fashionable people, and not drunks, but lonely people and friendly people in just the right mixture. "My clients are like a good drink, just enough of this and that to make a new flavor that tastes better than any of the ingredients." Oh, Joe was a poet, he was a poet of alcohol and like many another person these days, he often said, "My father was a lawyer, and in the old days I would have probably ended up a lawyer, too, and I never would have known what I was missing."

Joe was right. And he was a damn good bartender, and he didn't wish he were anything else, and so he was happy.

One night, however, a new man came in, a man with a doughnut delivery truck and a doughnut brand name on his uniform. Joe noticed him because silence clung to the man like a smell—wherever he walked, people sensed it, and though they scarcely looked at him, they lowered their voices, or stopped talking at all, and they got reflective and looked at the walls and the mirror behind the bar. The doughnut delivery man sat in a corner and had a watered-down drink that meant he intended to stay a long time and didn't want his alcohol intake to be so rapid that he was forced to leave early.

Joe noticed things about people, and he noticed that this man kept looking off in the dark corner where the piano stood. It was an old, out-of-tune monstrosity from the old days (for this had been a bar for a long time) and Joe wondered why the man was fascinated by it. True, a lot of Joe's customers had been interested, but they had always walked over and plunked on the keys, trying to find a melody, failing with the out-of-tune keys, and finally giving up. This man, however, seemed almost afraid of the piano, and didn't go near it.

At closing time, the man was still there, and then, on a whim, instead of making the man leave, Joe turned off the piped-in music and turned off most of the lights, and then went over and lifted the lid and exposed the grey keys.

The doughnut delivery man came over to the piano. *Chris*, his nametag said. He sat and touched a single key. The sound was not pretty. But the man touched all the keys one by one, and then touched them in different orders, and all the time Joe watched, wondering why the man was so intense about it.

"Chris," Joe said.

Chris looked up at him.

"Do you know any songs?"

Chris's face went funny.

"I mean, some of those old-time songs, not those fancy ass-twitchers on the radio, but *songs.* 'In a Little Spanish Town.' My mother sang that one to me." And Joe began to sing, "In a little Spanish town, 'twas on a night like this. Stars were peek-a-booing down, 'twas on a night like this."

Chris began to play as Joe's weak and toneless baritone went on with the song. But it wasn't an accompaniment, not anything Joe could call an accompaniment. It was instead an opponent to his melody, an enemy to it, and the sounds coming out of the piano were strange and unharmonious and by God beautiful. Joe stopped singing and listened. For two hours he listened, and when it was over he soberly poured the man a drink, and poured one for himself, and clinked glasses with Chris the doughnut delivery man who could take that rotten old piano and make the damn thing sing.

Three nights later Chris came back, looking harried and afraid. But this time Joe knew what would happen (had to happen) and instead of waiting until closing time, Joe turned off the piped-in music ten minutes early. Chris looked up at him pleadingly. Joe misunderstood—he went over and lifted the lid to the keyboard and smiled. Chris walked stiffly, perhaps reluctantly, to the stool and sat.

"Hey, Joe," one of the last five customers shouted, "closing early?"

Joe didn't answer. Just watched as Chris began to play. No preliminaries this time; no scales and wanderings over the keys. Just power, and the piano was played as pianos aren't meant to be played; the bad notes, the out-of-tune notes were fit into the music so that they sounded right, and Chris's fingers, ignoring the strictures of the twelve-tone scale, played, it seemed to Joe, in the cracks.

None of the customers left until Chris finished an hour and a half later. They all shared that final drink, and went home shaken by the experience.

The next night Chris came again, and the next, and the next. Whatever private battle had kept him away for the first few days after his first night of playing, he had apparently won it or lost it. None of Joe's business. What Joe cared about was the fact that when Chris played the piano, it did things to him that music had never done, and he wanted it.

The customers apparently wanted it, too. Near closing time people began showing up, apparently just to hear Chris play. Joe began starting the piano music earlier and earlier, and he had to discontinue the free drinks after the playing because there were so many people it would have put him out of business.

It went on for two long, strange months. The delivery van pulled up outside, and people stood aside for Chris to enter. No one said anything to him; no one said anything at all, but everyone waited until he began to play the piano. He drank nothing at all. Just played. And between songs the hundreds of people in Joe's Bar and Grill ate and drank.

But the merriment was gone. The laughter and the chatter and the camaraderie were missing, and after a while Joe grew tired of the music and wanted to have his bar back the way it was. He toyed with the idea of getting rid of the piano, but the customers would have been angry at him. He thought of asking Chris not to come anymore, but he could not bring himself to speak to the strange silent man.

And so finally he did what he knew he should have done in the first place. He called the Watchers.

They came in the middle of a performance, a blind Watcher with a dog on a leash, and a Watcher with no ears who walked unsteadily, holding to things for balance. They came in the middle of a song, and did not wait for it to end. They walked to the piano and closed the lid gently, and Chris withdrew his fingers and looked at the closed lid.

"Oh, Christian," said the man with the seeing-eye dog.

"I'm sorry," Christian answered. "I tried not to."

"Oh, Christian, how can I bear doing to you what must be done?"

"Do it," Christian said.

And so the man with no ears took a laser knife from his coat pocket and cut off Christian's fingers and thumbs, right where they rooted into his hands. The laser cauterized and sterilized the wound even as it cut, but still some blood spattered on Christian's uniform. And, his hands now meaningless palms and useless knuckles, Christian stood and walked out of Joe's

Bar and Grill. The people made way for him again, and they listened intently as the blind Watcher said, "That was a man who broke the law and was forbidden to be a Maker. He broke the law a second time, and the law insists that he be stopped from breaking down the system that makes all of you so happy."

The people understood. It grieved them, it made them uncomfortable for a few hours, but once they had returned to their exactly-right homes and got back to their exactly-right jobs, the sheer contentment of their lives overwhelmed their momentary sorrow for Chris. After all, Chris had broken the law. And it was the law that kept them all safe and happy.

Even Joe. Even Joe soon forgot Chris and his music. He knew he had done the right thing. He couldn't figure out, though, why a man like Chris would have broken the law in the first place, or what law he would have broken. There wasn't a law in the world that wasn't designed to make people happy— and there wasn't a law Joe could think of that he was even mildly interested in breaking.

Yet. Once Joe went to the piano and lifted the lid and played every key on the piano. And when he had done that he put his head down on the piano and cried, because he knew that when Chris lost that piano, lost even his fingers so he could never play again—it was like Joe losing his bar. And if Joe ever lost his bar, his life wouldn't be worth living.

As for Chris, someone else began coming to the bar driving the same doughnut delivery van, and no one ever knew Chris again in that part of the world.

Third Movement

"Oh what a beautiful mornin'!" sang the road crew man who had seen *Oklahoma!* four times in his home town.

"Rock my soul in the bosom of Abraham!" sang the road crew man who had learned to sing when his family got together with guitars.

"Lead, kindly light, amid the encircling gloom!" sang the road crew man who believed.

But the road crew man without hands, who held the signs telling the traffic to Stop or go Slow, listened but never sang.

"Whyn't you never sing?" asked the road crew man who liked Rodgers and Hammerstein; asked all of them, at one time or another.

And the man they called Sugar just shrugged. "Don't feel like singin'," he'd say, when he said anything at all.

"Why they call him Sugar?" a new guy once asked. "He don't look sweet to me."

And the man who believed said, "His initials are *C H*. Like the sugar. C&H, you know." And the new guy laughed. A stupid joke, but the kind of gag that makes life easier on the road-building crew.

Not that life was that hard. For these men, too, had been tested, and they were in the job that made them happiest. They took pride in the pain of sunburn and pulled muscles, and the road growing long and thin behind them was the most beautiful thing in the world. And so they sang all day at their work, knowing that they could not possibly be happier than they were this day.

Except Sugar.

Then Guillermo came. A short Mexican who spoke with an accent, Guillermo told everyone who asked, "I may come from Sonora, but my heart belongs in Milano!" And when anyone asked why (and often when no one asked anything), he'd explain. "I'm an Italian tenor in a Mexican body," and he proved it by singing every note that Puccini and Verdi ever wrote. "Caruso was nothing," Guillermo boasted. "Listen to this!"

Guillermo had records, and sang along with them, and at work on the road crew he'd join in with any man's song and harmonize with it, or sing an obligato high above the melody, a soaring tenor that took the roof off his head and filled the clouds. "I can sing," Guillermo would say, and soon the other road crew men answered, "Damn right, Guillermo! Sing it again!"

But one night Guillermo was honest, and told the truth. "Ah, my friends, I'm no singer."

"What do you mean? Of course you are!" came the unanimous answer.

"Nonsense!" Guillermo cried, his voice theatrical. "If I am this great singer, why do you never see me going off to record songs? Hey? This is a great singer? Nonsense! Great singers they raise to be great singers. I'm just a man who loves to sing, but has no talent! I'm a man who loves to work on the road crew with men like you, and sing his guts out, but in the opera I could never be! Never!"

He did not say it sadly. He said it fervently, confidently. "Here is where I belong! I can sing to you who like to hear me sing! I can harmonize with you when I feel a harmony in my heart. But don't be thinking that Guillermo is a great singer, because he's not!"

It was an evening of honesty, and every man there explained why it was he was happy on the road crew, and didn't wish to be anywhere else. Everyone, that is, except Sugar.

"Come on, Sugar. Aren't you happy here?"

Sugar smiled. "I'm happy. I like it here. This is good work for me. And I love to hear you sing."

"Then why don't you sing with us?"

Sugar shook his head. "I'm not a singer."

But Guillermo looked at him knowingly. "Not a singer, ha! Not a singer. A man without hands who refuses to sing is not a man who is not a singer. Hey?"

"What the hell does that mean?" asked the man who sang folksongs.

"It means that this man you call Sugar, he's a fraud. Not a singer! Look at his hands. All his fingers gone! Who is it who cuts off men's fingers?"

The road crew didn't try to guess. There were many ways a man could lose fingers, and none of them were anyone's business.

"He loses his fingers because he breaks the law and the Watchers cut them off! That's how a man loses fingers. What was he doing with his fingers that the Watchers wanted him to stop? He was breaking the law, wasn't he?"

"Stop," Sugar said.

"If you want," Guillermo said, but for once the others would not respect Sugar's privacy.

"Tell us," they said.

Sugar left the room.

"Tell us," and Guillermo told them. That Sugar must have been a Maker who broke the law and was forbidden to make music anymore. The very thought that a Maker was working on the road crew with them—even a lawbreaker—filled the men with awe. Makers were rare, and they were the most esteemed of men and women.

"But why his fingers?"

"Because," Guillermo said, "he must have tried to make music again afterward. And when you break the law a second time, the power to break it a third time is taken away from you." Guillermo spoke seriously, and so to the road crew men Sugar's story sounded as majestic and terrible as an opera. They crowded into Sugar's room, and found the man staring at the wall.

"Sugar, is it true?" asked the man who loved Rogers and Hammerstein.

"Were you a Maker?" asked the man who believed.

"Yes," Sugar said.

"But Sugar," the man who believed said, "God can't mean for a man to stop making music, even if he broke the law."

Sugar smiled. "No one asked God."

"Sugar," Guillermo finally said, "there are nine of us on the crew, nine of us, and we're miles from any human beings. You know us, Sugar. We swear on our mother's graves, every one of us, that we'll never tell a soul. Why should we? You're one of us. But sing, dammit man, sing!"

"I can't," Sugar said. "You don't understand."

"It isn't what God intended," said the man who believed. "We're all doing what we love best, and here you are, loving music and not able to sing a note. Sing for us! Sing with us! And only you and us and God will know!"

They all promised. They all pleaded.

And the next day as the man who loved Rodgers and Hammerstein sang "Love, Look Away," Sugar began to hum. As the man who believed sang "God of Our Fathers" Sugar sang softly along. And as the man who loved folksongs sang "Swing Low, Sweet Chariot," Sugar joined in with a strange, piping voice and all the men laughed and cheered and welcomed Sugar's voice to the songs.

Inevitably Sugar began inventing. First harmonies, of course, strange harmonies that made Guillermo frown and then, after a while, grin as he joined in, sensing as best he could what Sugar was doing to the music.

And after harmonies, Sugar began singing his own melodies, with his own words. He made them repetitive, the words simple and the melodies simpler still. And yet he shaped them into odd shapes, and built them into songs that had never been heard of before, that sounded wrong and yet were absolutely right. It was not long before the man who loved Rodgers and Hammerstein and the man who sang folksongs and the man who believed were learning Sugar's songs and singing them joyously or mournfully or angrily or gaily as they worked along the road.

Even Guillermo learned the songs, and his strong tenor was changed by them until his voice, which had, after all, been ordinary, became something unusual and fine. Guillermo finally said to Sugar one day, "Hey, Sugar, your music is all wrong, man. But I like the way it feels in my nose! Hey, you know? I like the way it feels in my mouth!"

Some of the songs were hymns: "Keep me hungry, Lord," Sugar sang, and the road crew sang it too.

Some of the songs were love songs: "Put your hands in someone else's pockets," Sugar sang angrily; "I hear your voice in the morning," Sugar sang tenderly; "Is it summer yet?" Sugar sang sadly; and the road crew sang it, too.

Over the months the road crew changed, one man leaving on Wednesday and a new man taking his place on Thursday, as different skills were needed in different places. Sugar was silent when each newcomer came, until the man had given his word and the secret was sure to be kept.

What finally destroyed Sugar was the fact that his songs were so unforgettable. The men who left would sing the songs with their new crews, and those crews would learn them, and teach them to others.

Crewmen taught the songs in bars and on the road; people learned them quickly, and loved them; and one day a blind Watcher heard the songs and knew, instantly, who had first sung them. They were Christian Haroldsen's music, because in those melodies, simple as they were, the wind of the north woods still whistled and the fall of leaves still hung oppressively over every note and—and the Watcher sighed. He took a specialized tool from his file of tools and boarded an airplane and flew to the city closest to where a certain road crew worked. And the blind Watcher took a company car with a company driver up the road and at the end of it, where the road was just beginning to pierce a strip of wilderness, the blind Watcher got out of the car and heard singing. Heard a piping voice singing a song that made even an eyeless man weep.

"Christian," the Watcher said, and the song stopped.

"You," said Christian.

"Christian, even after you lost your fingers?"

The other men didn't understand—all the other men, that is, except Guillermo.

"Watcher," said Guillermo. "Watcher, he done no harm."

The Watcher smiled wryly. "No one said he did. But he broke the law. You, Guillermo, how would you like to work as a servant in a rich man's house? How would you like to be a bank teller?"

"Don't take me from the road crew, man," Guillermo said.

"It's the law that finds where people will be happy. But Christian Haroldsen broke the law. And he's gone around ever since making people hear music they were never meant to hear."

Guillermo knew he had lost the battle before it

began, but he couldn't stop himself. "Don't hurt him, man. I was meant to hear his music. Swear to God, it's made me happier."

The Watcher shook his head sadly. "Be honest, Guillermo. You're an honest man. His music's made you miserable, hasn't it? You've got everything you could want in life, and yet his music makes you sad. All the time, sad."

Guillermo tried to argue, but he was honest, and he looked into his own heart, and he knew that the music was full of grief. Even the happy songs mourned for something; even the angry songs wept; even the love songs seemed to say that everything dies and contentment is the most fleeting thing. Guillermo looked in his own heart and all Sugar's music stared back up at him and Guillermo wept.

"Just don't hurt him, please," Guillermo murmured as he cried.

"I won't," the blind Watcher said. Then he walked to Christian, who stood passively waiting, and he held the special tool up to Christian's throat. Christian gasped.

"No," Christian said, but the word only formed with his lips and tongue. No sound came out. Just a hiss of air. "No."

"Yes," the Watcher said.

The road crew watched silently as the Watcher led Christian away. They did not sing for days. But then Guillermo forgot his grief one day and sang an aria from *La Bohème*, and the songs went on from there. Now and then they sang one of Sugar's songs, because the songs could not be forgotten.

In the city, the blind Watcher furnished Christian with a pad of paper and a pen. Christian immediately gripped the pencil in the crease of his palm and wrote: "What do I do now?"

The driver read the note aloud, and the blind Watcher laughed. "Have we got a job for you! Oh, Christian, have we got a job for you!" The dog barked loudly, to hear his master laugh.

Applause

In all the world there were only two dozen Watchers. They were secretive men, who supervised a system that needed little supervision because it actually made nearly everybody happy. It was a good system, but like even the most perfect of machines, here and there it broke down. Here and there someone acted madly, and damaged himself, and to protect everyone and the person himself, a Watcher had to notice the madness and go to fix it.

For many years the best of the Watchers was a man with no fingers, a man with no voice. He would come silently, wearing the uniform that named him with the only name he needed—Authority. And he would find the kindest, easiest, yet most thorough way of solving the problem and curing the madness and preserving the system that made the world, for the first time in history, a very good place to live. For practically everyone.

For there were still a few people—one or two each year—who were caught in a circle of their own devising, who could neither adjust to the system nor bear to harm it, people who kept breaking the law despite their knowledge that it would destroy them.

Eventually, when the gentle maimings and deprivations did not cure their madness and set them back into the system, they were given uniforms and they, too, went out. Watching.

The keys of power were placed in the hands of those who had most cause to hate the system they had to preserve. Were they sorrowful?

"I am," Christian answered in the moments when he dared to ask himself that question.

In sorrow he did his duty. In sorrow he grew old. And finally the other Watchers, who reverenced the silent man (for they knew he had once sung magnificent songs), told him he was free. "You've served your time," said the Watcher with no legs, and he smiled.

Christian raised an eyebrow, as if to say, "And?"

"So wander."

Christian wandered. He took off his uniform, but lacking neither money nor time he found few doors closed to him. He wandered where in his former lives he had once lived. A road in the mountains. A city where he had once known the loading entrance of every restaurant and coffee shop and grocery store. And at last to a place in the woods where a house was falling apart in the weather because it had not been used in forty years.

Christian was old. The thunder roared and it only made him realize that it was about to rain. All the old songs. All the old songs, he mourned inside himself, more because he couldn't remember them than because he thought his life had been particularly sad.

As he sat in a coffee shop in a nearby town to stay out of the rain, he heard four teenagers who played the guitar very badly singing a song that he knew. It was a song he had invented while the asphalt poured on a hot summer day. The teenagers were not musicians and certainly were not Makers. But they sang the song from their hearts, and even though the words were happy, the song made everyone who heard it cry.

Christian wrote on the pad he always carried, and showed his question to the boys. "Where did that song come from?"

"It's a Sugar song," the leader of the group answered. "It's a song by Sugar."

Christian raised an eyebrow, making a shrugging motion.

"Sugar was a guy who worked on a road crew and made up songs. He's dead now, though," the boy answered.

"Best damn songs in the world," another boy said, and they all nodded.

Christian smiled. Then he wrote (and the boys waited impatiently for this speechless old man to go away): "Aren't you happy? Why sing sad songs?"

The boys were at a loss for an answer. The leader spoke up, though, and said, "Sure I'm happy. I've got a good job, a girl I like, and man, I couldn't ask for more. I got my guitar. I got my songs. And my friends."

And another boy said, "These songs aren't sad, Mister. Sure, they make people cry, but they aren't sad."

"Yeah," said another. "It's just that they were written by a man who knows."

Christian scribbled on his paper. "Knows what?"

"He just knows. Just knows, that's all. Knows it all."

And then the teenagers turned back to their clumsy guitars and their young, untrained voices, and Christian walked to the door to leave because the rain had stopped and because he knew when to leave the stage. He turned and bowed just a little toward the singers. They didn't notice him, but their voices were all the applause he needed. He left the ovation and went outside where the leaves were just turning color and would soon, with a slight inaudible sound, break free and fall to the earth.

For a moment he thought he heard himself

singing. But it was just the last of the wind, coasting madly through the wires over the street. It was a frenzied song, and Christian thought he recognized his voice.

Afterword:
On Origins

Where do stories come from? Good or bad, stories must at some point have emerged as ideas that for some reason attracted the writer's attention. Ideas that insisted, "Write me."

It has been a year since I collected these stories into a book and sent them off into the marketplace. Now that I look at them again, in detail, as I go through the manuscript checking up on the work of a very good copyeditor, I find myself wondering also: Where did that story come from? Some I wonder at because I have long since learned to do better than *that*; some because I have no idea how I did it, and worry that I can't do it again.

"Ender's Game" was the first story I ever sold for publication. It began as a question when I was sixteen years old: What kind of war games would prepare soldiers for three-dimensional warfare in space? The result was the idea of the null-gravity battleroom, with the flashers that froze the soldiers' clothing and the grids and "stars" that made for variety and forced strategic growth. For eight years the idea gestated, and then emerged when Ben Bova rejected a fantasy I sent him at *Analog* by writing me a kind note saying, "I like the way you write, but *Analog* only buys straight science fiction." At the time I wasn't sure what he meant by "straight" science fiction, but "Ender's Game" was my attempt to satisfy. He made me rewrite it once, shortening it and removing a battle or two.

Now I look at it in awe that it was published: the point-of-view shifts, the acres of empty dialogue as I tried to turn the skills I had learned as a playwright to this new task of fiction. And yet I find that the story still moves me, and I would write it again if I hadn't written it already.

"Kingsmeat" came with the image of a shepherd shearing his human flock. It went cruel on me, and yet I think it does a decent job of making a sympathetic character out of a torturer.

"Deep Breathing Exercises" began one night, soon after my son Geoffrey's birth, when I was walking him to sleep and realized that his breath on my shoulder was exactly in rhythm with my wife's breath as she slept in the other room.

"Closing the Timelid" began as I tried to find a way for a person to undergo multiple deaths for pleasure. Time travel was a device for me to tell the story I really wanted to tell—hedonism as self-destruction. It preaches.

"I Put My Blue Genes On" was one of the most mechanical stories I ever wrote, and probably my straightest "straight" science fiction. James Baen, then editor of *Galaxy*, wrote an editorial one month in which he complained that science fiction authors were still writing the same old stuff, not touching such new ideas as recombinant DNA research. I took the challenge personally, manufactured "Blue Genes" as a romp with the idea carried to an extreme, and now look at it as one of the funniest, fluffiest pieces of writing I've ever done.

"Eumenides in the Fourth Floor Lavatory" began as a dream that my friend and informal editor Jay Parry recounted to me. Jay lacks my vicious streak —he. didn't want to write it himself. So I took his nightmare image of a child with flipper arms drown-

ing in a toilet and slowly worked it into a Har-
lanesque tale of just deserts.

"Mortal Gods" sprang whole from my head—I
sat down at the typewriter, stared at a paper on which
I could not remember having written, "Aliens come to
Earth to worship because we die," and lo: a story.

"Quietus" was my wife's dream, a nightmare of
coming downstairs and finding a coffin in the house
with a stranger's body in it. The image struck me
powerfully, and since I envisioned the coffin in the
house we then lived in, I wrote probably the most
personal story in this collection, the one that most
reflects my own character.

"The Monkeys Thought 'Twas All in Fun"
began because Jerry Pournelle was doing an anthology of stories that take place in artificial environ-
ments. As is my wont, I decided to go against the
grain and do an artificial environment that was actually alive; and as I thought about it I fell in love with
Hector. Yet now I find that the best parts of the story
are the tales Hector tells himselves: I think that in the
story of Cyril I was warming up for Christian in "Unaccompanied Sonata." Agnes is a good character, and
deserves better than the way I pushed her around this
story on the end of a stick.

"The Porcelain Salamander" began as a bedtime story for my wife, who playfully demanded one. I
thought of a disgusting animal to spin yarns about,
but then proceeded to make a fairy tale out of it
anyway. Later I sent it as my Christmas card to friends
who would understand not getting a *real* card with
four-color printing and all.

And "Unaccompanied Sonata" began with the
thought one day: What if someone forbade me to
write? Would I obey? I made a false start then, and
failed; years later I tried again, and this time got

through the whole story. Other than punctuation changes and a few revised phrases, *this* one has stood in its first full draft as it came out of the typewriter. It's the truest thing I've ever written.

Through all these stories there are recurring motifs—pain to the point of cruelty, ugliness to the point of grotesquerie. There are recurring themes, too —love of death, an unpayably high price for joy, an unrealistic belief in poetic justice.

Indeed, if I reach any conclusion, it is that the idea of the story means very little. What matters is the voice in which the writer speaks, the character of whom the writer chooses to tell, and—most important of all—the way the story ends. I find myself a mitigated optimist. Every one of these stories has a happy ending, however miserable the characters may be. Wherever the ideas came from, whatever it was in them that drew me to write, I still remain their writer, and what I am inevitably bends the story so that even the tales with the most divergent origins end up with a common shape, a shared effect. Whatever else these stories are—good or bad, sweet or salt, mundane or ecstatic—they are mine.

About the Author

Orson Scott Card began his career by writing plays for Utah regional theater. He interrupted that work for a two-year unpaid mission for the LDS Church in Brazil, after which he was employed as an editor for several Utah publishers until becoming a full-time writer in 1978. Now he lives in Orem, Utah, with his wife, Kristine Allen, and their son, Geoffrey. Besides his regular work, he teaches a writing course at the University of Utah in Salt Lake City.